The Cruel Romance

The Cruel Romance

A Novel of Love and War

Marina Osipova

THE CRUEL ROMANCE
A NOVEL OF LOVE AND WAR

Certain characters in this work are historical figures, and certain events portrayed did take place. However, this is a work of fiction. All of the other characters, names, and events as well as all places, incidents, organizations, and dialogue in this novel are either the products of the author's imagination or are used fictitiously.

iUniverse books may be ordered through booksellers or by contacting:

iUniverse
1663 Liberty Drive
Bloomington, IN 47403
www.iuniverse.com
1-800-Authors (1-800-288-4677)

ISBN: 978-1-4917-8547-8 (sc)
ISBN: 978-1-4917-8548-5 (e)

Library of Congress Control Number: 2015920915

Print information available on the last page.

iUniverse rev. date: 03/02/2016

For my parents

Note on Russian Names

In Russia, a person is identified by three names: an individual, given first name, a patronymic middle name in honor of one's father, and a family surname.

It is customary to call a person by both the given name and the patronymic, which implies a mark of respect–for example, Serafima Petrovna Krivenkova, Victor Ivanovich Kholodov, or Anna Konstantinovna Troyanovskaya.

Russian forenames have several diminutive forms derived from the given name, of which there are many–for example, Victor – Vitya, Ivan – Vanya.

In order to express affectionate feelings towards a person, Russian names have endearing forms–for instance, Serafima – Serafimushka, Victor – Viten'ka, Vanya – Vanechka, Anna – Annushka.

Calling a person after one's patronymic name – Semenich, for example, implies a slight tone of mockery or familiarity.

It was and still is common in Russia, to call an older woman, not necessarily a family member, aunt or aunty, and an older man – uncle.

PART I

THE DAMNED WAR

October 1941, Russia, a small village about 80 miles from Moscow

Serafima stole into the anteroom and halted, listening closely. The buzz of the spinning wheel was muffled from behind the closed door. She lowered the milk jar onto the table and then slipped from the house. For a second, she held her breath. No, the door did not screech, and no angry shout followed—only a flock of wild geese that sped over the clouded sky marked their flight with anxious cries.

Behind the barn, the field stretched to the west and the east restrained by the impenetrable green of a pine forest. Its serrated outline hemmed the horizon. She stepped into the squashy mud and hurried toward the trees.

Dusk had already set in, but across the sky, in the distance, thick reddish clouds passed as though escaping from a fire. Above the faraway treetops, a swarm of airplanes floated towards Moscow in triangular ranks like small, silent birds. At the yapping of a dog, Serafima looked back. The silhouettes of the huts lining the village's only street loomed in the haze.

The rain had begun again, falling in delicate drops. The air was redolent of damp earth mixed with the odor of uncut grain left to rot in the furrows.

Some hundred yards away from the fringe of the forest, she caught a glimpse of motion through the trees.

Her heart raced. *Vitya*. She saw him take an abrupt step from the thicket of the bushes, and she broke into a run.

Large-boned and of medium height, he was encased in a well-fitting officer's uniform, dark with wet spots, as though spattered with shots. The mist hung in his warm blonde forelock from under his peaked cap and the pale light glittered on it. "I thought you weren't coming," he said, his voice low and hoarse.

She wiped away the tear the wind had brought to her eye and said quickly over her choking, beating heart, "How could you think that, Vitya?"

He took her work-worn hands in his and pressed them to his face. "They smell of goat milk."

Her fingers became moist in his as the undisguised joy pierced through her, immediately changing to incomprehensible fear. Just thinking of him going to the front shattered her. "Viten'ka, when?"

"Today."

"Today," she echoed. "Today?" She stared at him for a long moment as if not comprehending. "Why? Why did you refuse your exemption?"

"I could not live with myself if I took the coward's way out. I could not live with the shame. Should my country demand sacrifice of blood, then I will make that sacrifice." He squeezed her fingers so tightly they cracked. "I will be back–don't you fret. We will drive the damned fascists away, and all will be as before. You and I, together."

He leaned over her and pressed his temple to hers, singing softly, his breath hot against her ear:

Dark eyes, burning eyes
Passionate and splendid eyes …

"As though this romance was written about your beautiful eyes. How I will miss them."

She only half listened. A shudder ran through her at the thought of parting from him. "I only ask you, please, please, be careful. You must, for my sake. For our sakes."

She rose up on her tiptoes to put her arms around his neck but lost her balance for a moment before he caught her and pressed her into the strength of his arms. "You are shivering. We must get out of the wind. The dugout is not far away."

The dugout. She stiffened, momentarily abashed. She was aware of the rumors that crept through the local villages about the infamous place.

"No, Victor." She backed out of his grasp.

A shadow of displeasure crossed his handsome face. "You might get warm inside it." Gripping her hand, he led her into the depths of the forest. Tormented by conflicting emotions, she did not resist.

The creased, ruddy pines rose straight and slender as ship's masts, while the birches, paper white and marked with varying lesions of black, tilted slightly in every direction. A chilly October breeze blew over the rustling trees, creating a colorful snowstorm of leaves on the soft pine-needle-sown ground. Thin, fallen branches crunched under their feet. Overhead a crow flew with a full, throaty cry.

Where trees thinned out, exposing the withered grass to the sky, a dugout emerged. Massive logs loomed several feet above the ground, and steps led down into the earth.

He swept her into his arms and plunged into the semidarkness of the hollow, which was fragrant with the sodden pinecones and the cloying sweetness of damp straw. In the dim light, she could make out a pair of rough-hewn benches and a table made from birch.

He turned her around to face him and stroked her escaping curl gently away from her forehead. Against the diffused light from outside, his gray eyes were full of passion.

"Serafima, do you understand what you mean to me? Do you?" His hands trembled as he tried to push her down onto the pile of flattened hay by the wall. "Say yes." His voice, deep and sensual, sent a ripple of awareness through her body.

"To what?" She heard her own voice, tense and panicked. Suddenly, she had a feeling that she must protect herself against his panting, his eyes, his fingers pulling buttons off her jacket, touching her in places he had never dared before. Guilt and fear of what she would go through if *that* happened to her flooded her from inside.

"To being mine." He was fighting his belt, breathing in shallow, quick gasps.

"No, Victor." She twisted and leaned back.

"Please, my darling," he said hoarsely. "Please."

She managed to break away from him, but he caught her elbow, his fingers hurting her through the material of her jacket. She pushed against his chest and flung back her head. "Let me go!"

He was looming over her now. "Don't push me off. Don't, my darling. I will love you forever. One time. Just one time."

She shook her head, over and over, and the desire in his usually imperturbable eyes changed to fury.

She squirmed at his wide-open mouth with spasmodic breathing. "Victor, please, let me go. I'll wait for you, I swear, but please, let me go now, I beg of you." She watched his eyes narrow and harden as if he was fighting something, and she thought she saw something ugly in them that she did not recognize and could not understand.

Little by little, the fury drained from his gaze, and his mouth pressed into a hard line. He stepped away from her and glanced at his wristwatch, which gleamed in the dusk. "It is time. I am due at the station at eight."

A cold knot formed in her stomach. "Where will you go? Directly to the front?"

He nodded.

She looked in his eyes, at his strong jaw, the lips that had kissed her a moment before, and saw him going to the war, to the sound of cannonade on the horizon. Despair shook her, and at the same time like a cloudburst there descended on her a fatal tenderness, to which she dared not yield because she felt she would be torn to pieces once she admitted to it. She had to wait until it passed.

"You could stay—"

He cut her short. "I am not a shirker. Anyway, it will soon be over. I'm sure of that. Then we will be together, to the end of our lives. Take care of yourself while I am gone." His voice was quiet, and there was a hardness to it that made her shiver. "Remember that you are mine. Only mine. Don't forget it." He took her hand in his, but his eyes were cold as they climbed out of the dugout.

"Go," he said. "Don't look back." But instantly he pulled her to him, crushing her in his embrace, and kissed her with a kind of cruel farewell tenderness. She held onto him, refusing to release him, and whispered, "Vitya, Viten'ka …"

With trembling fingers, she removed a small copper cross from her neck and slipped the string over his head. "Wear this, Vitya. Oh Lord, defend him and save him, cover him with Thy wings, he is all I have in the world …" She threw her arms round his neck, bending his head down to her face, biting her lips to control the sobs.

"Serafima, I must go. I will return soon. I promise it." He unfastened her hands from his neck and ran.

Through a film of tears misting her eyes, she caressed his silhouette as it grew smaller, smaller, and finally disappeared. Even when she had lost sight of his figure, she seemed to see him in the haze. She called his name in a whisper, "Vitya, Viten'ka, Vitya."

The rain continued to drizzle as she trudged home.

The village was obscured by fog and only the poplar, like a nighttime ghost, rose above Serafima's house, the empty crow's nest swinging in its brown top.

At the creak of the door, Glafira turned her head. "Where have you been, idler?" Her voice always seemed to be on the edge of anger.

Cornflower-blue-eyed, with a small, bulbous nose and smooth, flaxen hair gathered in a heavy knot at the back, she could be considered good-looking if not for the angry furrow between her brows and the deep lines at the corners of her mouth.

"I w-was at D-dunyasha's, Mother," Serafima stammered.

"Oh, good gracious, at Dunysha's. In the woods? Surely with her brother. Think I don't hear whispers going round the village?" Her gaze darkened, grew sharper, and bore into Serafima's face. "You watch out! I am warning you—if I see you flirting with him, I will whip you. Not a step will you stir away from me. How am I to give you away in marriage? A dog won't touch a gnawed bone."

"Mother, how can you—?"

"Surely you have erred with him." Her eyes narrowed at the sight of the little round hole left by the missing button in Serafima's jacket. "You disgrace me!"

Serafima ran from the house. *You disgrace me.* The words rang in her head like the crack of a whip. *As though I don't know the story of my own birth.*

In the barn, it was dark and soothingly silent. In the farthest corner, the goat's body gleamed white. Serafima squatted in front of her. "Zor'ka, Zoren'ka."

Zorka lifted her head, warm and silky under Serafima's hand. Tears rolled down Serafima's cheeks as she stroked Zor'ka's soft coat.

The screeching of the door struck against the silence and her mother's angry shout followed, "Serafima!"

"Soon, Mother." Brushing away her tears, she dragged herself through the yard back to the house.

Washed clean by the rain, the sky was stern and clear. In the north, the Polar Star gleamed piercingly. The horned and spotted moon poured down a flood of uncertain light—the withered wormwood seemed to smell more strongly and the wet soil to breathe more coolly.

With all the men at the front, Serafima and Glafira, together with other local women, spent the next week digging defense lines and anti-tank ditches. At night, the sky showed red from dozens of distant fires. During the day, a gray screen of smoke from the raging battle hung all along the horizon. Fierce autumnal winds blew, and the mud hardened.

After eight days of strenuous work, Serafima felt so ground down by exhaustion that every gesture made her grimace with pain.

"Here." Serafima put a small aluminum basin on the table in front of her mother.

They dipped their badly blistered hands into the lukewarm water and groaned simultaneously, "Ooh, God."

The birch logs crackled in the stove. The reflection of the flames flitted up the walls and flickered off the icon of the Savior, darkened with time.

Silently, they munched on rye bread, washing it down with sips of goat milk.

A far-off drone of aircraft came nearer, like bees humming in a wood. They froze, listening closely.

"Germans," Glafira half-asked, half-declared.

"No, Mother, those are ours."

The anti-aircraft guns began barking furiously in the distance. A dog joined, whining uneasily somewhere behind the farmstead.

"Do you think they—?" her mother asked.

"No, Victor said they won't let the fascists—"

"What can he do, your fighter?" Glafira snapped. Her eyes shifted to the icon and her lips moved as if in speech, but no words emerged. On unsteady legs, she went to the corner of veneration, kneeled, and bowed, beating her forehead against the wooden floor.

From time to time, a deep silence blended with the rumble of guns and the drone of engines. During those sudden streaks of quiet moments, she could hear her mother stubbornly demanding safety and preservation from the God who, as Serafima imagined, stared down at her with arrogant indifference.

Serafima averted her face from the icon and sank onto the bed. She closed her eyes but could not sleep. Restrained during the hours of labor, anxiety for Victor's life burst all dams at night. The thought that he might be killed haunted her, unwelcome and too painful to contemplate. *Why did I not yield to his desire?* she thought, abandoning herself to the bitterness of regret. *At least then I might have his child.*

At night, her mother tossed and turned, moaning in her dream, and her metal bed creaked under her light body. When she quieted down, Serafima got up. She slipped her feet into her old felt boots, took the padded jacket off the hook, and pulled it on over her heavy flannel nightgown. In the dark, she reached for a notebook and tiptoed to the anteroom.

She struck a match and held it out to the stump of a tallow candle. The worm-like wick amid the melted wax thawed out and took light. The flame flickered and danced in the breeze coming through the cracks in the walls. A fly buzzed, caught in a spiderweb on the ceiling.

Serafima tore a lined piece of paper from her notebook and dipped a pen in the inkpot bottle.

October 31, 1941

My beloved Viten'ka,
I think of you always. Praying you are safe. Where are you now? Are you already in the action?
The damned fascists! I hate them with all my heart because they took you from me.

Suddenly, she was overcome by the urge to recite the text of the lost prayers. "Supreme Ruler, Holy Mother of God, and our Lord Jesus Christ. Bless, Lord, Thy slave of God, Victor, entering battle. Wrap him in a cloud, with Thy heavenly, stony hail protect him … Amen."

It felt good to pray, to unburden her heart.

I know you will be angry with me, but I pray to God that He may hold His hand over you and protect you from all the horrors at the front. Although you do not believe in God, I know my prayers will reach Him and He will spare your life, for me. I believe that eventually there must be defeat over the damned fascists, and then all our dreams will come true.

Darling, darling Vitya, I love you so that it makes my heart ache. I beg you to take care of yourself. You are everything in the world I hold dear. If anything should happen to you, I think I should go insane.

Return safely from the war, and I promise you a son.

She looked lovingly at the sheet of paper and then at the candle flame—a yellow moth of fire fluttering and throbbing when she let out a breath.

Closing her eyes, she dreamed of the kisses he had pressed on her lips, the smell of his skin, his strong arms, his body yearning for her.

The tongue of the candle swayed violently as the door was flung open.

She hurriedly folded the letter and hid it on her lap.

"Have you lost your mind?" her mother hissed at her, angrily baring her small teeth. "What are you doing wasting the candle! Go to bed. Have you forgotten? At daybreak we report to the check point."

"Yes, Mother, yes. You go, please. I will be there in a minute."

Glafira mumbled something under her nose and closed the door behind her.

Serafima blew out the candle and stared at it while the wick glowed until it faded to nothing. She went to the room, silently kissed the letter and put it into a book on the shelf. When she finally drifted into a heavy sleep, she dreamed of Victor's pleading eyes and his voice, whispering against her lips, "You are mine." It was both a promise and a threat.

The front door banged, striking against the silence. "Aunty Glafira! Serafima!" Dunyasha gasped for breath as she stumbled into the house. She resembled Victor, with her fair hair, gray eyes, full, heart-shaped lips, and rosy cheeks. Only now, her beautiful face was a chalky white, distorted by boundless terror.

Disheveled, her kerchief thrust on the back of her head, she leaned against the wall. Words burst forth in a tremulous whisper. "They are in the town! All in black uniforms, with death's head insignias … They have herded together all the men and boys into the old church. They have already built two gallows. People say they are for those who were in the Communist Party."

"How is it that they are in the town? It's only four kilometers from here. How is it possible?" Serafima said.

"They are taking over our houses. They are taking our cattle!" Dunyasha's strong hands trembled.

"So they'll be here soon." In a single glance, Serafima took in the bookshelf with her old school books, her mother's leather-bound, grease-stained copy of the Gospels, the icon of the Savior in the corner of veneration and their shabby dressing gowns, dangling from the clothes hooks hammered into the wall by the door.

Glafira, who had been listening in stony-faced silence, sprang up as if emerging from a stupor. "The devil curse them!" she cried, brandishing a hatchet she had pulled from the drawer. "They won't have our Zor'ka!"

"No, Mother. No." Serafima seized her mother's arm and tried to snatch away the hatchet. "Mother, please, please, I will hide Zor'ka in the woods, in the dugout. Mother, please!"

Glafira ran from the house and moved toward the barn, Serafima and Dunyasha falling in step after her.

The goat was peacefully munching hay in her corner.

Serafima dashed forward and sank to the ground. She pressed the goat's head to her chest. "Zor'ka. Zoren'ka."

"Out of the way!" Glafira thrust her aside.

The meek creature bleated pitifully when Glafira knocked her to the ground and tied her front and rear legs together with a rope.

A wild look, quick and violent with something wrathful and cruel in it, glittered in Glafira's eyes. She thrust downward with the hatchet and instantly, a fan of dark blood spattered her face. Recoiling, she squeezed her eyes shut. The hatchet dropped from her hand with a thud. For a moment, she stood stock still then, jerkily, tore her white kerchief from her head and wiped her face—two uneven stains the color of rotting cherries prominent against her pale cheeks.

Zor'ka cried out with a horrifying guttural sound as the blood poured from her neck.

Serafima shuddered and threw her hands over her ears.

"You'd better go. I'll help your mother." Dunyasha put her arm around Serafima and led her out into the open. The sky was full of stars. They looked cold and dead.

When she reached the house, Serafima collapsed onto the floor. "I hate you! I hate you!" she cried out again and again, not knowing at that moment who she hated more, those who she did not face yet, or her own mother.

The clock hands spun around. The wind cried outside, bringing the sound of the whinnying of horses from somewhere far away.

Serafima sat on the floor with her back to the stove, oblivious to her mother bustling about, and in her delirium she heard Victor's voice saying, "Don't fret, we will drive the fascists away, and all will be as before." With painful clarity, she acknowledged to herself that she did not believe his words anymore.

Glafira blew out the candle and lay down on her bed. For a long time, Serafima heard her pattering. "Our Father, who art in heaven … on earth as it is in heaven … and forgive us our trespasses … deliver us from evil …"

The booming sound of distant explosions beat against the window.

Not much before midnight, Serafima realized how the room had cooled. She sank onto her cot as she was, dressed in her jacket, resolved on fighting off sleep to be ready for what would happen. Yet she must have fallen asleep, for she woke suddenly to the bubbling roar of engines, followed shortly by the guttural sound of commands shouted in German.

An icy shudder ran through her. Throwing her blankets off, she bolted up from the bed. "Mother, get up! We must go, this instant!" She fought into her felt boots.

Glafira rubbed at her eyes and yawned noisily. "What?" she said, sitting up in bed when a burst of machine-gun fire reached them distinctly.

Serafima jerked her mother up by the shoulder so roughly she almost fell. "Get up! Follow me!"

"Follow you—to where?"

"We'll go through the backyard—into the forest."

"We shan't get out of here. It is as I thought." Glafira pressed her hands to her forehead. "I had a terrible dream ... As if I was lying in the grass—and ants were crawling over my face ..." The words came out in a hoarse whisper.

"Not a word more! Is it clear? Not a word more!" She saw her mother start as though before a blow. "Forgive me, Mother. For God's sake, get up. Let's go, before it is too late."

Glafira shoved her feet into her big felt boots, threw a sheepskin overcoat over her shoulders, and held out an arm to Serafima.

They walked to the door and into the anteroom, Glafira, hanging on her, embracing her around the waist.

"Faster, Mother, faster. We must get out of here. Faster, faster." She kicked the street door with her leg but stopped short at the cry.

"*Halt!*—Stop!"

They were face to face with a soldier. He wore a dust-stained uniform, a green coalscuttle helmet and boots coated with layers of dirt. A heavy bundle of grenades hung from his belt. Next to him stood a black German Shepherd dog, tenaciously holding them in its glare.

"Commissar? Partisan?" The soldier jerked his machine-gun, leveling its barrel at their chests.

Mute with fear, they stared fixedly into the dark hole of the barrel.

"Commissar? Partisan?"

"N-nein Com-missar. N-nein p-partisan," Serafima said in a choked voice.

He pushed them aside and stepped into the anteroom, then kicked open the inside door.

They could hear the sound of heavy boots stomping and a metal bucket clattering to the ground, then a rattle of plates. An angry voice shouted, "Scheise!" and he stepped out of the room.

He strode to the barn, let the dog inside and peered in. Then, without another glance at Serafima and Glafira, he jumped onto his motorcycle. His dog followed him into a sidecar, and they sped away, joining the other four vehicles on the outskirts of the village.

Serafima and Glafira stood in the doorway, staring blankly in front of them. At the crack of a rifle shot from somewhere behind the village, a flock of crows shot up into the sky like ash from a fire.

Serafima drew a deep breath. "We can hide in the woods, Mother. You gather whatever food we can carry.

The hen, too. I will bundle the blankets, some clothing. Hurry." She disappeared inside the house.

She thought it was only a moment that passed when she heard her mother's cry, "They are coming!"

Glafira ran into the room. Her face was bloodless, and her left eye winked nervously. The hen, which she held by its legs, clucked and twitched in her hand.

With a chilling emptiness in her chest, Serafima pressed her nose against the window. In the uncertain dawn, the glare of headlights crept closer and closer. A military jeep stopped in front of their house. An officer—she judged him to be about twenty—climbed out of the car. He was tall, with a femininely slim waist, and walked with easy, long-legged grace. He opened the passenger's door. A glossy knee boot appeared first, hanging suspended in the air for a moment as if hesitating to grant the frozen mud its spotless elegance. Then a peaked cap emerged, and a man rose. He was an inch or two over six feet, lean, and a mouse-gray overcoat fit close to his straight back. He stretched his arms above his head, flexed his legs in quick kicks then turned to the house. He said something to the younger officer who walked quickly to the front door ahead of him.

Serafima turned away from the window and saw Glafira staring at the icon of the Savior in the corner of veneration, illuminated by the icon-lamp's single candlelight, her lips forming the words to her prayer. At the scrape of the door, she went white.

The older German stooped and stepped inside. He sniffed with distaste and pulled up the collar of his greatcoat to cover his nose. His steel-gray eyes roved over the room. As his gaze fell on the tall stove and the tarnished samovar, a barely perceptible smile turned up the corners of his mouth. It disappeared when his eyes moved to the unmade wooden cot pushed against the whitewashed wall of the stove, the table with a greasy kerosene lamp and unwashed utensils, the worm-eaten wooden bench at the small bare window, and the spinning wheel. His eyebrows shot up in surprise at the sight of the iron bed with sophisticated lace-like headboard that was set against the wall. As he halted in front of the photographs, soiled with fly-specks, and a scrap of yellowed mirror on the wall, his lips twisted into a cynical smile.

"*Russischer Schwein! Alle sind Schweine! Schweinedreck!*—The Russian pig! All of them are pigs! Pigs dirt!"

The old boards screeched sonorously while he walked round Glafira indifferently, as if she were an extraneous object. He halted in front of Serafima and stared hard at her.

She resolved not to look away.

With only a twitch of his brow, his cold expression unchanged, he turned to the younger officer. "*Der ganze Dreck muß weg!*—Out with this filth!" he said.

Serafima thought she recognized the word "filth."

He made a sweeping gesture with his elegant whip with a carved ivory handle and short black tassels, as though including the women as well.

"*Jawohl, Herr Major!*—Yes, Sir Major!" The younger officer clicked his heels and spun round. He glanced at the women briefly before taking a small book from his pocket and flipping through it. "Remove," he said in broken Russian, pointing to the bed. "Please," he added, stumbling over the word.

The iron bed, a Revolutionary forfeiture from a local landowner, had been implanted into the earthen floor in 1918, before Serafima's grandfather had even put down the wooden planks.

They bent and pulled at the bed. It creaked and hardly moved. "Let's first draw it aside from the wall, Mother," Serafima said.

The young man stepped up and grabbed it at the headboard. Serafima watched his thin, delicate white hands with elongated fingers grip the frame and wondered how a man could have such hands.

The major's face immediately transformed into a steel mask. Smacking his whip against the leg of his polished boot, he said something to the younger officer.

"Jawohl, Herr Major!" The young man stepped away.

Serafima and Glafira grabbed hold of the bed from opposite sides and dragged it to the door. It left long, uneven scratches on the wooden floor.

By noon break, the house was empty; all their possessions had been heaped on the straw in the corner of the barn. They returned to the house and stood side by side in the doorway, not daring to look at the Germans.

The young man flicked through his little book again. "Clean."

"*Los! Los! Schnell!*—Move! Move! Quick!" The major snapped his fingers three times.

"Quickly," the young man said after he had found the right word, and averting his eyes, made for the door after the major.

"I hope you choke, you brute," Serafima said through her teeth.

Carefully, Glafira unhinged the icon from the wall. It slipped through her fingers and fell to the floor face down. "God Almighty, God Almighty." She made the sign of the cross and picked it up with shaking hands. She wrapped the icon in a kerchief and pushed the bundle in Serafima's hands. "Hide it. I will go to fetch water."

On her hands and knees, Serafima removed a loose floorboard behind the stove and slipped the icon inside.

For hours they dusted and swept and mopped and scrubbed the floor and the walls. Every movement of their fingers opened up the cracks in their hands, which oozed blood.

The younger officer walked in and out, carrying traveling bags and suitcases. He brought in a radio, and a flood of brassy words poured out, taking turns with barking marches and choruses of "sieg heils." An alcohol burner appeared and a foreign, bitter aroma wafted from the pot.

Soon an oil painting of Hitler in a wide gold frame replaced the Savior in the corner of veneration.

The major came in. "*Du.*—You." With his whip, he pointed first at Serafima then at the stove. "*Einheizen!*—Heat the stove!"

"I will do it." Glafira stepped forward.

He made a dismissive motion with his hand without casting her a glance and poked Serafima on her chest with his whip.

Again, he said something to the younger officer and laughed. Serafima watched him lewdly licking his lips as if calling to mind some particularly amusing adventure. Stains of scarlet appeared on the younger man's cheeks.

Glafira paled and bowed her way out of the door backwards, and Serafima followed her to fetch the firewood.

Soon the blazing logs were crackling and spitting gently, but the blissful, healing fire burned now for the intruders and the room seemed alien and strangely revolting to her.

The younger man had covered the table with a blue and red checked tablecloth and laid out platefuls of sliced white bread, strong-smelling cheese, and a kind of sausage Serafima had never seen.

The major reclined on his camp bed, barefoot, his tunic open. Reaching now and then to the table, he sipped something from a bottle, licking a little rim of white foam from his top lip. They talked in their terrible, strident voices, so different from the tone of her German language schoolteacher. Amid the torrent of foreign words, Serafima caught some familiar ones—girl, house, mother, Moscow, partisan—but she could not string them together into something that had meaning. *I heiße Serafima. Ich gehe in die Schule,—*My name is Serafima. I go to school, ran in her head.

She returned with more firewood and squatted down to put the logs by the stove.

The major raised his eyes, and his stare crossed with Serafima's. Aiming his cigarette-holder at her, he clicked his tongue to imitate the sound of gunfire.

"Damn you," she said, almost inaudibly.

As though he grasped the meaning of the word, his face clouded and his hand darted to the whip.

Tripping over the threshold, she rushed out of the house.

Serafima stepped into the early new-moon night. The top of the poplar loomed black in the sky over the roof of their house. Buffeted and drenched, it had been holding on to a last few brown leaves. A large, blue star winked enchantingly in the dark emptiness over it.

Overcome by exhaustion, the muscles in her shoulders and neck aching, she entered the barn and lay down beside her mother on the iron bedstead. Buried in the mound of coats and jackets, breathing the pungent scent of the musty straw, they huddled, each drawing warmth from the other.

Minutes of silence passed with only the sound of the mice scurrying about at ease, squeaking and scratching.

A clammy cold crept into Serafima's chest, drawing tightly in a ring round her heart. "Are you asleep, Mother?"

"How could I sleep?"

"Mother, we cannot allow this. We cannot take orders from the Germans. We would do better to slip off into the forest."

"We would freeze to death."

"We can stay in the dugout until we can join the partisans."

"How would we find them? Do you know where to go?"

"No. But we will find them somehow. We must."

"And if we cannot? We will die of hunger."

"We will take everything we have and the hen. And the Germans have a lot of foodstuff. They won't even notice." She rummaged under her jacket and pushed into her mother's hand a small, boxy glass jar, warm from the heat of her body.

"Gipsy blood," Glafira muttered under her breath.

"Huh?"

"Nothing. What is inside?"

"I don't know. I didn't have time to examine it," she said with a childlike, thief-like joy. She untwisted the metal lid and sniffed. It smelled vaguely familiar. "Try it, Mother."

"You first."

Serafima scooped out the jelly mass with two fingers. It was sweet on her tongue. "It is strawberry jam." She pressed the jar into her mother's hand.

Glafira dipped her forefinger into the syrupy mass. "Almost like the one we make," she agreed, smacking her lips.

"Do you not think we should go?" Serafima asked, after they had licked the jam clean.

"I think it is better to wait. We've got to think it over—think it over, I say."

If only I knew where to find them. Serafima firmly resolved to desert to the partisans at the first opportunity.

The booming sound of distant explosions tore the heavy silence. Then silence again, and suddenly the wind carried a muffled melody of a Strauss waltz. Serafima's heart clenched at the vivid image of Victor that the waltz conjured in her mind.

Her memory urged up the fragments of the past—the first meeting of the eyes as he, the Secretary of the District Committee of Komsomol, the Young Communist League, handed her the membership card and a red and gold badge with Lenin's profile.

She remembered stolen glances during the Komsomol meetings, going out of the way to be at a place where she knew from Dunyasha he would be passing, the celebration of the 23rd anniversary of the October Revolution in the city club. That was where after the inflamed long speeches that ended with a solemn prayer, "Long live Comrade Stalin and our glorious Communist Party!" she first heard him singing, *Dark eyes, burning eyes,* at the concert, leading the chorus. And of all the voices, she heard only his voice, powerful yet warm, simmered with barely-checked passion.

After the concert, they danced.

Was it only one year ago? Nearly to the day.

She recalled that evening clearly. "Blue Danube Waltz by Strauss," came the announcement through the loudspeaker.

"A waltz, Comrade Krivenkova?"

A waltz … Is it possible? She was inwardly trembling, gazing at him, so strong and handsome, with his warm blond hair carefully parted on the side and his gray eyes smiling at her.

He put out his arm to encircle her waist. Bending her left hand, she laid it on his shoulder and they began moving rhythmically over the floor in time to the Strauss' waltz. She felt the little willful tendrils of her curly hair break free about her neck and temples and flushed, unwilling to free her hand from his shoulder to smooth them. He was a better dancer. The more they moved, the more tightly he grasped her hand, as if encouraging her not to be embarrassed. After the waltz, she went to Dunyasha, and she hardly had time to say a few words before he came up again for a foxtrot.

In her haze, she was once again seeing him bending his head as though he would fall at her feet, and in his eyes, there was nothing but humble submission and she had wondered, what had become of his always self-possessed, resolute manner and the severe expression of his face?

She recalled how later she was sitting with him under the damp hayrick, trembling and fighting her overwhelming need to be crushed within his embrace, and how she had realized with an inward tremor that she was inseparably bound to this man already. It was only the seventeenth spring of her life, but her heart had chosen him.

Despite the cold, her hands grew warm as she remembered how his strong hands used to seize hers. She dozed for a while, the melody going round and round in her ears. Humming softly to herself helped her to suppress the anguish at the thought that Vitya might be killed.

She was jolted awake by a screech of the barn door, her heart pounding when she perceived where she was and what was happening. A voice came, "Light the stove." Then, "Freezing," almost apologetically.

Outside, the yard, the fields, the village seemed wrapped in drowsy slumber. To the east, right on the skyline, an uncertain gray light lurked over the wood. Her teeth chattering, Serafima grabbed a load of firewood with stiff fingers and tiptoed into the silence of the house. The younger man sat hunched on his cot, his back pressed to the stove. The major seemed to be asleep. He was stretched over the length of his camp bed, his woolen blanket up to his chin.

Soon, merry flames danced inside the stove, sending waves of warmth onto Serafima's face and her hands. A beam of the firelight fell on a dull surface of the gun that lay on the bench close to the major's bed. Her heart sank within her. *If only I knew how …*

Almost involuntarily, her hand crept toward the gun. Suddenly, the major's leg darted from under the blanket, blocking her way. She leaped and lost her balance, hitting the back of her head hard against the stove. The major shouted something, but she was already at the door.

It seemed as if the sun would not rise in the morning, as if darkness had spread over the earth forever. However, the sun did rise at its predetermined hour, and the sky turned blue and cloudless. And a proclamation appeared, nailed to the lid of the draw well:

IN CASE OF DISAPPEARANCE OF A SINGLE PERSON, ALL INHABITANTS OF THE VILLAGE ARE SUBJECT TO IMMEDIATE ANNIHILATION.

Serafima and Glafira stood with their backs toward the barn wall, frozen, still holding the buckets. Glafira's hands trembled, sending the water spilling over the brim.

The young man stood stock still, his little book ready, while the major paced in front of them, striking his boot with the whip. "Now we will teach you how to work, you filthy Bolsheviks," he said in German. "Every day, you will light the stove before sunrise, at noon, at sunset, and in the middle of the night. You will clean the house inside and shovel away the snow. You will do the laundry."

The younger officer, his brows drawn together in concentration, turned pages, looking for the right words, supplementing them with gestures.

The major patiently waited as his subordinate translated. He kept his eyes on the women, a look of disgust marring his face. When the young man finished, the major said, "Teach this swinish rubble to say 'Jawohl!' to every order of ours."

"Please say 'Jawohl,'" he translated.

"Jav, jav," Glafira stuttered, her head nodding like a doll on a spring.

Serafima made no answer.

The major moved closer. "Jawohl!" His curt voice lashed at her, saliva flying from his mouth.

Her breath burning in her throat, she carefully wiped her chin with the corner of her kerchief. Trying to control her voice, she forced herself to say, "Jawohl."

The young man beckoned them with his hand. "Go inside the house."

In the anteroom, underwear, shirts, and sheets lay in neat stacks on the bench. He made a gesture of washing laundry.

Glafira stared at a lilac, cube-shaped block. She took it with her tentative fingers, as if it were something fragile, and sniffed, wide-eyed. "Soap?"

The young man's eyebrows shot up in surprise. For a long moment, he stood motionless then shook his head and returned to the room.

"Look at it." Glafira fingered the stitched monogram *HS* on a handkerchief. "Look, the towels, too." She pointed to a blue, silky monogrammed *WL*.

"Mother, you light the stove. I will fetch the water." Serafima picked up the yoke and two pails and hastened out of the house.

Hardly had she stepped outside when she heard a clatter and her mother's shriek. She ran back into the hut.

The inner door flew open. The young man stood on the threshold, staring at Glafira, his right hand pressed to the pistol holster.

Doubled up, holding her right shoulder with her other hand, Glafira sat on the floor, the brass washtub next to her on its side. "I went to unhook the tub from the wall and it fell." She gave Serafima a long, pained look.

The young man let his hand slip from the holster and stepped toward Glafira. He encircled her back with his arm, and supporting her elbow, lifted her from the floor.

With an astonished glance, she allowed him to lead her to an easy chair. Then he picked up the tub, placed it carefully on the bench, and said something. They could not understand the words, but Serafima could read his face perfectly—his eyes were filled with the damp light of pity.

"*Danke schön,*—Thank you," Serafima said.

It seemed he was taken aback at her 'thank you,' and he gave her an uncertain smile. He brushed back his blond hair, revealing a high ivory-white forehead. For the first time, she noticed he had gray eyes like the major's, but his were gentle and filled with a veiled sweetness. As if embarrassed by her gaze, he spun around and strode toward the door.

"Mother, why didn't you wait for me to return? We have always unhitched the tub together," Serafima said with a touch of reproach. She hoisted the yoke across her shoulders and went back out.

The gleam on the snow made her squint. The houses, the trees, the ghostly, endless forest on the horizon—all seemed to shimmer in the cold light. Beneath her steps, the snow crunched loudly. On the farthest end of the village, a dog howled plaintively.

She passed a group of soldiers who clapped their hands together to beat off the cold, and she thought of the moment when she would put her hands into warm water.

All day, Serafima and Glafira soaped and rubbed, fetched water, rinsed and wrung out and hung the lilac-smelling items outside on the clotheslines strung between the house and the barn. They did not talk much. Only now and then Glafira would utter, "Why? It is clean." She would crumple the garment in her fingers before throwing it into the tub. "It is soft like a baby's jacket." Or, with a distorted face, she would say, "This is the major's."

The air was damp and warm. The lilac aroma lingered about the anteroom. Through the little window, a beam of the setting sun blazed off of the copper tub.

At last, Glafira straightened. With a groan, she wrung out the last sheet and turned her face to the tired light of sunset.

"We are done for today, Mother," Serafima said.

"Thank God," Glafira echoed, nodding her head wearily.

Hardly had they lowered themselves on a bench when the major stepped in, a tunic in his gloved hand.

"*Die Schweine!*—Pigs!" He tossed it back in the tub and went off.

Breathless with rage, Serafima's lips moved in a silent whisper. "Damned, damned you are."

A strange light shone in Glafira's eyes. Pulling herself to her feet with an effort, she gripped the edge of the tub. With great deliberation, she spat a gob of saliva onto the tunic.

Her bitter face relaxed.

Subjected to the strict German order, two weeks passed by. The days came and went with humiliating dependency. The first day of December was no different.

In the afternoon Serafima entered the room, bringing a hand load of firewood and a breath of cold air with her. She breathed in the savory aroma of roasted meat and glanced at the major who was sitting at the table with his back to her, sipping his beer and chewing slowly at a fatty shining sausage followed by white bread. She halted to fight down spasms of nausea. In a burning disgust, she watched his ears rising and falling as he ate.

Without turning her head, she darted a side-glance at the youth. Lying on his cot, he played the harmonica. The notes, fleeting and light, floated in the air. Pale and remote, he gazed fixedly at the ceiling as if the music held him tied in its charm.

It seemed they ignored her presence as though she were a ghost.

Soon, a nice fire of fir twigs crackled in the grate; a pleasant resinous smell spread in the warming air.

Taken by the tenderness of the sounds of *her and Vitya's waltz,* Serafima forgot where she was and who they were. She was stirring up the embers with the poker, looking vacantly at the cloven tongues of fire. Whether because of the leaping flames in the opening of the stove or of the kind warmth that was slowly spreading around her or maybe the tender sounds of the music she was slightly swinging to the rhythm of the melody.

A sharp "Halt!" forced her to turn. The poker slipped from her hand and leaped aside, hitting the major's polished to the shine boot. A speck of ash imprinted clearly on its glossy surface.

After a momentary pause, he said heavily, indicating the boot with his eyes, "So-o?"

Sideways, she moved to the anteroom and returned with a rag. When she squatted in front of him, his boot kicked up meeting her chin, sending her to the floor backwards. She got up, helping herself with her hands, feeling the hot blood surging to her face.

He waited till she wiped the gray speck from his boot then turned to the youth. "These red bastards must be taught how to respect their masters. Werter, let's teach this filthy Russian cheek some German words. Tell her to repeat after me."

She thought she understood the meaning.

Avoiding her eyes as though he himself was guilty of the offence against her, the young man said, "Repeat after the major."

"*Entschuldigen Sie mir, mein Herr.*—I beg your pardon, my master." The major bared his teeth with an atrocious grin.

"Entsch—" Revulsion made her choke on the word.

"Hmm, she does not want to learn how to apologize." The major stepped closer to her. "Let's try another way. No translation needed. She'll understand." Screwing up his left eye as if taking aim, he raised his whip, pointing at her and pulled an imaginary trigger. "Bang-bang. Repeat after me, 'Mauser.'"

"Mauser."

"Good girl. Now say, 'partisan, gallows.'"

"Partisan." She did not catch the other word.

"Gallows." He produced an up-movement with his right hand.

She plunged into the cold of his eyes and clenched her fists.

"Even an animal can smell when he is hated." In a lightning-fast motion, he flung his hand with the whip and a sharp-tongued, spiteful, at once cold and burning, stinging, penetrating sensation assaulted her hand.

She jerked to one side, almost gluing her back and palms to the wall and surveyed him anxiously.

"*Raus! Raus!*—Out! Out!" he shouted.

Outside, the sun hung in the sky peacefully as if nothing had happened. On the roof close to the chimney, rooks were chattering. Startled by Serafima's footsteps, they flew off, circled round the house then flew to the forest clearly outlined against the clear morning sky.

The wind of the preceding days had swept across the snow, piling it up against every barrier, filling in hollows, and leaving brown patches of bare soil in other places.

"Oh no." Serafima stared at a small stack of firewood covered with frozen snow. *Hardly enough for two days.*

She rushed to the draw well to meet her mother who trudged facing her, balancing two pails on a yoke over her shoulders.

"Mother, no firewood left."

"So now this. Cholera take them, damned Fritzes," she muttered curses to herself.

"I'll go to Aunty Anna, maybe she has some extra."

"It's a mere trifle. Don't bother. She just complained to me that she had spent all she had stocked for the winter on *her* Germans. Let's carry the pails to the house, and then we'll go to the forest. But how do we get enough firewood now?" she continued to grumble.

As ordered by the Germans, Serafima knocked the inner door twice, and at the major's "Herein" stepped into the room chilled by the strong wind that rattled the window.

Bent over the table, the major and two other officers were sitting. They turned toward her and their eyes ran over all of her, from her scarf-covered head to her feet in the soft felt boots.

With his usual grin, the major said something. "Ha-ha-ha!" they burst into a loud laugh as they threw themselves back in their chairs.

She tensed, guessing from their glances and the major's gestures that the remark was related to her. Holding a log in her hands, she stood there waiting.

They continued talking amongst themselves, poring over a map and jabbing their fingers at it.

"Yes?" At last, the major said glancing sidelong at her.

"No." She indicated the log in her hands. "Forest," she said, taking steps in the air with her fingers.

The major turned to the youth who was waiting at attention and told him something, cocking his head on his right shoulder and closing his left eye, as if he were taking aim.

"You here. Mother firewood." The youth searched for more words in his phrasebook. "If your mother doesn't return, he will shoot you," he said and instantly dropped his eyes.

A burst of a sharp 'Sieg Heil!' and the rumble of the major's car mowing away reached Werter's ears from behind the window. He sat in silence for a moment then switched on the army radio transmitter. Lili Marlene's raspy voice sounded so painfully nostalgic that he shivered. *How quickly the hut cools off. How cold this country is ... I wish the girl would come soon.*

He shot a quick glance at the door, then shaking his head as if driving the thoughts away, refilled his fountain pen.

The Eastern Front
Den 5. December, 1941

Meine liebe Mutter,

I received your very nice letter and was very glad to hear that everything is well with you and my lovely sister, my dear Gerdi. I am fine and well myself.

Never before could I imagine that I can be so far away from you. And yet, I'm here, thousands of kilometers away, in this God abandoned country.

Huge fields lay around. The horizon touches the vast dark forest on all sides.

I have joined the motorized squadron to which I was assigned when it was on its way to our current position.

We are stationed in a hamlet some four kilometers away from an old city with many beautiful churches, which I was told, were used as storehouses by the Bolsheviks. The village is of thirteen shacks with rotten straw roofs, all set on one side of an unpaved road.

Major Schuette and I quarter in the house that is in some degree habitable. It has a broad, brick, white washed Russian stove that is the best thing in this hut. It quickly warms the room and wards off the icy winds pretty well—except towards mornings.

I consider it an honor to be Major Schuette's aide-de-camp. He is a hero. He got his first Iron Cross for the campaign in France. The second, for Poland, he received from the hands of the Führer himself.

He teaches me life. His favorite expression is 'All is permissible that leads to experience.'

You cannot imagine how fond he is about my playing harmonica. He says it reminds him of our beloved Germany.

I miss my violin so much, but here it would not survive this dreaded weather and the roads. My thoughts turn to my beloved Berlin, and I have a great wave of homesickness for you and my lovely Gerdi. I remember our quiet evenings when we used to play violins with her and you accompanied us on piano.

He took his mother's picture from his breast pocket and laid it in front of him. Involuntarily, his hand rubbed against his heart.

I have to shoo these sweet thoughts away. First, we have to free the poor people of this country from the bloody Bolsheviks.

The village looks uninhabitable. Only now and again, one can see a woman. I did not see any children. I wonder where they hide them. Neither have I seen any men. I surmise they all are at the front or hiding in the woods. There is a lot of talk about partisans.

The peasant women I saw all are dressed in the similar quilted jackets the color of something between gray and brown and they wrap their heads in drab headscarves. I did not see a single friendly face.

The hostess and her daughter stay in their cattle-shed. They kindle the stove for us, fetch water, clean the house, and launder our clothes.

A German-Russian phrase book helps me to convey Major Schuette's orders to them and besides, I learn new Russian words every day.

The girl—I think she is about seventeen— may know German; I have found a besmeared German language schoolbook in the house, but she pretends not to understand.

There rose in his mind how the other day when he, hearing her busying with laundry in the anteroom, could not suppress the urge to see her and opened the door.

She turned to him with a start and all her curls quivered. From her hands, still warm after the wash, a faintest wisp of steam uncurled. Questioning, she raised her eyes at him. She looked especially pretty like this, with her curls damp from the vapors.

His eyes involuntarily passed over her small girlish breasts, usually hidden under her clumsy quilted jacket but now clearly discernible as she leaned over the tub.

A dim feeling that it was wrong to have such thoughts disturbed him. He sighed and returned to the letter.

> *We get our hot meal twice a day from a kitchen in another village a kilometer away. Also, I can't help mentioning that the hostess spared a chicken so we can enjoy fresh eggs. How nice of her.*
>
> *We have no shortage of anything and still I miss your cookies, especially with pink icing, and coffee. The way you brew it.*

The outer door creaked and there was a sound of footsteps in the anteroom. He knew it was the girl. He heard her brushing the snow off her boots with the twig broom at the door.

"Come in," he said, even before the knock came.

She stepped in, bringing a breath of cold air with her. She swept a frightened glance around, and visibly relaxed, edged towards the stove. Moving cautiously, she pressed a bunch of firewood to her chest. A fine fluffy curl escaped from her kerchief.

How nice it would be to run my hands through it, to touch her curls and stroke them. But that was out of the question. He loosened his collar.

As she was busying herself about the fire, stirring the logs in the flame, deliberately, as it seemed to him, prolonging her time to stay in the warming room, he glanced from beneath his eyelids at her.

Her neck twisted continually in the direction of the table as though by a strange force. The plate with a thick piece of white bread richly spread with butter and marmalade, missing one bite at the corner seemed to magnetize her. Two rosy blushes in her cheeks and a hungry glitter in her eyes betrayed her.

He reached to her shoulder. She flinched and looked up with her wonderful blazing eyes, and said with her lips, without any voice, "Bread."

He understood and he felt how the color spread thickly through his face. *"Wie heißt Du? Die Name, die Name. Ich heiße Werter.*—What is your name? The name, the name. My name is Werter." He pressed his index finger against his chest then pointed at her. "We heißt du? Mariya? Anna?"

"Serafima."

"Serafima, Serafima," he repeated while cutting off a thick piece of bread and then covering it with butter and marmalade.

With her eyes, she followed every move of his fingers, breathing in shallow, quick gasps.

At the sound of the opening door, she turned abruptly.

"Herr Major!" Werter started and a blob of marmalade fell from the knife to the floor.

The major's lips twisted into a cynical smile. "You seem to have a good appetite, today." He strode to the table, bent down, and pushed the plates and a saucer with butter aside. "You, Lieutenant Lindberg, deliver a report to Oberst Martens."

As he wrote something on a piece of paper, Werter buttoned his jacket and put on his cap.

The major sealed the paper carefully and extended the envelope to him. "Confidential."

"Jawohl, Herr Major!" He raised his right hand to the brim of his peaked cap and made for the door.

The biting cold wind chilled him instantly. *Four kilometers to the headquarters and back. On foot, it'll take at least two hours,* he thought, all at once feeling a shaft of ice in his chest.

Behind the house to the right, shielded from the howling wind, a group of soldiers gathered around the bonfire, smoking. Although they drew their shoulders up and jumped from one leg to the other, they laughed loudly and cheerfully.

Beside the outermost hut, he saw a soldier checking the ignition of his motorcycle and ran, waiving his hands. "Hey, Obergefreiter! Where are you to?"

"Nowhere, Herr Lieutenant." He tossed his hand to his temple. His face was almost hidden between his upturned collar and his cap, which was pulled down as far as it could go. His red nose projected long streams of vapor, which vanished instantly in the icy air. "Because of this merciless cold I have to warm it thoroughly every two hours. Otherwise, in case of battle alert it may not—"

Werter cut him short. "To the headquarters, there and back, I have an urgent dispatch."

On the move, it was even colder because of the strong headwind. They drove along the forest wrapped in snow and predatory silence. The vehicle skidded and jolted. The muffler banged and the gears stridulated as the motorcycle lurched off the snow bank and away. From time to time low mumbles emerged from the driver's covered mouth, protesting the condition of the *dreaded Russian roads.*

Sitting hunched in the sidecar, his knees drawn up to his chin, Werter rubbed his gloved fingers, grabbing convulsively the cold iron of the sidecar's handle when the motorcycle bumped into endless frozen ruts.

It seemed the minutes wore on agonizingly slowly, and a dull disquietude crept into his consciousness.

At last, they turned to a short street lined on either side with kitchen stoves surrounded by piles of charred logs. In front of a three-story brick building that housed a temporary regimental H.Q., the driver hit the brakes, bringing the tormented vehicle to a halt.

Some of the windows of the building were intact, some were bordered with plywood. Mantled with snow, a statue of a man with his hand stretched upward was headless on its pedestal.

A frost-bitten-faced sentry exchanged salutes with Werter and let him in.

"To Oberst Martens. From Major Schuette." He left the dispatch with the Oberst's orderly, and after raising his hand in the "Hitler" salute, hastened outside.

Stamping his feet, with his hands pushed deep into his pockets, the driver stared at the church that was hit, but the tower with its magnificent onion dome was saved.

Werter, too, halted for a moment, taken again by the beauty of the half-destroyed cathedral then jumped into the sidecar. "Back, Obergefreiter, step on the gas."

A vague unrest that something must be happening there and he could not, was not able to prevent it, scorched him.

Serafima swallowed hard and boldly met the major's gaze.

He stood in the middle of the room, rocking on his heels. Directing his whip at the gelatinous claret substance on the floor, he licked his upper lip expressively. "So-o," he said with conjured tenderness.

She did not move.

"*Laß uns etwas ganz anderes versuchen,*—Let's try something quite different," he said to himself and smiled. Indicating by the motion of his head that she must take a seat at the table, he sat down himself and patted the seat of the chair next to him with his palm.

She raised her chin with a cool stare.

Her reaction seemed to amuse him because he uttered a small laugh. He pushed the plate with white bread and the marmalade jar over the table closer to her and snapped his fingers indicating the invitation.

Biting her lips nervously, she shifted from foot to foot and then, as though not trusting she could resist the temptation, she took an abrupt step back.

As if propelled by an explosive force, he lunged at her.

She leaped from him and grabbed the chair, holding it in front of her chest as a shield.

"Don't come near me!"

"*Ruhig, ruhig, Weibchen.*—Quiet, quiet, little female." His voice sounded like it might break into laughter at any moment again. He pressed with his hands against the table and pushed it aside. In a blitz motion, he snatched the chair from her and sent it flying to the stove. It overturned and fell down with a thud.

She scampered towards the stove where the poker rested against its wall.

He followed the direction of her eyes and an ironical smile crept over his face.

Ready to fight, she bunched her fists and stepped sideways, and the next moment he caught up her arm as she darted to the poker.

She broke off towards the door.

He blocked the doorway, spreading his arms wide, murmuring something playful like a loving father pretending to snare his child but failing.

Watching him intently, she pressed herself side-on against the wall and waited.

As though tired of the cat-and-mouse play, the expression on his face changed. An inexplicable look of withdrawal came over it.

"*Darf Ich gehen?*—Can I go?" Suddenly, she remembered the words learned in school.

His eyebrows rose in amazement and he stepped away from the door.

"*Danke*,—Thank you," she said, and the next moment even before she could take a step, he snatched her jacket, his fingers biting deeply into her shoulder, his steel-gray eyes searching her eyes, pleading obscenely.

With a violent jerk, she tore herself from him, but instantly his hand fell on her head. Her hair slipped between his fingers. "*Süßes Weibchen, süßes*

Weibchen,—Sweet little bitch, sweet little bitch," he muttered hoarsely into her face, alcohol-breath coming from him.

She screamed, trying to free her hair from his grab.

He let her hair go and threw her to the floor, towering over her, stripping the belt from his trousers then lowering to his knees and pressing her with his elbow to the floor.

She wrenched and yanked, beating into his chest, pushing against his shoulder, "Damn you! I'll stab you through your heart in the night!"

Clutching at her skirt, he jerked it up. The sound of torn fabric was clearly audible. He flung himself violently upon her. His words were dense and indistinct, like those of a drunkard as he was struggling his breeches down.

The loud knock at the door drew him up like a steel spring released.

Werter stopped mid-stride at the threshold and straightened slightly from a feeling of suffocation in order to draw more air into his chest. He was frightened by the tormenting evidence of his vague misdoubts as he watched Schuette hanging over the girl, his bleary eyes fixed on the girl's leg that was seen in the rent of her skirt.

Panting curses, Schuette thrust his arm, yanking her to her feet, and taking two steps backwards, said hoarsely, licking the sticky foam at the corners of his mouth, "Ask her what she was looking for!" He took out his handkerchief and wiped his hands fretfully.

The girl—at this moment he could not recall her name—pressed her back against the wall, shook her head, her teeth chattering, gulping and repeating in a groaning whisper, "Be damned, be damned, be damned."

He remembered hearing this word before, trying unsuccessfully to find it in his phrase book but now, he had to execute the major's order—translate his question. At last, he had found the right words and stuttered, "What did you look for?"

"Nothing. He lies." Her glance was the glance of a hunted animal, ready to strike back, and at the same time, despair in her eyes shocked him deeply.

"Tell him you wanted something to eat."

"It's all a lie!"

The look of the disgusted revulsion on her face, her eyes, which apparently could not, did not know how to lie, aroused in him an awkward kind of pity and surprise, and a feeling like shame, unexpected, stunning, struggled inside him. And he, simultaneously despising and accusing himself for his position, his inability to defend her, felt how his hands, against his will clenched into fists. "Say this lie," he said with a single expiration of breath.

"Lieutenant, what are you conversing about?" Schuette stared at him with a stern expression tinged with suspicion.

"She said she was looking for a piece of bread," he replied.

"Ah so-o," Schuette said, drawing out the word and striding towards the girl. "*Sie war hungrich, armes Ding. Der Dieb! Raus! Raus!—*She was hungry, poor thing. The thief! Out! Out!" he shouted and shook his head wildly in the direction of the door.

She convulsively squeezed together the flaps of her skirt torn along her thigh and stepped backwards to the door.

Seeing her disappear, Werter sighed, relaxing his clenched jaws.

A pitch-black night had fallen outside. Werter shuddered, listening to the unhappy neighing of the wind. It was whistling, lashing against the corner of the hut. The poplar's branches beat on the roof.

Why does Schuette hate the girl? Because he thinks she is a Jewess? But why then does he call her a sweet spoil of war? And he recalled how the major's eyes went blank with remembered lust when he talked about the women in France, Poland, and West Ukraine and how nice they were to German soldiers. Suddenly, it dawned upon him. *He hates her because she is not like those women.* A slight nausea rose to his throat, and he was aware of the pen trembling in his hand.

> *Dear Mutti, I had to lay my letter aside to carry out an urgent order from Major Schuette.*
>
> *It is barbarically cold here and I feel like thinking about our lovely house. Sometimes, in my dreams I think I feel the smell of violets that grew in the pot on the windowsill in your room. Do you still have them?*
>
> *Despite the fact that I have had no contact with the enemy yet, I have a high fighting spirit. We know what we are fighting for, and confident of the Führer, we will win. This is our duty to our land and our great people, our duty to the Führer and our God. Be proud that your son takes part in this greatest war in history.*
>
> *In the hopes of a victorious return,*
> *Your son Werter.*

He stared for a long time at the last sentences then carefully folded the paper above "*Despite the fact …*" and tore it off.

In the hopes of a soon return, Werter. He squeezed into the meager space that was left.

On a bitterly cold day of the second week of December, no usual chuckle from the henhouse was heard.

And sure enough, left without the every day treat of eggs, Werter peeked into the barn. "*Yaiki.*—Eggs."

"Nein yaiki," Serafima said. "The hens don't lay eggs in wintertime, what can I do?"

He expressed his incomprehension by twisting his face into a plaintive grimace and shook his head before closing the door.

Glafira looked at Serafima in fear. "He'll report to the major."

"Don't call him Major. Damned, that's what his name is!"

"God save—" Glafira crossed herself and broke into a spasm of coughing.

Soon after dusk had set, a beam of light fell through the cracks of the door, and then it screeched open. Werter poked his head forward. The circle of light wandered along the floor to the bed on which Serafima and Glafira rested and stopped its flickering for several seconds on Serafima's face.

He made two steps toward them then squatted to move aside planks under their bed. The next moment, his hand was clenching the pitchfork's round handle.

Serafima watched his eyes widen with alarm.

For a moment he studied her intently then got up and stepped to the corner where a jumble of sackcloth bags, a compressed pile of hay, sheaves of dried sunflower stalks, and ropes heaped up.

He pronged the hay here and there.

They waited. Stiff and silent, they followed the progress of his search.

Suddenly, he struck on something that rang.

They exhaled an audible "ah."

He shot an alerted side-glance at them and cautiously disjoined the wisps with his free hand. The earthed metal box they used as a cooler in summertime revealed itself.

"Eggs there?" He directed the flashlight into their faces.

Not getting any answer from them, he pulled the box at the handle and opened it.

They knew what he saw there: a few frozen potatoes and bulbs of onions, two corn-cobs, an empty small boxy glass jar that had held German strawberry marmalade some days before, and all that was left from Zor'ka—the last lead-like chunks of meat, and …

Despite penetrating cold, sweat was running down Serafima's spine. Glafira doubled on the bed, fighting an onset of coughing, clutching to her chest.

From the depth of the box, Werter pulled the hatchet at its shortened handle. With the pitchfork in one hand and the light and the hatchet in another, he exited, his steps faltering, as if he were drunk.

"Queen of heaven, forgive me my sins, our last day has come," Glafira said in a hissing whisper.

Surely, this is the end, Serafima thought and felt as empty as though only her skin was left and everything else was squeezed out of her. "Now I have only one dream, Mother. To get a hold of some hand grenades. Then I'd show those Fritzes …"

A cackling of the disturbed hen and a noise of shuffling was heard from the chicken-house and then heavy silence fell.

Serafima fought off sleep, for the darkness and her funk brought bitter regret. *I could kill them … Any night … Why did not I think of the hatchet?*

At four in the morning, scared cold, aware of the tiny hairs stiffening on the back of her neck, she slunk into the house with an armload of kindling. Wrapped up into their covers to their foreheads, the Germans seemed sound asleep.

The starting fire breathed out warm air. She briefly closed her eyes and immediately the pitchfork and the hatchet began to flash through her mind, and Zor'ka's chunks of meat, grayish, frozen chunks of meat. Keeping away from the major, she stole away on tiptoe.

"Wake up, wake up!"

Serafima awakened sharply, seeing her mother, blanched, pulling herself to her feet heavily. "What's there?" she wheezed, her eyes darting back and forth between Serafima and a linen bag with an imprinted eagle symbol at the door.

Teetering with fatigue, Serafima approached the bag and pulled at the knot, her fingers trembling. She looked inside. "Mother—" With difficulty she opened her frozen lips.

Glafira anxiously studied her face.

Tearing her gaze away from the contents of the sack, Serafima said again, "Mother—"

"What? What's there?" With fidgety small steps, Glafira approached her and bent over the bag. After she recovered from a fit of coughing, she smiled a simple, childlike smile. It was as though a ray of sunlight danced across an autumnal, rain swept field. "A manna from heaven."

They wolfed down some hefty bites of bacon covered with salt and chased them with a crust of real, fragrant white bread.

Eating just made them hungrier than ever. They kept putting the bag aside, but their hands always returned to it, and they would start supping again. Everything seemed a bit unreal.

"Enough. We leave the apple cake for tomorrow," Glafira said resolutely and tied up the lace. She pressed the bag to her chest, and so she sat unmoved for a minute or two. Then she jerked the lace open with a repressed urgency.

After swallowing two pieces of cake dusted with powdered sugar, their shrunken stomachs rebelled at the sudden onslaught of food.

Beneath their hurried steps, the snow crunched loudly like the grinding of teeth as they tried to shorten the distance to the outhouse.

When they returned to the barn, they both sat down on the bed, the empty bag lying between them. All of a sudden, they exhaled simultaneously. "He didn't denounce us."

A beam of a sunlight came through a chink in the wall. For a moment, they had an illusion of being free and … that they wouldn't be hungry again.

"He is not bad, this young lad, even if German." Glafira's face glowed.

Serafima looked at her. *Grateful for a meal from the hands that may be blood-stained.* It seemed to her that she suddenly felt nauseated again. She straightened up. "Why fool ourselves with dreams? We are captured and accursed!" She was silent for a time then got up slowly and dragged to the door. "Time to kindle the stove."

"I'll fetch brushwood." She heard her mother say.

The wind came in at once as she opened the door. The sun was rising, distended and red, over the bare poplar. She grabbed a load of branches and twigs, and as always, stopped before entering the house, feeling cold terror.

She let out a huge breath as she saw Werter alone in the room.

Their eyes met.

She grew embarrassed under his glance. "Th-thank you," she said.

Pressing one hand to his chest and coughing artificially, he shoved a tiny flat metal box in her pocket. "For your mother."

Deeply shaken, she looked at him. *Do they have human feelings, the Germans?*

December 13, 1941

At dawn, the booming sound of distant explosions came. This stopped, began again a few minutes later, then stopped, then began again.

Serafima peered through a chink in the barn wall. Aunty Anna, from the furthest house on the street, was running bent double under her bundles toward the forest. At her heels, the old Grunya who neighbored Anna's house hobbled, assisting herself with her knobby stick. The dry one-time sputtering of a machine gun sounded after them; the snow splashed up high from the impact of the bullets and dissolved into the sunlight.

She noticed a group of Germans by Anna's house. Suddenly, something blazed inside it and almost instantly, the entire hut was in the grip of greedy, whirling flames.

"Mother, they set Anna's house on fire!" Serafima shouted as she ran out the barn and to the house.

The front door stood ajar. She stepped hesitantly in. Some newspapers were strewn over the floor, the empty glass bottles lay overturned every which way about the table.

She lowered on the bench and half-closed her eyes as if charmed by the emptiness of the house. Almost immediately, at the troubling thought that the Germans may return, she pulled herself together and stormed outside.

"Mother, quickly to the forest, quickly!"

They ran over the field, stumbling and falling, scraping their hands over the frozen crust. The crackling of the shots lent wings to their feet.

Some fifteen paces away from the fringe of the forest, Glafira halted. Her face changed as though suddenly torn by helpless anguish. She dropped on her knees and raised her arms toward Heaven. "It's a sin. It's a sin, God won't pardon us."

"What's the sin, Mother?"

"We can't let them burn the image of our only God. My mother prayed in front of it and my grandparents, and theirs, too. Think of God, *he* won't overlook it. Run back, save the icon, save us from the mortal sin."

Serafima flinched.

The same moment, Grunya's hut went ablaze.

"Why do you stay as if struck dumb? You'll manage before they—"

The words lashed Serafima like a whip. She listened with grating teeth, struggling with herself. With faltering step, she turned to the house.

There was no wind. Not a breeze, and two smoke pillars stood like props between the snowy slush of the ground and the sky of hazy blue. After an unexpected thaw of the previous day, the fog was settling in, becoming rapidly denser. It already reached to the neck and was billowing and seething coldly.

She bent forward, sank into the protection of the fog, and with uncertain, stumbling feet ran toward the village. The sharp sound of accursed tongue reached her indistinctly and then the next hut flashed. Burning embers flew in all directions above the fog's surface. In all her being, she felt that something terrible, irreparable would follow.

Another short run and she burst into the house. She thought she heard the noise of a motor outside, close, very close. For a long moment, she stood stock still listening. No, it was blood hammering into her ears.

She darted to the stove, bent to pull a plank, and there it was, The Christ Almighty. She jerked the icon out from below a plank, got up, and looked around. A beam of light reflected from a smooth surface of the harmonica that lay carelessly upon the cluttered table. For a second, she forgot why she was here and she grinned. Without hesitation, she seized harmonica and slipped it into her pocket.

"Ah ha!" A voice that sharply enunciated "a" struck at her neck, ringing with harsh power and something predatory.

She jerked her head, cringed, turned, and saw *them* in the doorway. A momentary burning wave of dark horror and blinding hate for these Fritzes, their mouse-gray greatcoats, their eyes, full of a cold gray light, the open smirk of the major scorched her.

"Now we'll roast this sweet little chicken. Aah, what do you say, my boy?" the major shifted his gaze from her to Werter.

She didn't understand what he said, but what she saw were his flung open arms and his hands bristled with blond hairs right down to the knuckles.

"Don't come near me, you!" she hissed. Suddenly, she knew that in an instant the life that pulsed strong and healthy through her veins would cease forever—but she stood there calmly as if it were nothing, and she were only a little chilly in the cold room.

She heard the youth stuttering, "Harmonica." He stretched his hand to her with his palm up. Something arose in his face, something humble and despairing.

"We have something better here, sonny. You'll enjoy it." The major winked at the youth and took a step to her.

She threw back her head and spit square in his face. The spittle did not hit its mark, but stuck in a white spot on his chest.

He wiped it away with his white handkerchief. The skin on his temples tightened as he gave a half-grin. "Little bitch." He turned to Werter. "Take her. Take her as a sweet present of war!"

She did not understand what they were arguing about and only saw Werter's face pale, heard his stammering, "Nein, Herr Major, nein."

Clutching painfully at the icon, gripped by an unfamiliar savagery that had exploded in her, catching only a glimpse of the major's narrowed eyes, his wolfish expression, as if aroused by the sight of blood, she threw herself at him. She smashed him with hatred and enjoyment on his bony, chattering jaw, injecting into this blow something hot and bubbling in her heart that had boiled in her since the very first day he intruded into her life.

The icon broke in two and fell with a dull bang on the floor.

His mouth distorted by a spasm of fright or by surprise at the sight of her sudden resistance, and for a brief moment she saw a thin streak of blood on his jaw, black in the dim room.

Instantly, his right hand fell with implacable insane speed to his waist, tearing the pistol from the leather of his holster. Strange—the steel glitter of the pistol did not arise fear in her—on the contrary, some spring of hate compressed to frenzy, and flung her blindly, irrepressibly and furiously toward him again.

A terrible blow on the head tore the ground from her feet and flung her towards the floor. The walls swayed sideways, shadows darted above her, and someone's ferocious yell transfixed her. Instantly, the face and a wildly gaping fish-like mouth vanished somewhere behind the blanket of fog reeking of gunmetal.

When booming sounds of distant explosions, separate and distant, reached Serafima's consciousness, the barely visible objects around her began anchoring her to the sensible world.

Her head spun. Round and round the floor beneath her tilted. Round and round reeled images of the day, a windmill whirl of them—the houses on fire, the harmonica, the major's inflamed eyes, bulging with malice, and his black, open, gasping mouth staggering forward, grinning victoriously to reveal strong healthy teeth.

The smell of burning seeped in.

With an effort, she drew her hand up to her temple and felt her blood-clotted hair. *Why this terrible headache? It is so cold here. Why am I on the floor?* This went through her mind in a shadowy stream. *No, it isn't all a dream. After all, that did happen. That young German with gray eyes, like Vitya's, wanted to have his harmonica, yes, yes, I took it from him.* And then the face—repulsive, loathsome—blinded all other images. *The major!*

At last, she struggled onto her hands and knees. Her trembling arms could hardly bear her. Swaying, she scrambled to her feet.

In the washbasin, she found some clear water. Her face stared back at her from the surface. It looked strange. She splashed it. The water turned red. Then she looked down at herself—her skirt was torn, a thin trickle of blood making its way on the inner side of her thigh into her high boot. She washed it too.

She stepped out into the street that was dismal and dead. The disabled carcasses of Wehrmacht vehicles lay scattered in a haze of whirling smoke. In the rents of the murk, slightly parted by the freshened current of air, what was left of the huts and the charred trees loomed. Their twigs and smaller branches had been burned away; the stumps and a few of main branches still rose into the air. They looked like immense black hands stretched up out of the earth toward the sky.

In the entire village, only two houses were spared by fire. *What if they come back, the damned Fritzes? To burn these houses, too?*

She heard heavy breathing, listened closely, and then realized that it was she herself who was breathing so loud. The field, pock-marked with shells, plunged and shook beneath her, throwing her from side to side. She fell, gashed her knee, then stood up on unsteady legs, and dropped again on all fours. The last meters to the forest, she crawled like a half-killed animal, her face almost touching the ground.

Somebody's arms stretched out, helping her to get up to her feet. "What happened? We thought they killed you."

"Give me the icon!" Glafira demanded in a shrill voice.

Serafima turned around. "What icon?" She heard a strange, sobbing sound resembling laughter mixed with suppressed tears in her throat. The irrepressible weeping was choking her, tearing her chest apart. Suffocating, swallowing this weeping, she saw in the middle of the gray, fluid emptiness the cold face of her mother and another face … the major's.

"Glafira, let her alone. Don't you see she isn't quite …" a woman said.

No longer able to stand, Serafima leaned against the trunk of a pine, feeling a trembling of her legs and the iron bitterness in her mouth. With swimming eyes, she saw women gathering around her, and it was beyond her will to understand how and why she was there.

She heard them speak, but their words floated away from her. It was as if her brain, already choked by the day's horrors, had refused to absorb any more. She felt a strong hand seizing her elbow and a voice reached her consciousness: "For goodness sake, you are wounded. Let's go inside."

The same hands helped her to crawl into the dugout and lowered her down on the hay. The women, sitting on the benches, huddled against each other. Their faces looked gray and hollow, as though frozen.

The woman returned with a snowball wrapped in a piece of fabric. "I'll press it to your temple. You try to sleep," she said softly.

Serafima closed her eyes. As if from a long distance, she heard women howl their prayers—"God is merciful, all-bountiful ... infinitely kind and just, and for us carried his heavy cross ... God show yourself. Save us, God. We believed in you ..." and those pleadings to God mixed with crude curses, "Oh, blast them! The devil curse them!"

An indistinct thought spun like a monotonously flickering roundabout in the dim emptiness, dizzy, revolting, leaving an unresolved desire to understand. Why, where it had come from and why this feeling as though she had done something shameful, disgraceful, for which there was no forgiveness or justification?

She gathered herself up into a ball, hunched, inhaling the scent of sodden pinecones and the cloying sweetness of damp straw that reminded her of something familiar, but she could not perceive of what.

"Vitya! Beloved," she groaned, tossing herself about. "You see … you said they wouldn't come … dearest, you left the harmonica …" Striving to master her pain and horror, she began talking unintelligibly, as though oppressed by something. "Our waltz … Oh God … it burns … I feel … I am dying."

"Lord Jesus …" someone sighed in the darkness of the dugout.

An impenetrable darkness closed over her and not a single human voice stole in.

The day dawned gray and wet.

The front had suddenly come alive. From behind the woods, on the right, came the sound of an outburst. Three more followed, quick and nearer. Artillery shells arched across the sky. The fire got heavier and more regular. The banging of mines could be heard. Soon the wind brought the smell of explosives.

The women huddled to each other at the entrance of the dugout. Their eyes moved in the same direction. They listened and it was not only their ears that listened—it was also the bowed shoulders, the thighs, the knees, the braced arms and hands. They listened motionlessly, and only their eyes followed the sound as though they were obeying an inaudible command.

Suddenly, six planes with red stars flying wing to wing appeared in the sky—six fighters.

"There they are!"

"It's our boys!"

The women crossed themselves and kept praying, "Our Father, Who Art in Heaven, Hallowed be Thy Name, Thy Kingdom Come ..." their voices trailing into whisper.

Behind Serafima's head and her ears, ringing with fever, the battle went on. By late afternoon, the vehicles of rear-guard artillery companies and the carts and wagons of the medical corps packed the only street of the village.

Serafima lay in a big tent among the wounded soldiers. A dead-weary doctor came, looked at her, and left without doing anything.

The field hospital stayed in the village for two days and then moved on.

*E*astern Front
Den 19. Dezember, 1941

Liebe Mutti,

I received your package. Thank you for your cookies with pink icing. I enjoyed them immensely. The warm wool socks and gloves are more than needed here. My special appreciation for them.

Several days ago, a flame-throwing unit of two arrived in the village where our squad was stationed. The order was that, while moving to another position, everything had to be destroyed. The Ivan's' offensive was so fierce that there was not enough time to burn all the houses. The house we occupied was spared from fire if only the artillery attack of their own did not destroy it later.

At least, I got my baptism of fire. A hot wave of blood shot through my heart and pulled me forward. I do not remember the details of the butchery. We ran forward like homicidal maniacs, Major Schuette in front of us, with his handgun over his head. We shot, slashed, and beat. We fell down, got up, and stormed forward again. When we beat the Russian attack off, a series of explosions ripped through the air beside us. My

*first sight of a dead soldier was an unexpected
shock, but the death of Major Schuette ..."*

He set the pen aside and buried his face in his hands.
I cannot and may not write everything.

Schuette. In his mental eye, he could still see him
with absolute clarity. His peaked cap and a piece of
his head were sent flying, and he fell backward with
a horrifying cry. Schuette's shattered skull crashed
into his hands, and he, and others close to him, were
splattered with blood and fragments of flesh.

Holding back a scream, he had buried his face in the
dirt. He had a feeling the shrapnel that killed Schuette
might have been intended for him.

*He has fallen like a hero on the field of honor
for Germany and for the Führer. My heart aches
when I think of his loved ones—his mother, wife,
and his teenage son. He had just shown me the
new pictures of them, received that very morning
with a letter from home.*

He caught himself frowning, feeling as though
somebody or something made him write these words
despite their falseness, like a man who defends something he does not believe himself any more. From either
the cold or his disquieting thoughts, he shivered.

The weather turns cold rapidly. The thermometer gradually creeps to twenty degrees below zero.

It must be still warm in Berlin. Is your rose geranium blossoming? I remember rubbing its dark green leaves between my hands smelling its strong perfume. I hope to be back home soon, having breakfasts with you and Gerdi at our kitchen table with a blue and white checked tablecloth, drinking your exceptional coffee with hot milk and munching your honey rolls. Lately, we have ersatz coffee but were told the good one will soon arrive.

I will write you more as soon as we have a stable position.

For now, I send you and Gerdi my love.

Dein Sohn Werter.

December 20, 1941

The howling storm broke again and again on the frosty windowpanes with a harsh violence, but inside the house, the stove was glowing, the dying fire cracking and spitting.

Dunyasha ran in, breathing heavily, sweeping off the lumps of snow from her padded jacket and headscarf. "How is she, Aunty Glafira?"

"She won't make it ..." Glafira was silent for a while then repeated. "She won't. Don't you see she's not long for this world?" She turned from the stove. "There is a letter from your brother to her. Look up there, on the table. Want to take it?"

"Sure." Dunyasha shifted her feet then darted to the bed. "Later. I'll take it later." She put her hand on Serafima's forehead and gasped. "Aunty Glafira, I think she has no fever."

"Oh yeah—" Glafira stirred up the smoldering coals with a poker then headed to the exit, unhooking her sheepskin overcoat and the scarf while moving. "I'll bring more kindling."

Their words did not reach Serafima through the dark shroud swathing her consciousness, deadened by the beautiful melody of the Strauss' waltz. *Harmonica*, a thought broke through. She swallowed air and half-opened her eyes. The room was enveloped in a spider of uncertain whitish light. Things grew slowly out of shadows, so slowly they seemed distorted. Her eyes wandered over The Christ Almighty icon in the corner of veneration—its two parts tied up with a rope, then to a small window faintly lit by a beam from the thin scythe of a new moon, and then to a girl who perched upon the edge of her bed with her head bowed. She wept silently, rocking back and forth.

Serafima tried to recall all that was associated with her. "Who are you? Where am I?" She heard her own voice coming from far off.

"Oh God." Dunyasha lifted her face and clasped her hands to her chest. "Serafimushka, home, home you are and I'm Dunyasha, don't you know me?" She grabbed Serafima's hand then jumped and ran to the table whooping with joy.

Against her will, Serafima's eyes turned to The Christ Almighty again and as if to work free of the view of the icon and the pictures that were called up by it, she passed her hand across her eyes.

"Look, there is a letter from Vitya!" Dunyasha said.

"Vitya?"

"Yes, Vitya, your Vitya, our Vitya. I will read to you, let me read to you." Brushing the tears away, Dunyasha unfolded a grayish three-cornered piece of paper that was not sealed. "Listen.

Serafima, not a single letter from you. Dunyasha does not write me, too."

She stopped, shaking her head. "Not true, not true, I've sent him three letters. He must just not have received them. Oh what I'm talking about. Listen.

"*The Sovinformbureau reports recounted that your area has been occupied by Germans. Can you imagine how heavy my heart was? Are you alive? Yes, you are! I know. I feel this. Now that your village is free from the damned fascists, I hope to receive your letter soon.*"

She read in patter, gulping words, then going back to repeat.

"*If you bear me a grudge for what happened in the dugout the last time, please forgive me.*"

She stopped suddenly, holding her breath.

"Give me the letter." Serafima almost snatched it from Dunyasha's hand then sat up, ever so slowly, holding still until the thumping in her head beat more quietly.

Every day, I think about it. The images flow into my mind. But if I return home, then I know one thing: as long as I live, you'll be the only woman I'll ever love.

We pursue the enemy away from Moscow and we will turn them out of our country.

Soon life will change and I will do my best for you to forget what evil tried to destroy our lives and I cannot wait till I call you my wife. We will have many children but first you will give me a son. Promise?

Something else: be assured that I love only you. I remember every minute of our time together and long to get back to you. Please think of me often, and know that in my life I have only done my duty, nothing but my duty.

Now, I have to finish. If you see my sister tell her my reproach for not writing to me.

Your Victor.

"Send him my letter immediately. He must be worried to death," Serafima's voice broke miserably. "Look up on the shelf. It must be there, in a book."

Dunyasha went to the bookshelf. She rummaged through the few books and the Gospels, muttering under her nose, "Not here … Not here." She turned to face Serafima. "There is no letter."

"But how is it possible! Why do you say 'no letter'? I've written a letter, I remember!" She got up to her feet, swayed, a purplish haze with light and dark circles floating before her. "I remember." Weak with her effort, she fell back on the bed and instantly fell asleep, pressing Vitya's letter to her chest.

Eastern Front
Den 24. Dezember, 1941

Meine liebe Mutter!

You can't imagine how delighted I was today: in the morning, we marched into a village, and in the prepared quarters lay on a table two of your letters. They tore me away from the reality of the war, if only for a brief time.

It's the most beautiful night of the year. From the army radio resound the familiar Christmas melodies. In the course of this one forgets reality, the earth frozen solid, the desolate villages, the noise of battle. In the bunker stove, a warming fire crackles. We even have a glittering, decorated Christmas tree. We drank a bottle of wine, ate some cookies, smoked a cigarette. We showed each other the photographs of our loved ones. All our thoughts were at home. Then my comrades asked me to play mouth harmonica, and we sang, "Silent Night, Holy Night."

My God! How wonderful this holy night at home would be. As always, Gerda and I would play violin and you accompany us on piano. All dreams. They are so sweet if you can stretch your hands closer to the burning oven. The reality is that we are brutalized and defeated by the cold, at minus 25 degrees Celsius and snowstorms such as no one in Germany knows. The flesh on our faces and ears would freeze if we left it exposed for very long, and our fingers freeze even in gloves. My hands are ruined for music.

Mom, you write that you admire my strength, but you don't know the whole, what inundates me in the nights. My thoughts keep returning to the events at that village that was set afire, to that girl, her name is Serafima. It hammers at me in my sleep and I am haunted by the feeling that I am no longer the "good" person I once thought I was. I know they are subhumans, Bolshevik subhumans. This idea is pressed into my mind and soul. One must not allow any sympathy to grow for these people. I have to be pitiless and relentless. However, I can't stop thinking that there is punishment for every person who does evil to others. And that shrapnel that killed Major Schuette might very well have been intended for me.

Sorry, Mama; instead to unburden your heart from concerns about me I make you worry even stronger.

Dein Sohn.

He sealed the letter and looked dully at the envelope.

At first, he did not realize that he was dreaming. Slowly the room assumed a different shape; it began turning into a street with filthy huts and charred trees, then into a barn fragrant with rotting straw. He recognized the girl with black blazing eyes lying on the floor and heard her saying gently, "Prokliaty. Prokliaty." And he thought, he knew the meaning of the word: "The damned one." In his dream, he lived again and again through that day and even felt the shuddering convulsion in his body. He would awake and drive the dream off violently, shading his painfully screwed-up eyes with his hand. "The damned one, the damned one," he repeated silently.

A terrible crushing raised him from his uneasy sleep.

Toward the end of March of nineteen forty-two, the weather turned mild. For a week a southern wind blew, warming the earth. The thaw had eaten away the snow; a month earlier, it was four yards deeper. April brought sluggish, sultry winds. Suddenly it froze again for several days and then melted. The first timid snowdrops showed their blue buds, here and there.

At an unearthly hour, Serafima would go off to the neighboring little city where at the war-effort factory, in a twelve-hour shift seven days a week, together with other workers, she produced details for armored troops.

Every day was the same.

In the early morning of April 17, tearing her eyes from the lathe, Serafima caught sight of Semenich, nicknamed "One-legged," their supervisor. He approached Aksyushka, shouting something in her ear against the roar of the grinding machines and smiling the tender smile he always kept for women. It instantly changed into an angry frown as the girl shook her head in denial.

She saw him move his fur cap to scratch the glaring bare patch on the top of his head then touch his Stalin moustache as though adjusting it on his face. He did not conceal how proud of it he was and kept it carefully brushed. Whenever he passed a mirror or a window, he always stopped to look at it, provoking the women-workers' smiles or sneers. He had a pug nose, a tawny shade of brown eyes and girlishly lascivious lips, which added to the appearance that had nothing to do with a commanding manner utterly purposeful for a post he was assigned to in the first month of the war.

Lucky, if only missing a leg was a right assumption, he was spared from the front by a misfortune that sent him under a tram in his rowdy youth, about twenty years ago.

His wooden leg, stamping and creaking, announced he was behind her back. "Serafima, come with me."

She stopped her lathe and screwed up her face. "What is it, Semenich?"

The next moment, his hand darted and pinched her on her butt. "Oh what a tempting girl you are. Would I meet you one day on a dark street—" His lips parted by a half-smirk that exposed his tobacco-stained front teeth.

"Semenich, stop it," she said, annoyed, sliding out of his reach.

"Let's carry that box to the foundry."

They strode to the metal box pressed against the wall and each grabbed one handle.

"One, two, three!" he gave out an order.

They lifted it up a bit.

"Oh!" She felt a twinge in her belly, right under her heart and let the handle go. In a delirium of terror, she leaned against the wall and slowly slipped down on the floor. Her eyes were swimming, and she saw Semenich as a blurred and shifting silhouette.

"Serafima, stop playing games with me. Come on, girl, come to yourself." She heard the stamping of his wooden leg, then, "Hey, somebody, *yob*, —fuck, bring liquid ammonia from the portable medicine chest!" He added a few more strong curses.

Serafima felt his hands working her cheeks, heard his shriek voice, felt the other women join him, but the shock of comprehension was unbearable—the morning sickness that turned her weak and dizzy, those strange moves inside her stomach, which she had attributed to the constant hunger. *God, no, no, please!* She tried to persuade herself that none of *this* was happening, that it was all a nightmare from which she would wake up to see another normal day.

As if she had cotton in her ears, women's voices came from a great distance off.

"She is with child."

"No, that's from hunger."

"Don't think so. Looks like she put on some weight lately."

"Hunger, you say? Look at her middle."

"One can swell up from hunger, too," another insisted.

"Stupid woman you are. You who have reared four children."

They laughed discreetly.

"Her husband must be on the front, I fancy."

"What husband? She's not married. What, you didn't know?" another interrupted mockingly.

"The child can be Vit'ka's, I fancy."

"From the hardware shop?"

"No, from the District Komsomol Committee. The good-looking one. What a guy! And what could he have seen in her? She's got no bottom or belly."

"I don't care that he is such an important figure. If they are not married, she is a shameless hussy!"

"Ha, what do you expect? She's Glafira's daughter. Herself out of wedlock. Like mother like daughter."

"The whore, her bitch of a mother didn't beat her enough." One clicked her tongue disgustedly.

"Dear, oh dear, oh dear. How awful," another female voice said sympathetically, but with a certain gloomy relish.

Again, she heard the creaking of Semenich's artificial leg. "*Yob!* Cut your jawing and go back to work," he snapped irritably.

He waved an ammonia stick under her nose.

She moved her head away and glanced up from a half doze. Several pairs of eyes peered at her from above. She rose onto all fours, pushing her hands down to the hard cold floor, wobbled to her knees, dizzily, got up, and waded back to her lathe.

The women dropped away.

"Need something to lift, call upon me." Semenich stumped after her. "And don't listen to these goddamned magpies."

When the siren announced the end of the shift, she rushed out of the shop. Everyone seemed to be staring at her, and she fancied hearing them whisper behind her back.

Serafima stepped out into the street. It was getting dark, and all of a sudden, her fear for a decision she had to make came upon her. All day she tried to escape from it. But now, in the uncertain light, it seemed to creep upon her out of every corner.

All at once, her heart seemed to beat so loudly that for a moment she feared the women who caught up with her might hear it. Behind her back, she heard a whispered, "Ah, my dear, a dog doesn't worry an unwilling bitch," and a muffled giggle followed.

The calculated insult came like a blow. Stumbling over the uneven stones, she quickened her steps to the gatekeeper's office with her head sunk on her breast.

She walked aimlessly down the street, turning over an unformulated decision in her mind.

At the far end of the town, dogs, disturbed by her presence, barked in chorus. Where the road forked to Gamishovo, she stopped, chewing the ends of her kerchief, choking with tears, with torment, with the dreary emptiness that lashed through her heart.

It had grown foggy. The trunks of the trees stood in the haze as dark as though made of coal.

What should I do? A quiver in her stomach shook her from her stupor. She ran stumbling over the muddy road.

After half an hour's wandering, she halted before a small, dilapidated straw-thatched hut. Time had set its hands upon it—the roof was sinking, the walls were awry, the shutters hung loosely.

In the darkness of the hall, she banged her knee against something. Unconscious of the pain, panting with agitation, she raised her hand several times to knock at the inner door, but each time, her hand fell as though struck away. When at last she did knock, she tapped at first with her finger, but then, resolutely, beat at the door with her fist.

"Come in," a weak voice reached her ears.

With her heart violently beating, she bent down and stumbled over the doorstep. Inside, it was warm and smelled of over-sour hops and old human flesh. A flickering glow of a candlestick produced weak light. "Good health to you," she said.

"Who's this?" The old woman rose up a bit from her bed, staring at her askance, squinting.

"Serafima, Glafira's daughter. Good health to you, Aunty Agafia."

"Holy fathers! Serafima! Come closer, my angel," she replied. "Why, Serafima, the devil himself wouldn't know you! Look at the girl you've turned out to be. But now, what do you want at this time of night? Don't tell me, you …"

Blinking her tear-filled eyes and trying to restrain the irresistible trembling of her lips, Serafima put a small parcel on the slimy unclothed table with unwashed utensils. "Here is my week's ration. Aunty Agafia, dear, help me." She fell on her knees. "Whatever it costs, I'll give you … My last piece of bread I'll give you, only help me!"

The old woman chewed away with her withered mouth. "My little girl, I'm done with helping girls out. I'm almost blind. No, no, no such things any more." She rose from her ragged bedclothes, crossed herself to the black icon and smacked her lips disconsolately. "Like mother like daughter … As if it was yesterday, I remember your mother exactly at this very spot, of a mind to get rid of you after she sinned with that gipsy man …" She shook from side to side and sighed dreamily. "The best blacksmith in the vicinity he was. The men took their horses to him to shoe, the men as far as Kalinovka and Gradikovo. Horses liked him, were not afraid of him. Not only that, handsome he was! The girls from the neighborhood … Oh, and when he took the guitar in his hands—" She tsked and closed her eyes as if savoring the picture in her mind. "The girls marveled at him. And what could he have seen in your mother? We've got better looking girls going …" Her voice trailed. "Ooooh, jealous the local men were of him. Ivan, you may know his son, Vit'ka. I've heard he's a big figure now, a leader of something, don't know what. That Ivan, he, the blockhead, thought his Katherinka became pregnant from the gipsy. When angry, he completely lost control of himself, beat Katherinka, the fiend. Once the blacksmith saw it, he stood up for her. Showed his greatness. That was a hand-to-hand fight!" She chuckled. "But what for? She was not guilty, Katherinka, I mean, God's truth. I myself delivered the baby. Dunyashka, you may know her, she was born a month after you appeared on this earth. Both Vit'ka and Dunyashka, in face and figure are like their father, Ivan. Katherinka was not guilty, your mother was. That I can say. You are after him, the gipsy—at least I don't know anybody else in the neighboring villages with such beautiful gipsy eyes as yours." She smiled, displaying her crooked black teeth beneath the pucker of her lips. "Glad I refused to rid Glafira of you. But what for? As he learned about her pregnancy, he vamoosed. So what, why are you here? Did your cavalier disappear too?"

Serafima jumped up as though on springs and ran out of the room.

"Your bag!" Agafia's voice calling reached her indistinctly.

On the porch, Serafima vomited violently.

The wind had suddenly sprung up and the fog began to heave and roll like a noiseless, ghostly sea. A few crows flapped about like dark rags.

A terrifying realization washed over her. She had known it, the way one knows many things—without actually realizing them or completely feeling them— that there was no other way, and the decision was there at once, big and full of a chill horror and at the same time a relief.

At the barn door Serafima took breath and then entered, stumbling over the doorstep, biting her lips till the blood came. Through the lilac darkness, counters of the overhead beams and a bench emerged uncertainly out of the gloom, and the musty aroma of hay came to her nostrils. A mouse making its way through the straw broke the drowsy silence. Just for a fleeting moment, she remembered what fun it was as a child to climb over the haystack at the end of the summer and snooze in its fragrant warmth. Only for a second, she forgot about her decision.

Slut, returned hammering as a metronome to her head. *Like mother like daughter. Slut. Like mother like daughter. Slut …*

With evil determination, she gathered her last strength and gropingly, in a somber yearning, which scratched at her shamed and despairing soul, made her way to a corner. She picked up the cord with which they used to tie Zor'ka. It proved to be too short. She went outside, unfastened a linen rope strung from the house to the barn, tied it together with the cord, testing it for firmness, and made a noose. Back into the barn, she lowered herself on the old bench.

Her head seemed to be filled with a milky fog, which suddenly had everything make no difference to her. She could think of her own death without flinching, as a soothing veil that would fall slowly over her and all her terrors of the past, present, and future.

At least it will be over. No more scornful looks, shrewd tongues, and most of all, no damned bastard.

With all the force and resolution that possessed her, she threw the rope over the cross-beam, mounted the bench beneath the noose, and climbed on its shaky surface. She unbuttoned her collar, and without the tremor of a muscle, set the rope around her neck. Suddenly, a violent shiver engulfed her whole body and the bench slipped from beneath her feet. The knot, gripping her throat, choked her. The sound of the breaking cross-beam crawled into the silence of the moment. The cold floor hit her hard. She felt herself gliding and falling, down, down through the ground.

Mournfully realizing that she had not completely carried out her intention, she struggled on to all fours.

"Serafima! You there?" Dunyasha's joyful voice came from outside. The barn door creaked. "Serafima?" The light of the new moon penetrated the dimness. Dunyasha's face glimmered pale in the darkness as she peered inside. For a second, Serafima thought she saw Vitya there.

And then, "No! No! Oh-h-" died away in a gasp. Dunyasha threw herself on her as if trying to defend her from a blast of a bomb. "Why? Serafimushka, why?" she cried with incomprehension. "Vitya will marry you. You'll see, he comes back, he will marry you. And he'll be so happy indeed. So happy." She was caressing Serafima's hair, her face, seeking her hand as if wanting to assure herself her friend was alive. "I know, I've already heard. Don't give a damn for anything the wives are chattering about—in one ear and out another."

"No, no, no … He won't marry me, he won't." Serafima's teeth chattered and her throat was closed by dry spasms of irreparable guilt and despair.

The incident at the factory caused a great deal of talk. The rumors spread like wildfire. And though no one had seen where, under what circumstances and when Serafima and Victor met outside the Komsomol meetings, womenfolk guessed from the outset she had sinned with him—as though someone had set a mark, burned a brand on her face.

In no time, the gossips reached Glafira's ears.

Serafima winced as the front door banged open.

"You goddamn little tramp! Wasn't it enough for me to carry my own sin?" Glafira's voice, trembling with boiling rage, entered before she herself was in the room. "Now I have to carry yours!" She went right up to her. "Stupid! Fool! How do you get rid of it? Go, get to Agafia. She can help you."

"She didn't help you," Serafima shouted.

"I wish she did!" Glafira swung her arm and slapped Serafima across the face. "You'll go through it yourself, you are branded, and your unborn bastard is already branded, too. That's all your goings off to the woods." She stood in thought a moment, looking at her hand, her lips moving silently as she counted fingers. "Too late. Stupid! Stupid!"

Her words hung in the quiet room like a fog over a damp field.

Serafima raised her eyes, and her stare crossed with her mother's hateful, scornful gaze.

"Here, from your Romeo." Glafira jerked something from her pocket. She thrust into Serafima's hand a piece of gray, pulp paper folded in a triangle with their address in the handwriting that she knew so well. "My own one, my good one," she said in a voice chocked with angry mockery. "Pray to God that he comes from the war alive and that he marries you." She glared at Serafima as if to imprint her words on her brow, then made off toward the door. On the threshold, she stopped and without turning back muttered, "Heaven help you."

Serafima unfolded the letter.

Xx Field Post, 1ˢᵗ Unit

Serafima, my own one, my good one. Today, I received Dunyasha's letter dated December 24. It grieved me deeply and was a great relief at the same time because you are alive! If you would be taken away from me, I don't know what I would do. Do you know that you mean everything to me?

Hard battles with the enemy everywhere. I'm not afraid of anything—I have you. I'm the most fortunate man in the world and I can't see how I deserve it at all. With your love, I feel as if I could go through the seven fires of hell and come out alive.

I am longing to see you, if only for one hour, but it is out of the question until we win the war.

You will never, never know how I love you. Please take care of yourself; you'll do it for our sakes, won't you?
Your Victor.

She read the letter again and again, first with her eyes then aloud. *Maybe he will*—She shuddered the thought and the hope away.

In the following two months, Serafima went about, did things, ate and slept, but always as if in a stupefying, narcotic daze.

Every morning, with unseeing eyes, she walked along the same rode to the blocks of the red brick factory buildings with girdered rooflines and the sooty dark gridded windows. Strangely, only the cold metal of the lathe handle and its buzz, and the monotonous movements of her hands helped her to forget—forget what was coming.

On one of these days, with a side-glance, she saw Semenich approach one woman-worker after another, yelling something over the noise of the turning instruments, bending over the boxes with scrap.

"Serafima!" She suddenly heard his voice close by, and the next moment he seized her by the sleeve. "Stop the machine. Let's go out to have a talk."

"What about my work plan, brigadier?"

He made an annoyed jerk with his head.

"As you order, Semenich."

Shoulder to shoulder, they went off to the corridor followed by ironical glances of the women.

"Such a thing, girl. Er … tomorrow, I'll send you an apprentice, Mashka, my wife's younger sister. It's not fair—" He cleared his throat and looked expressively at Serafima's midriff. "She is a strong girl. Teach her, and then … Well, I've settled it for you."

"What did you settle?" Serafima stiffened.

"Er … that you take Mashka's place in the Quality Department."

Tears sprung to her eyes, hot, unexpected. "You're the only one who likes me here, Semenich." She leaned forward and placed a peck on his cheek.

He flinched away and went purple in the face. "Leave it, you stupid girl!" He twisted his head round. "Now go. Complete your output. And don't you pay attention to the old wives' nonsense." He tugged his gray row linen cap down and repeated with an edge to his voice, "The stupid old wives' nonsense."

The next day, the round-faced Mashka, a short girl of sixteen, stood in front of Serafima with an air of resentment. She did not say a word through all the time Serafima demonstrated to her how to grab a metal strip from the big wooden box, then quickly pull it under the cutter, move the handle down, and instantly push the part away and into the other wooden box. Instead, she studied Serafima from head to toe through her narrowed eyes.

"Want to try?" Serafima looked at her sidewise.

"I wonder why is Semenich so fond of you?" she said contemptuously and glanced at Serafima's bump hardly noticeable under her heavy padded jacket.

"Blockhead you are. Come closer, here, try." She stepped aside, giving way in front of the lathe for the girl. "Tomorrow, you'll be on your own."

"And you … you are stealing my place," Mashka snapped out.

The following day, Serafima went to the factory management, got her new assignment to the job, and was met with a dead silence by the women at her new work place.

During the 12 p.m. break, she went to find Semenich.

"Here." She pushed a little parcel into his hand.

"You don't come close to me, girl. Had I not enough quarrel yesterday with my wife? What's that you are shoving onto me?" Demonstratively, he put his hands behind his back. "What's that? Bread?"

"Vodka."

"Are you out of your head, girl? Don't shame me. Barter it for bread or … whatever. You have to eat properly. Properly!" Half concealed by the cap, his forehead shone with abundant sweat. "And don't approach me any more. They denounce, in no time, daughters of the bitch!"

With trembling lips, Serafima watched him stumping away.

Through a soft fabric of his tunic, Victor fingered the small copper cross hidden in his breast pocket. *Serafimushka.* The image slashed as a razor's edge—her imploring eyes, her trembling fingers as she slipped the string with the cross over his neck. He thought he could still feel the warmth of her whispered entreaty, "Oh Lord, defend him and save him, cover him with Thy wings …"

I'm still alive. Does her charm really work? A cold shiver spread over him.

He slipped his greatcoat over his shoulders. The early May sun could not penetrate the thick of the pinewood, and the forester's hut kept the coolness of the unheated space and an earthy smell of decay.

From his map case, he took out a sharp lead pencil and opened the notebook at a blank page.

May 11, 1942

My dear, cherished, darling!

He stopped, listening closely to the indistinct rumbling and thunder of the battle somewhere fifteen miles away where the front line had stalled for the last two days.

An uncertain beam of the sunset came through a tiny window. From behind the doorframe curtained by a piece of tarpaulin, the rustle of the sentry's measured steps reached his ears, then a gust brought an echo of a command, then a dull metallic sound of a mess kit bumping at a rifle.

I keep moving from one place to another all the time, that's what life at the front is like. Maybe that's why I did not receive a single letter from you since March. Or probably it was lost somewhere on the way to me when I was in the hospital.

He halted, contemplating if he had to write more about his wound then immediately another thought followed. *Why are the scouts late? Is it possible the reconnaissance mission went wrong?* Consulting his wristwatch, he rubbed his eyebrow. *Eight hours seventeen minutes since they have left.* And as if answering his troubled question, Sergeant Polonyuk's voice came from behind the door curtain. "Comrade senior lieutenant, may I come in?"

Involuntarily, he covered the letter with his bandaged left palm and reached to his peaked cap with the other hand. "Come in, Polonyuk."

The stocky, lop-eared sergeant with apple-pink spots on his broad cheeks entered sideways. He drew himself up and came to an abrupt halt, bringing his hand to his temple.

"At ease, sergeant. You are a perfect scout. I didn't even hear your approaching."

The round peasant's face of the soldier with dark snappy eyes lightened up to the praise of the superior. "May I report to you, comrade senior lieutenant?"

Victor nodded.

"As ordered, the reconnaissance unit brought a prisoner for interrogation," he shot proudly.

"Have him over here."

Polonyuk half turned, lifted the curtain, and shouted, "Bring him in."

Two scouts in camouflage jumpsuits with carbines in a state of semi-readiness lead in a tall, clean-shaved German, an artillery colonel judging by his epaulettes. The gleaming silver eagle with outspread wings and a brand-new Iron Cross on the left breast pocket adorned his tightly fitting, buttoned-up mouse gray tunic.

"A distinguished murderer, I see. Good catch, comrades. Did he have a map with him?"

"Here's what he had on him," Polonyuk said, somewhat apologetically. From his tarpaulin camouflage bag he pulled out and placed on the table one object after the other—a Mauser with an inscription on it's handle, an implacably white handkerchief, a lighter with swastika, and a silver cigarette case with a geometric engraving. A narrow white band held together a three-letter stack and a photograph of a woman. "We turned out his pockets. Nothing important. And here is his identity card, I think." He peered into a piece of paper wrapped in cellophane, moving his lips silently, puckering his brows at the effort and then shaking his head. "In school, did I know I would need this damned German language?" He smiled crookedly.

"Sergeant, call up the interpreter and we'll make this German bastard indulge in talk. I'm sure we'll shake out enough secrets from him," Victor ordered.

As if nothing concerned him, the German stood there looking fixedly in front of him, straight over Victor's head.

A minute or two passed and the interpreter still was not there. A silence ensued, made especially long by the frequent glances the scouts cast at Victor. He guessed they wanted nothing more than to be able to hit the hay.

Victor consulted his watch, and at the same moment, a youth in a wide soldier uniform that did not fit him ran in, breathing heavily, grains of some kind of gruel sticking to his full childish lips and chin. He shot his hand sharply to his field cap from under which a forelock of a shiny mix between red and brown escaped. "Private Berman!"

"Well, private Berman, don't yell at the top of your lungs, no one is deaf. You'd better tell this Fritz to take off his peaked cap. He is a prisoner of war, and he is in front of a Soviet officer."

"*Nehmen Sie die Mütze ab. Sie sind vor dem Sovietischen Offizier.*"

Not a single muscle moved on the German's strong, gray-eyed face with a thin stubborn mouth.

The scout to the right of him tore the peaked cap off the prisoner's head, revealing a big red scar stretching above his temple, hardly concealed under the close-cropped grayish hair.

"What's his name?" Victor nodded to Polonyuk to hand the document to the interpreter.

"Franz von Stauffenheim."

"Oh-ho-ho, that's the bird that must fly high." Victor mockingly singled out the word "high" by his intonation. "Tell him we need information about their communications, the number of units, reserves, the depth of defense, flanks—panzers, artillery ..." He continued his innumerate questions, waiting patiently till the interpreter wrote them into his little notebook and then translated.

All this time, the German stood cool, gazing over Victor's head with a faraway look.

"So he had swallowed his tongue, the fascist vermin. If he doesn't answer, repeat the questions and repeat them again," Victor said, trying to keep the fury that was swelling with increasing persistence off his face.

With stubborn concentration, the interpreter repeated his questions one after another.

The German remained motionless.

Victor clenched his fists and ground his teeth to overcome the piercing pain in his left hand. He glanced at the nails of the remaining fingers, stained with iodine, and the white bandage with a rapidly spreading stain of red. *One of the stitches must have broken apart* went through his mind.

"Comrade senior lieutenant, let me re-dress your wound." Polonyuk took a step to him, jerking a First-aid kit from the pocket of his camouflage tunic.

"Cancel!" Victor cut him off coldly.

"Sorry, comrade senior lieutenant." The sergeant stepped back.

"What's the matter, lost your tongue, German scum?" Victor rose at a jerk, sending the easy chair flying to the floor, crossed the room in two quick bounds, and drawing his pistol, shouted into the German's face, "Speak up!"

The German barely lifted his chin.

With an inner tremor, Victor noticed that the German's hands were not trembling and nothing changed in his erect posture. He stared in the hard gray eyes of the man in front of him and saw that these eyes did not implore and there was no cowardly submissiveness in them. On the contrary, they were repulsively cold and proud.

All of a sudden, the hut trembled from a terrible blast. It seemed to tear the earth. Everyone in the room hunched their shoulders except the German. With a sharp turn, he broke away from the scouts and his hand lunged to his Mauser that lay on the table.

As if propelled, the soldiers threw themselves at him, pinning him to the earthen floor, then seized him roughly by the arms and thrust him up to his feet, all the while swearing elaborately under their noses.

Ignoring the machine-guns pointed at him, the German straightened his uniform. He fastidiously shook the specks of soil from his tunic and the bridges, and for the first time met Victor's gaze.

"Tidying himself up, the fascist! Polonyuk, twist his hands behind his back," he ordered, boring into the German's imperturbable face and feeling a fuming flush spread up his neck.

The high-pitched sobbing and the rising whistle of Dr. Goebbels mortar-rockets was heard closer, closer. One explosion merged into the next, shaking the hut, tearing the earth some three hundred yards away.

A satanic smirk spread across the German's thin lips.

Then shots rang, meeting the high white forehead. "For every blast of your rockets!" Victor screamed.

The German's head jerked back, and it seemed there was a glint of unsuppressed hatred in his light eyes before two thin crimson trickles flooded them. In falling back, he thrust his right hand, "Heil Hitl—"

As though unaware of the empty revolver, Victor continued pulling the trigger, shaking with his entire body in a sensation akin excitement. Only when Polonyuk's voice, repeating over and over hoarsely, "Comrade senior lieutenant, he's dead, he's dead," reached his consciousness, did he notice that his hand clutched convulsively to the German's Mauser.

Relentless rumbling and thunder indicative of the heavy battle moved somewhere to the northeast.

His boots crunching, Victor walked about the room, turning on his heels with mechanical precision at each corner. With surprise, he noticed that the moon was high in the sky, in the upper corner of the frame, and the night lay behind the small soot-covered window. Involuntarily, his eyes kept returning to the spot where the German had stood. *I wonder if blood is still there.* The thought did not go. And though he couldn't see in the dusk, it agitated him, magnetized.

He lighted the kerosene lamp. It smoked a yellow flame that gave off a stink. Holding it in his hand, he squatted in the middle of the room, looking closely at the floor. To his disappointment, he didn't see any stains.

This was his first German shot at close range. Maybe he had killed more enemies but how could he know? During the attacks, he shot at the figures moving in the distance as did his comrades and saw them falling, but he couldn't know if it was his bullet that sent the Fritzes to their hellish fascist heaven.

At the thought that he had to describe his actions in his report to the Division Political Commissar he grimaced. He dug into his pocket and got a cigarette, lighted it, and sucked greedily on it, letting ash drop to the floor.

The superiors won't approve of me. And what will my subordinates think of me? I probably should have behaved more calmly. But why? Surely I am not sorry for him? He continued pacing the room, stopping on the fifth step before turning abruptly. One scene after another rushed through his mind—the shattered forehead no longer white, blood flowing over the lids; the scouts, dragging the long soft body by both arms, one of which just some seconds ago was raised in a fanatical Hitler salute; the helpless legs in gleaming, polished, chrome-leather boots disappearing behind the tarpaulin curtain. He tried to recall the expression on the German's dead face, secretly hoping for a grimace of fear or pain and not finding it in his memory. The feeling of helpless rage that had engulfed him then choked him again.

He reflected on that and suddenly, with surprise, understood that independently of his initial feelings, and opposed to them, the memory of that moment was instead bringing him intoxicating pleasure, akin to that of an adrenalin rush. He stopped, savoring the new sensation, then shook his head. *Enough, now it's time to prepare the report.*

He returned to the table and pulled the German's things toward him. Squeamishly, he tossed the handkerchief to the corner of the table then opened the cigarette case and emptied it on the table, twisting and crushing one cigarette in his fingers and finding nothing suspicious. At the strange sweetish aroma, he wrinkled his nose. *How can they smoke this junk?* He removed the remaining cigarettes from his half-empty Kazbek soft pack, stacked them in the silver case carefully, and slipped it into the pocket of his britches.

"Sentry! Come in!" he called.

A noncom with a silver moustache and slightly bowed back entered, saluting.

"Help yourself." Victor indicated the scattered cigarettes with a nod, watching with delight how the man's eyes lit up with narcotic gleam.

"What a present, comrade senior lieutenant, what a present," he mumbled under his nose, picking them up one after another with his trembling, calloused fingers and shoving them into the pockets of his soldier's greatcoat. He carefully collected tobacco flakes into a small piece of newspaper and smiled, showing off a gap where one eyetooth should have been. "May I return to my point-duty, comrade senior lieutenant?"

"On your way," Victor said, and after the sentry withdrew in a flurry of "thanks, comrade senior lieutenant," he picked up the stack of letters. *Berman will translate. Surely, I don't find anything worthwhile in them. Their military censorship is as brutal as ours is.* He smirked to himself.

The photograph lay face down, with *Zu meinem geliebten Gatte* in a calligraphic handwriting. He flipped through his German-Russian soldier's phrase book. *Gatte, gatte. Aha, husband.*

He turned it over. A blonde woman in her thirties dressed in a dazzling-white embroidered blouse looked into the camera with dignity. *What an arrogant bitch.* Frowning, he tore himself away from the picture. *She will never know who sealed the fate of her husband.*

Suddenly, he caught himself humming,
Sometimes at night
We kissed each other good-by …
No more nights!

With a jolt, he remembered about his letter to Serafima.

The Mauser gleamed dully, resting on the notebook. Holding the pistol cautiously by the rough handle, he lifted it up and lowered it on the photograph covering the German woman's arrogant face.

His eyes ran over the lines on the paper.

May 11, 1942

> *My dear, cherished, darling!*
> *I keep moving from one place to another all the time, that's what life at the front is like. Maybe, that's why I did not receive a single letter from you since March. Or probably it was lost somewhere on the way to me when I was in the hospital.*

He took the pencil and continued.

> *Two fingers on my left hand were torn off by shrapnel. Of course, I shouldn't write you about this. But don't worry too much, I can fight the damned fascists without these fingers, and my arms are as strong as before to hug you, my love. There are only two sacred words left to us. One of them is "love," the other one is "revenge."*

"Was it revenge?" he asked as if talking to somebody else. "Of course, revenge," he answered himself in a whisper, shooing away a feeling of pleasure he experienced again in remembering the German's white forehead torn by bullets.

Do you remember the song "The Little Blue Shawl"? In a rare quiet moment between the attacks when my yearnings for you become unbearable, I sing it for myself. Do you still remember my voice? How much I would like to sing it to you, just to you, tenderly and quietly into your ear.

The victory will be ours. Each day brings me closer to you, my darling, my one and only.

Your Victor.

Summer had arrived almost overnight. The grasses and wild flowers grew with abundance, making a thick lawn scattered with pink and white clover, humble field daisies, and a variety of aromatic plants. The earth, engaged in the process of vigorous germination, exhaled a subtle but nonetheless powerful odor.

When Serafima was hungry—it was most of the time—something living, turning, knocked timidly inside her, time and again. Something would happen, she hoped, and in some miraculous way, she'd be freed of *the damned major's brat.*

At the factory, during the short breaks for meals, the weary-faced women conversed about their children or husbands. What other talk could there be, other than of the war and front?

"Mine is in the hospital, somewhere in the rear. Wrote he's coming home." The woman's eyes lit up.

"After mine had lost his leg, like our Semenich, only his is the left one, he's not fit for battle anymore," another said and sighed rather happily.

"Lucky you. I wish mine too—" one of the women cut herself off abruptly and dropped her gaze.

"I received two letters from Aleshka lately. Says, all is well. Ours are pushing," someone said, a trace of uncertainty in her voice.

The widows who by that time had received the laconic notice "killed while defending his country" were clearly identified by black kerchiefs and the constantly wet eyes.

Between these two groups, there were women over who "vanished without trace" was raised as a sword of Damocles.

Over Serafima alone hung the dark shadow of shame, separating her from others as though she were plague-stricken.

She slept and awoke and went to the factory to only collapse fourteen hours later on the dirty sheets, without undressing.

Occasionally, Dunyasha met her after her shift on the way home, pushing into her hand a parcel with a slice of bread or a tin of canned fish.

"Did you eat something?" she would ask, searching her eyes with concern. "The little one must have his supper."

Serafima always refused the giving and looked away, provoking Dunyasha's angry, "Vitya won't forgive you if …"

At home, Serafima winced as she noticed on the table in the anteroom a folded three-cornered letter with the seal broken.

June 20, 1942

> *Serafima, I am mortally upset that I did not have a single letter from you since March.*

I did receive a letter from Dunyasha but not from you. What is it she is hinting at? What is it that, she writes, will make me happy? I rack my brain all the time and can not imagine what it can be. Please, don't leave me in ignorance, what is it, dear?

My dear one, we shall see each other again, remember this. I hope for it and believe in it.

Your ever loving Victor.

She stroked the letter with her trembling fingers, running them over the sentences one after another as if seeking the warmth of his touch on the paper. *He really loves me. He will understand.*

Unconsciously, she pressed her left hand to her belly then jerked it back as if scorched.

I should tell him the truth. I have no right not to, she thought, beginning again to impress this upon herself.

But will he forgive? Her heart whispered back.

She opened the window. A fresh smell entered softly and a faint redness of the fading sunset died away over the edge of the pine forest. A landrail called with a single screeching note.

Suddenly anxious to put an end to her uncertainty, she stepped to the table and lighted a kerosene lamp. A shadow swayed slightly with her every move.

July 14, 1942

> *My dear Vitya,*
> *I received your letters that you have written on May 11 and June 20. Sorry I did not respond promptly.*
> *Your every letter is such a joy to me. I pray to God to spare you for me and I know He hears my pleadings.*
> *There is something very important I have to tell you.*

The pencil slipped from her fingers and fell on the floor with a sharp sound. She drew in a deep breath, as if after a struggle. Hoping a relief would come after she wrote the truth, she bent down and resolutely grabbed the pencil again.

> *I know I had to write you about it long ago.*

The tip of the pencil broke. Tortured and bathed in sweat, she squeezed the letter in her fist. Striking the table over and over again, causing the plates to rattle, she repeated obstinately, in time with the blows of her hand, "No, no, no. Oh God, I can't!"

July 17, 1942

A skylark danced in the air at the height of a telegraph pole. Over the rye fields, over the shells of the disemboweled huts surrounded by the yards overgrown with low blue-gray wormwood and scrub, hung a deathly sultriness. Already dried, yellow grasses did not hold down the dust, which was stirred up in clouds by the slightest movement, getting into nostrils and throat.

Serafima dragged along the road lined with a growth of prickly thorns, taking her usual way to the factory. Her eyes filled with tears because of the glaring sun. The hot sweat ran down between her swollen breasts, and the light cotton dress stuck to her back.

A column of trucks with the anti-tank guns hitched to them and the carts and a field kitchen caught her up and surpassed, leaving behind the smell of iron and petrol in the dusty air.

She saw the faces of the soldiers, their waving hands, heard their cheerful shouts above the noise of the vehicles. "Bear a soldier!" "We need more front people!" And something else, their voices lost in the continual groan and rattle of the wheels.

How is Vitya there? The thought barely crossed her mind before another followed. *Dammit. Let it happen, better sooner than later.*

The siren of the morning shift's start caught her entering the Quality Department. She hurriedly slipped on a black tarpaulin apron and pushed her chair to the long quality table.

Pain hovered inside her like a supplementary presence; but she was too busy to pay much attention to it. Suddenly, she felt as if something broke inside her. Breathlessly, she stared at a gush of liquid pattering on the floor around her feet.

"What's that?" she said slowly to herself.

"Eh, girl, your water's broke," Anyuta, a woman of forty, her only sympathizer said.

"Oh." Subconsciously, Serafima put both hands on her belly, feeling quite a faint, but definite tightening, gripping of muscles deep inside her.

Anyuta got up and put her comforting hand on Serafima's shoulder. "Don't worry, you still have a lot of time. Believe me, I bore three myself. But you better go to the hospital. Go, go."

"Go. We don't need you slinking here," someone said behind Serafima's back.

The local hospital was seven blocks away. The contractions only came at long intervals and in the spaces between them she felt gloating joy. *If only it would happen sooner … getting rid of the damned brat.*

In front of the brick two-storied building the color of old snow, a few gray-clothed attendants lifted stretcher after stretcher out of the ambulance and arranged them on the grass. The wounded soldiers followed Serafima with their wondering and puzzled glances as if an idea of a new life in times like this was out of place.

She held up to her swollen belly, tortured by the living being there inside her kicking and moving about.

For all those months, she had struggled against this being. She had jumped down heavily from a bank; at work, deliberately, with silent fury, she lifted huge buckets with scrap. She had drunk every kind of herbal potion and infusion she could get her hands on. But the child had obstinately gone on growing.

"Maternity ward is at the end of the corridor, where you'll see the 'head physician' plaque on the door." A nurse sent her on her way with an impatient wave of the hand.

Clutching on to the rough, white-painted wall, Serafima hauled herself along the corridor. From behind the open doors, there came such an overpowering smell that she took a deep breath as if about to dive into a pond. On the floors lay soldiers with bandaged heads, with arms in slings, with feet swollen by dressings. Some were howling at the tops of their lungs, emitting a sound, which combined fear, anger, and pain.

The last steps she struggled.

Four metal beds were squeezed into the room with the "head physician" plaque. A heavy plastic sheet partition kept a part of it out of sight. On the wall, there was a big clock.

She slumped to the bed by the open window and levered herself round and back onto the pillow. Surprisingly, the pain went away, as if it had never been there at all, and she looked through the window in amazement. The clouds, sulphurous, misty formed and reformed. They flowed together, they disintegrated, they turned from white to swollen purple to inky black. The dark gray sky threatened rain, and the next moment it poured. A pearl of thunder broke right over the roof and went rolling away.

A big woman in her late fifties with a face ironed slack by tiredness, almost ran in. "Oh, this suffocating heat. At last the rain." She swept sweat from her heavy eyebrows. "When did your contractions start?"

"Today, in the morning."

"Now of course today. What time?

"After eight a clock, I think."

"Let me go and fetch a doctor."

Serafima thought it was an eternity before, finally, a young woman appeared. She quickly did the exam. "So at eight, you said?" Her face showed she was elsewhere. "Your first pregnancy?"

Serafima nodded.

"Four hours, then," the doctor said, hoisting a tired smile. "Everything is going perfectly normally." In moving to the door, she turned her head to the nurse. "Give her instructions."

"Lie down." The midwife threw on a thin gray bedspread over Serafima's legs. "Now, just pay attention. When the contractions come breathe deeply. In through your nose and out through your mouth." She stifled a yawn with her hand and left the room.

After a while, feelings changed. It was not squeezing that she felt any more, it was a crushing, a pulping. It was not stretching now, but tearing. "Three times accursed, three times accursed," she hissed through clenched teeth.

She watched the clock. Gradually the respites ended sooner and sooner. And then … two minutes of pain, like eternity, and she understood that the respite wasn't coming this time.

"Nurse," she squeaked.

It seemed like forever before the midwife stepped in. She was wiping her big shovel-like hands on a towel, her apron spoiled with fresh streaks of blood. "What is it?"

Her lips writhing uncontrollably, Serafima said in a broken whisper, "How much longer?"

"You pull yourself together and breathe as I've told you, or you'll kill the baby," the nurse replied without inflection.

Serafima groaned, gripped in an iron band of pain. *For God's sake, if it has to be, at least let me die instantaneously! Finish me off. Bring me to the end. Just end it. I cannot take it any longer.*

Some twenty minutes later, the midwife helped her on the high chair behind the curtain and ordered, "Push, push, push …"

Serafima wanted to howl like a wolf. Her bones were cracking and breaking apart. A sticky, sickly sweat covered her forehead. Grounding her teeth and convulsively jerking her head, she gasped in air. *I shall die. And that's all there is to it.*

When the child, desperate for life, began fighting his way out, she felt not only the terror of the pain but also an uncertain joy: there was no getting away from this, so let it be quick.

The doctor appeared. "Delivering ... Delivering ... Breathe ... Push, I'm telling you! What, do you want your baby to choke?"

Serafima fixed her dilated eyes on the doctor. *Soon, soon, it'll be all over. No part of me any longer.*

For several minutes everything disappeared, everything lost reality—hot sweat ran down her inflamed face and her eyes filled with tears.

"A boy," the doctor said triumphantly, holding in her hands a slippery puny ball of red-and-blue flesh with tiny arms and legs like crooked, thin sticks.

Shielding herself from the sight of him, Serafima raised her hands to her face. She heard them talk.

"Prematurely-born. See how tiny."

"Nowadays, how can you know? Look at her—she's nothing but skin and bone."

Then a tiny cry came that sounded like a tinkle of delicate glass and yet so strong that it eliminated the quiet talk between the doctor and the nurse.

Serafima gave a long-drawn-out groan. Yet, she felt a profound release. A burden that oppressed her all the time and everywhere had dropped from her heart. She did not reflect that now she had to make another decision, she only knew that the *damned brat* was not a part of her any longer.

"Look at him, Mamma!" The nurse lifted the little creature with the wrinkled face. As though expecting a blow, Serafima shrank back and turned her head away.

Behind the window, the sun was shining again. Two yellow butterflies with black dots on their wings played around a bush covered with tiny white buds. *Soon they will bloom* was her last waking thought before she dozed off on billows of sleep, out of which she only awoke when she heard two women talking in undertones.

"Mine is on the front, somewhere at the Volga now. This boy is his last-day-at-home child." She giggled. "He'll go crazy, that's how happy he'll be to have a son. At last … We have four girls."

"Mine is not liable for call-up. Shortsighted. If I don't tell him he now has a daughter, he won't figure out." She broke out laughing, and it was clear that that might have been their in-house joke.

The nurse appeared with two bundles in her hands. "Mammas, time to feed your babies," she lisped. "The boy for you. The girl for you." She handed the newborns to the women and hurriedly went away.

She did not bring him. With a pang of joy, Serafima averted her eyes from one of the women who was giving her breast to the child dozing in her arms. She lay on her back and listened in fearful silence, broken only by the sucking sound of the babies and of women's cooing.

"Mamma, time to feed your sonny."

She startled and screamed.

The baby whimpered, very timidly.

"What, do you think I have time to stay here and beg you?" The nurse threw out the words angrily, her lisp more noticeable.

Only now, Serafima noticed that she had deep eye sockets under her gray cap and a mouth in which many teeth were missing. Serafima held her gaze silently.

"What's the matter? Have you mud in your ears? Or is something else wrong with you?" She did not get any response. "I'll report to the doctor of your—"

"Poor girl." Serafima heard a woman saying. "With my first child, it was the same with me. Hardly seventeen I was. What kind of a mother can you expect from a mere child?" she said without a shade of malice.

"Not too young to copulate—" The nurse's words hit Serafima's ears.

"Wait," the same woman said. "Take my Olen'ka. I'll give suck to him ... You, a little Blondie. Hungry, I see ... Suck, suck," her voice dropped to a soft whisper.

Four hours later, the same nurse came accompanied by an old doctor in pince-nez. "This one." She poked with her finger at Serafima.

"How do you feel, my little girl? Is something wrong? Why don't you nurse your child?" he asked, looking at her with bloodshot dark eyes full of pain and unquenchable warmth.

"I don't want him. I don't take him. Do what you want with him." Serafima half-raised on her elbow, pressing another hand to her throat. "Leave me alone, leave me alone," she repeated jerkily without recognizing her own voice, shaking with her entire body.

"You—" The nurse's features contorted with shock and anger.

The doctor shook his head and put his hand on the nurse's elbow. "Postpartum. Leave her alone. She'll come to her senses," he said with a touch of gentle softness in his voice and walked out.

The distant roar of a truck broke against the windowpanes. Serafima raised her eyes to the window. The larks fluttered in the warm sunset air. She followed them, chasing one another, gay and light. *Tomorrow, it'll all be over. I'll be free like these birds.* She glanced at the door.

The next morning, another doctor came with the same elderly nurse on his heels who held the medical charts and a bunch of papers in her hand.

The doctor took the women one after another to behind the partition. "You may be discharged today," he said to each of them.

"Ksenia Nikolaevna, give instructions to the new mothers."

The women giggled and said simultaneously, "What instructions, doctor? This is my fourth child." "This is my second."

The doctor's face eased into a smile. "You can get your excuse from work letter in the Registry. Good-bye." He hurriedly turned to go.

"Doctor, er—" The nurse followed him.

Serafima heard them whisper about something for a minute and then the doctor said, "I need the ward for the wounded."

The nurse returned. "Mammas, time to fill out the papers and then you are free to go." She plopped on the easy chair by the little table.

After she finished with the other women, she turned to Serafima.

"Now you. So … Serafima, last name Krivenkova. Right? Why is your father's name missing in the form?"

"No father." Serafima crossed her arms.

"Hmm. The baby's father's name?"

"No father."

"I see, I see. Your mother's name?"

"Glafira Petrovna Krivenkova."

The nurse raised her eyes to the ceiling as if searching her memory and muttered something under her nose, what Serafima could not hear clearly. "Here, take the paper to the Registry Department within thirty days. I'll bring the baby."

"I don't take him," Serafima replied curtly, holding her arms behind her back.

"What do you mean, you don't take him? You bang around yet somebody has to take care of your brat? Many legitimate children are without parents … their parents are killed at the front or died of hunger. And she, the slut, announces she does not want her baby!"

The nurse looked at her with such revulsion that it was as if she had seen a squashed woodlouse on her face. She rushed out and immediately returned, pushing the bundle into Serafima's hands. "Your mother should help you out. She knows how to handle bastards." She crossly spat on the floor, threw her one more glance full of abysmal disgust, and stood aside to let Serafima pass.

With the child in her hands, she felt fear again, stickier, heavier, and clammier than before. She had to decide what to do with *him*.

As she walked toward home along the main road, she halted occasionally to catch her breath.

The village came closer. It lay there dismal and abandoned. From afar, she saw a light frame of her mother standing by the poplar with her palm shading her eyes from the sun. On recognizing her daughter, she ran to meet her.

Serafima stopped.

When still some little distance away, Glafira shouted to her, "Now why do you stay there under the scorching sun like an idol? A girl? A boy?"

The baby fussed, and suddenly, she felt how heavy the bundle was in her arms. "A boy."

"So now you will write to him, will you? Happy he'll be, I fancy. The son. They all want sons as a first child. An heir, a helper in the household," her mother jabbered.

Serafima squinted in her direction, and stepping across the threshold, she at once fixed her gaze on their brass washtub. *We washed the Germans' dirty clothes in it. That's were the bastard belongs.*

"Help me to unhook the washtub, Mother, and please give me some linen."

"What do you need the tub for?"

"Hmm, to put him in."

Glafira shot her an accusing glare. "What? Are you going to put him into the trough like dirty things? I have something better for him till we manage to get a cradle. Look up by the stove and I go to bring the linen." She went hurriedly off.

A cradle? We won't need one, Serafima thought. She stepped over the threshold and instantly saw their soft osier basket with two handles sitting on a rug pressed to the stove. Freshly cut clover covered the basket's inside, making it look like a bird's nest.

She deposited the swaddled child square in the middle of the table. Deserted by the warmth of her arms, he gave a pitiful squeal.

"Here." Glafira ran in, breathing heavily, and pressed in Serafima's hands a sheet that was warm and gave off a delicate herbal fragrance.

Serafima threw it into the basket, lowered the child down and straightened up, turning toward the door.

The baby squalled now in earnest.

"And what, don't you hear he is crying? He's hungry."

"I don't care! I'm not going to nurse him!"

"Stupid! The people already branded you a slut. Want to be branded an infant-murderer?"

Serafima looked at her mother from under her brows and smiled grimly without parting her lips. "Children die. Especially now. Here is a wonder indeed. No one will ever suspect anything." To her dismay, her voice broke slightly.

"First, I had the same feeling about you, but I kept you alive, learned to love you." Glafira raised her eyes to Serafima before moving them obliquely away.

"Did you?" she shouted. And with a trembling that shook her body, she kept shouting and shouting, which she had never formerly permitted herself to do. There must have been so much pain and aversion in her voice and gaze that her mother drew her head down to her shoulders as though she wanted to disappear.

"Victor won't forgive you—"

"He will. He has nothing to do with this damned creature! *He* is not his!"

"You say he—" With the shock imprinted all over her face, Glafira flinched and retreated, crossing herself repeatedly.

With anger and hurt vying for dominance, bitter words came to Serafima's lips, and her effort to choke them back was useless. "It's you! It's all because of you! Your icon! Your God! What good did *he* do me? Why didn't *he* save me from them?" She looked at *his* image but instead she saw the steel gray eyes and the mouth twisted with a rapacious smile, and she knew that that damned image was inscripted into her mind forever. She felt a spasm of unburdened hatred against the one who had caused all this … and against the baby.

She tore the icon down. It fell with a thud and split in two as it did on that accursed day.

Glafira lifted her face, her lips moving as if in speech, a pained reproach lurking in her eyes.

The noise sent the infant into squalling fits, his puny legs kicking against the cover.

Serafima winced in renewed pain and rushed out of the house.

There was quiet, wonderful twilight peacefulness over the countryside. Tiny white clouds sailed west and the grass had a strong scent. Bumblebees and honeybees flew from flower to flower. A young cat stole by.

"Puss, puss, puss," Serafima called with a softened voice. "So thin you are, just skin and bones."

The cat stopped, her ears high, and then moved in her direction. It glided around her several times then came closer, rubbed against her feet, arched its back and began to purr. Serafima bent down and tickled behind the cat's ears. It lay on its back and stretched out, its dugs showing grey amid the fur of its heaping stomach. "It seems like you'll have kittens soon."

Suddenly, as if remembering her own business, the cat darted to the bushes, then halted, looked back with her scrawny, half-starved face before disappearing in the undergrowth.

The sun was going down. Along the main road in a distance, a string of carts piled with mowed grass moved slowly, the horses kicking up clouds of white dust with their hoofs. The men walked along, holding the reins, and a deep voice urging on the horses reached Serafima's ears. From a cloud of dust, she watched a woman approach and turn to the side-road leading to the village. Although not yet close enough to distinguish her features, by the light, crisp walk, she recognized Dunyasha in her new uniform of a medical orderly.

Serafima hastened to meet her.

Dunyasha hugged her friend then pushed a small bunch of timid field flowers into her hand. "Show him to me. I could hardly wait for the instructing to end to see him. I know it's a boy. I was told by the doctor. I was in the hospital first, to inquire about you." She almost dragged Serafima into the room. "Serafimushka, I'm so happy, so happy!" she cried out then threw her hands over her mouth. "May he be sleeping?"

Noticing the child in the basket, her face darkened for an instance. "Will you get a cradle for him?" She tiptoed closer and stretched her hand to feel the child's fair fluffy-haired head. The baby turned his head to her and fixed his alerted eyes on her face.

"Oi! He looks at me." She turned to Serafima, easing into a broad smile then bent to examine the baby's face. "He is the image of Vitya." She pressed her hands to her chest as though preventing her heart from jumping out of her chest. "Or, what do you think, does he look more like me?"

Serafima made a slight gesture of agreement and was silent.

"What name did you give him?"

Serafima thought for a while then made a vague gesture with her hand.

"What, you don't know? I've thought a lot about it. If a girl, she would be Katherina, like my mother. A boy—what about Vanechka?" Dunyasha's voice trembled a little. Not getting an answer, she stumbled out the words, "V-Vanechka, Ivan, like my and Vitya's father. What do you think?"

After a silence during which she studied Serafima's face and tried to catch her gaze, a sudden shadow overcast her brow. "How sorry I won't see him … maybe for a long time. I leave tomorrow morning."

"Directly to the front?"

She nodded. From her haversack, she pulled a loaf of dark bread and two cans of condensed milk. "This is for you."

Serafima shook her head in denial.

"Out there, they say we'll have more to eat than we have here ... Write Vitya about his son. I have written him before that happy news is coming. He'll be so happy, I'm sure."

As if discouraged by Serafima's silence, she added quickly, "Pass by the old wives' talk. You know my Vitya, he'll marry you. You take good care of our Vanechka." She squatted in front of the basket. It seemed she could not take her eyes from the child. "Let me hold him in my hands. Who knows when I will see him again?" She took him up. "So light you are, so tiny. You grow up my little nephew," she cooed to the fussing baby. "Lucky you are, Serafima ... Oh what a blockhead I am! I almost forgot—" She lowered the child on his linen and rummaged in her haversack. "Take this money." She put a carefully folded thin stack of banknotes on the table. "Out there I won't need it."

An unwelcome blush crept into Serafima's cheeks.

"So sorry I've got to go. Let me look at him one more time, one more time." Dunyasha bent down over the baby and crossed him in a blessing. Big, shining tears glistened on her long lashes and ran down her cheeks. "Why do I think I'll never see him again?"

Serafima followed her to the road. They walked on, barely saying a word to each other. At the road fork, they threw their arms around each other simultaneously. Not knowing why she couldn't find her voice, Serafima whispered, "Don't write Vitya about the child," and responding to Dunyasha's questioning gaze, she added, "I will. Myself."

"As you wish," Dunyasha said, gulping air in hard, shuddering sighs.

For a long while, Serafima stood there looking at Dunyasha's retreating figure. As if sensing her gaze, Dunyasha turned back, shouted something, waving her hands, then strode away, a mist of dry dust rising beneath her feet. A few crows flapped above her like dark rags—like the presage of death.

The thought that she had to return home made Serafima nauseous, and she turned to the wood. She walked listening to the endlessly repeating hiss of the grass against her legs. A hundred meters away, a bird suddenly took off, disturbed by the noise.

In the forest, it was peaceful. She could feel her thoughts settling into place and did not notice how her legs brought her to the dugout with its massive logs now rickety, blocking the entrance. Around it, a thin stripe of a meadow was abloom with red and yellow and blue wild flowers. The air was scented with thyme, spurge, and wormwood.

She stood still and listened inward. Somewhere there must still be a voice; an echo of hope must still linger. But she found nothing. There was only emptiness and nameless pain. The words came out in a whisper, "Vitya … What do I tell you? Do I tell you the truth?"

Shrouded by mist, Vitya's distracted face appeared, the way she had seen him last time. All his other faces were blurred; this one alone became clear. *Why do I think of him as someone who will come back to me? Or maybe he would if ... there is no bastard in my life.*

She sat on the old birch trunk, worn and withered by the sun and frost, and pumped out the milk from her breasts. Overcome by exhaustion, which ached in the muscles of her shoulders and neck, she lay down on her back.

Clouds wandered across the sky. Birds twittered in the birch trees. A yellow butterfly floated from blossom to blossom. After a while, a second one joined it. They played together, chasing each other, then flew united through the hot air.

If Vitya is killed ... She started at the thought. *Then I must explain nothing. Then I may let people think the child is his.*

The sky began to fade above the woods. Something like a shadow was gathering in the east, threatening rain, and thunder rumbled somewhere far away like the booming of explosions.

She pulled herself up but could not move. *I don't want to go there.* The terror returned in all its intensity, and she stood paralyzed, letting the minutes tick by.

Another thunder crack returned her to reality. "Come what may," she said to herself and started slowly toward the village.

Dunyasha's withered flowers lay on the workbench. The freshly washed swaddling clothes Glafira had cut out of the old sheets, danced on the clothesline with every gust of breeze. Not a single sound came through the open window.

She took a breath and forced herself to step through the door. "What, is he still—" She squinted in his direction and grimaced in disgust. The baby's tiny arms flailed and the clenched fists trembled.

"Don't play God Almighty. If *he* wants, *he*'ll take him … I've got some milk for the child. There is enough for another two times."

On the table, a stack of nappies lay next to a milk-filled half-liter glass jar. *With this hot weather, it will turn sour.* At the sensation of her breasts filling up again, she shuddered inwardly. She slipped outside, tore off one of the sheets and fastened it tightly across her chest.

The grassy scent wafted in a cool stream through the wide-open window, washing Serafima's face with a damp breeze. Beside the house the grass rustled. *The she-cat*, the thought came.

She listened to the silence from the basket. *He must have … died.* She pressed a hand over her mouth to cover a smile, feeling the sensual pleasure she took in being cruel towards the German bastard and in her powerless hatred.

Through the night, she woke with a start to find nothing had changed, then fell back again into a half sleep, only to be startled into wakefulness once again. At the first glimmer of daylight, the sound of a weak and plaintive squeak brought her crushing to her senses. Then, her mother's shuffling and a whispered, "Shoo." Another squeak, followed by a low sound of suckling for some time and a deep baby's wheeze.

"Sleep, little brat." Quietly, Glafira crooned a lullaby with a tenderness she had never heard in her mother's voice.

And again, Serafima dropped swiftly from consciousness into deep sleep.

"Do you recognize me?" A young German asked in a soft voice, dropping his eyes with shame.

She looked fixedly at him, trembling, sweating with anguish and fear. She wanted to rise and flee, but he stretched his arm across the table laden with delicacies and held her back.

"*Do you remember the day you tried to kill yourself in the barn? The bulk broke, do you remember? I sawed it.*" *He started laughing, drumming with his fingers on the table to the lilting rhythm of his laughter.*

"*Why do you revive those memories? I should not be thankful that you saved me.*"

"*Was I wrong in saving you?*" *After a long silence, he added,* "*Why did you want to die?*"

"*I was afraid.*"

"*I, too, was afraid.*"

"*Why? You were the masters.*"

He lowered his head to his chest and gripped the edge of the table with his white refined fingers. "*I was only following orders but I got what I deserve.*" *When he raised his head again, she saw his forehead split open, his eyes clotted with blood.*

A terrified cry escaped her lips. Her mind stayed blank for an agonizing moment, trapped by the images that crowded it. She sat up in bed and became aware that she was awake. An icy sweat dripped down her face, and the frightful sight of that bleeding ghost sitting at her table remained before her eyes until a soft laughing drifted in. *Who is laughing?* She rose to her feet and tiptoed to the door. *Mother?*

Glafira sat on the doorstep with the baby on her lap, his tiny legs and arms moving sporadically. She was fanning him with a folded newspaper, driving off the flies. At the squeak of the door, she turned. "How many days are you staying home?"

"I've got three."

"I'm staying with you."

"Why?"

"Enough that *I* know why. Run to Grunya, tell her to report to the brigadier that I'm not feeling well."

"But you—"

Glafira dismissed her with a wave of her hand. "And get a pot, a clean one I left on the table. She must have some milk for me, say I'll pay her back. She knows how."

To the right, the wheat field gleamed yellow in a slimy, heavy sun. Serafima raised her head at the throaty cry of a crow that took fancy to the old nest on the poplar and now was circling over it, holding in her beak a big worm.

With Serafima's every step, warm, silky dust floated to her ankles, covering them as fluffy gray socks.

When she returned, she saw the baby in the small aluminum basin in which they used to cook wild strawberry jam, and Glafira, supporting him by his head, splashed water on him with her free hand. She stopped, following Serafima with her gaze.

"Put fresh milk into the cooling box."

In the semidarkness of the barn, crickets chirped from the shadowed corners. Serafima could make out the cat sprawled on last year's bale of hay. Three tiny blind striped gray kittens pressed themselves to her bosom, sucking. The young cat-mother kept her in sight but did not move.

She went back to the house and found a small saucer among the utensils.

"What do you need the saucer for?" Glafira stopped playing with the child who was now comfortably swaddled. "To feed the cat? I've seen the brood."

"She probably can't haunt the mice now," Serafima said.

"Don't you dare spend the child's milk feeding a stray cat." Glafira got up, and holding the baby pressed to her chest, snatched the saucer out of Serafima's hand.

A nother night came and then the morning. Serafima leaned on the doorframe looking at the huge round summer sun slowly climbing up above the serrated outline of the fir wood. In the silence of the early hour, every sound was sharp and distinct.

Suddenly, she heard a strange noise coming from the barn. The cat's cry, squeaking so hard, almost like groaning. She jerked the door open. In the shadow of the corner, she saw a vague, dark knot of something moving, struggling. The first thing she was able clearly to discern were rats, their dark gray backs glittering oily under the fan of the uncertain sun light through the chinks.

Shaking uncontrollably, she stood there for a moment then shrilled, "Aaaa!"

Two huge rodents darted aside, holding something in their teeth. The third one was fighting the cat, which was sheltering her kitten with her body.

Serafima grabbed the pitchfork, and the next instant, with a wolfish cry, she thrust it into the dark body of the rat. It let the cat go. "Damned! Damned! Damned!" She speared the rat repeatedly until it ceased to whirl and shriek.

Her knees buckled and she leaned over the cat. Blood trickled from her neck. She seemed to seek her baby with her glazing eyes but in a moment, all was over.

Serafima took the lifeless little ball into her hands and could still feel the living warmth. She put the kitten by the cat's side. *She fought bravely for the life of her babies.*

And suddenly, scorched by a burning inner shame, feeling nagging guilt towards her own child like a rough, new pain, she understood that something very unnatural happened to her, something that resembled treachery, an inadmissible breach of something, a crime against nature.

Sprinting through the yard and the anteroom, she burst into the room, gasping.

"Why did you scream at the top of your lungs?" Glafira said in an angry whisper. When her gaze fell to Serafima's blood sprinkled canvas shoes, her eyes widened in horror.

Disturbed by the thud of the door and their talk, the child gave his voice; a timid whine of hungry demand.

With fingers that did not obey her, Serafima tore the buttons of her blouse, hurriedly jerking the sheet strap from her chest. She took the baby into her hands and pressed him to her freed breast, inhaling the milky tender scent of his neck.

His eyes moved up toward her face and gazed at her with what looked like a profound concentration. He managed to catch the nipple, sucked once, another time, and let it go. An angry howl erupted. His cry ended with a shuddering gasp for breath. Lungs filled, he wailed again.

Glafira looked from the child beating Serafima's breast with his tiny fist to a strap of fabric on the floor and back again. She leaned forward, almost hissing her words at her. "Idiot! Idiot. Idiot. Your milk grew rancid."

Serafima turned away from her hard, disgust-filled eyes to fight off tears. She'd be damned if she would cry in her mother's presence.

Glafira walked out to bring milk from the barn then snatched a piece of dark bread from the table, pulled out a crumb from its middle and chewed it carefully for some time. She put the chaff in a piece of gauze, making it a little ball and dipped it into the milk. Her eyes imperceptibly changed. "Hold him." A ghost of a smile seemed to relax her face. "Let him get used to his mother."

Too surprised to speak, she looked at her mother in astonishment—her new gestures, the voice full of tenderness, the smile unfamiliar to her. *How perceptibly this tiny alien creature changed my mother in just three days*, she startled at the thought.

Pressed to Serafima and getting hold of his meal, the baby quieted down and started moving his little mouth. She brushed his little fist and his hand claimed her finger. Her heart leapt at the contact. She found herself caught in the warmth of her son's grip.

"You don't tell anybody what you've told me ... Don't ruin Vanechka's life. Let people think he's Vit'ka's. Who knows, maybe he won't come back from the war ..." Her eyes were suddenly full of tears.

"For Christ's sake, will you kindly shut up, Mother." She was shocked how her mother's words gave expression to her own secret thoughts.

The next day, Serafima left the Registry office with a small, double folded greenish paper of the Birth Certificate that read, "Ivan Victorovich Krivenkov."

A one-story shabby structure hid behind a production shop. Above a faded signboard, *Reading-room*, in white uncertain letters *Kindergarten* was painted.

Serafima readjusted Vanechka in her hands and halted, surprised to hear sounds of music coming through the half open door. Without daring to enter, she peeped in. Her eyes ran over the empty bookshelves pressed all to one side, a row of a variety of beds along the opposite wall, the portraits of Lenin and Stalin, a grand piano, and a woman with her back to her, playing. On the mismatched stools sat children from about two to nine years of age, hollow-cheeked, with pale lips, looking like old emaciated dwarfs.

A boy, aged about eight or nine, got up on his stick-like legs, his knees jutting out like gnarled bumps, and tapped the woman on her arm. "There is an aunty there."

The woman stopped playing, rose, and moved swiftly from the piano. She was quite tall. An elegant summer dress that hung loosely around her waist accentuated the slenderness of her figure. "Come on in. You are welcome," she said in a soft, warmly melodious voice and smiled. Her teeth gleamed milky in her narrow face creased by hardly noticeable wrinkles, and her eyes, with dark shadows underneath, seeming unnaturally large because of her thinness, shone with a warm sad light. "My name is Anna Konstantinovna. And you must be Serafima and this must be Vanechka. Right? Your father—"

"My father?"

"The one-legged man—" With her thick blonde hair streaked with silver, brushed back and wound into a tight knot, her forehead was completely bare and her embarrassment was plain to see. Recovering from her confusion, she said, "The man ... He had told me you'd come. Let me show you your son's cot. See, he nailed planks so the child won't fall out."

Serafima looked around, uncertain where to lay Vanechka down.

"May I hold him?" Anna Konstantinovna stretched out her delicate hands covered with a mesh of fine wrinkles and her arms took a natural curve around the child.

Serafima could not help but notice the long spotless fingers with pale transparent nails. "Here." She put her assignment, the ration card, and a little bundle with swaddling clothes on a small shaky table.

"The swaddling clothes, we'll need them, I'm sure," Anna Konstantinovla said, her gaze beaming kindness. "Your shift must have started already. Don't worry about anything, go and work."

They both turned as the entrance door opened with a bang. A woman stepped in, holding a steaming pot with both hands. "Uh, you, the kingdom of the hungriest, here is your cabbage soup," she said lovingly and lowered the pot on the table, blowing on her hands and fanning them in front of her mouth. From a pocket of her besmeared apron, she pulled out a little bottle. "Milk. Is he the one who gets it?" She glanced at Vanechka in Anna Kostantinovna's arms and a beginning of a smile tipped the corners of her mouth.

Eastern front
Den 20. September 1942

Meine liebe Mutter,
First of all you must excuse this letter—there
is no table in the trench so my knees must serve
as a desk.

I did not write you about my furlough that
was scheduled for the end of the month for not to
give you a hope that may be uncertain. Something
unprecedented is going to happen that everybody
is sure will be the last offensive of this war. The
name of it is Stalingrad and the city of the biggest
enemy of our country.

The eastern campaign is practically decided.
The remnants of the Red Army are one step away
from annihilation. I feel, I believe, after this last
battle I come home for good.

"Achtung! Get ready!"

Werter hid the letter on his chest and looked up
from the ditch.

Intermittent flashes from the battle being fought
somewhere to the west of them, through the outer
fringes of the town, lit the darkness. The firing kept
stopping and starting, sometimes very close. The series
of explosions made him hunch his shoulders and then
a shock-wave seized him and hurled him several yards

backward. Lumps of sticky yellow clay pelted down like rain. The smoke and the rotten eggs' reek of exploded soil choked him. Then the shrill cries, "Hurrah! Za Stalina! Za rodinu!" which he knew meant "For Stalin! For the Motherland!" deafened him.

A hail of fire rained on the German positions, from right, from left.

The next few hours were horrible, indescribable. The front shifted to the streets. They fought for every house, every staircase, and every cellar. They bombed each other with grenades. There was a ceaseless hand-to-hand struggle, bodies torn to raw chunks in a flash all around.

In all this angry barking of machine guns, he suddenly discerned the hissing of shrapnel, the humming of shells.

Of all that followed, he remembered one moment indelibly and palpably. The trousers at his left knee were ripped to pieces, blood pouring. He jumped to his feet, half-delirious with the shock but doubled-up with pain and fell headlong. The burning, lacerating agony prevented all movements.

Everything swam before his eyes and he came to his senses when a medical orderly bent over him, cleaning the wound with a solution and then dressing his knee up. "You have to wait till your turn comes to be attended by a doctor," he said and ran to a soldier who lay about twenty yards away, flat on his stomach in a flood of blood moaning for help.

It must have been hours later when he noticed the pallid light of a sickly dawn seeping through the cuts of the tent and the medical orderlies bending over the stretchers placed on the sand floor. "Dead," he heard them say now and then, or "There is nothing more to do."

The far-off drone of the Russian aircraft spread like a hum of bees in the warm evening air. Flies crawled over his face—an ant crept up his leg, but he had no energy to whisk it off.

At last, he got a splint on his leg, one injection against tetanus, and a shot of morphine against the pain. They decided not to operate, otherwise his knee would have remained stiff. Whether it would ever regain its full use was doubtful. "Time will tell," the doctor said. "Prepare him for the evacuation." Werter heard him order.

It was a jolting, painful ride—an ambulance train that was under constant fighter attack … a horse-drawn cart … a medical train that waited for hours on sidings … an airplane … endless moans, groans, screams, and whimpers, the smell of pus, urine, stomach and lung wounds, and his own pain that pressed in wild waves. In the state of semi-consciousness, he dreamed of somebody giving him injections, bandages, tablets, and something to drink.

Suddenly, the strange silence lifted and a voice came through a fog in his head. "Well, are you doing better?"

He raised his head over the edge of the stretcher. Two medical orderlies carried him along a quiet, long corridor full of hospital air and into a bright room with beds pressed to the wall with their headboards.

"One more to your company. Which one is unoccupied?" Werter heard the orderly say, and the next moment they lifted him up from the stretcher and pushed the crutches under his arms.

Three men lay on their beds, two sat at the table in the middle of the room. A tall man stood at the window with his hands concealed in the pockets of his gray hospital tunic.

For a moment, he saw them very small and far away in the dirty gray light—then he was there again and the room stood still. Werter wavered. Nobody moved to offer him help. Yet, six pair of eyes slid inquiringly over him.

"What's happened to you?" One of the men lying on the bed shot an unfriendly glance at him.

"I have been shot in the leg."

"They patch you up and send back to Russia," said the one who was sitting on his bed propped up to the wall with pillows on both sides. Where his torso ended, the sheet lay flat.

Werter winced and felt almost guilty at being whole.

"I'm a gone man," the same man continued stubbornly and somehow matter-of-factly. He was in his middle years, not more than forty, yet his dark blond hair was already graying. "After the war I'm not a hero anymore but just a cripple, sitting on a pushcart and selling matches like the men after the first war."

"That's not important. The most important thing is that you are alive," Werter said, instantly aware of a flush creeping across his cheeks.

"Alive? You call it alive?" The man who was the first to address him tore a sheet down and lifted his legs without feet.

A mine or frozen, Werter thought automatically. "They have wonderful prostheses."

In the dead silence that ensued, they stared at him and the pained reproach in their haunted eyes was beyond endurance. He turned away, and suffering from the hurting pressure of the crutches and a bitter, sad anger, which was arising in him, hobbled to the vacant bed and lumped down.

"Prostheses? Are you saying prostheses?" A lad in his late teens jumped from his bed. He drew in his breath sharply as though to shout something and waved his short stumps. His nostrils quivered and his eyes flashed. His angry movements made his wavy blond hair drop in curls on his sweaty forehead. Looking straight at Werter with his bright, cornflower-blue eyes he asked, "How can I hold my fiancée with prostheses?"

"You make me sick, you milksop, whining and slobbering incessantly." One of the men at the table made a gesture of annoyance with his right hand that was missing four fingers. The sleeve of his hospital tunic ended with a knot below the elbow of his other arm.

"I'm afraid she'll be cheating on me." Tears slowly slipped down the youth's cheeks.

"You'll find another one," the same man said rudely.

For a fleeting moment, Werter remembered the desire to hold that Russian girl, Serafima, in his arms, but it was instantly erased by another recollection. *I have seen more crippled and mutilated bodies in Russia, but they were lifeless.*

As if reading Werter's thought, the man at the table, who all this time had not uttered a single word spoke, "We are lucky. Others became prisoners of war or are under the crosses. God grant they *have* the crosses in that accursed Russian soil." With his cracked and chafed hands, he caressed the crutches that rested against the table with the same tenderness with which he just a moment ago fingered the photographs in front of him.

"Stop it, please." From the window, the tall man detached himself. For a fraction of a second, his face contorted and then it was gone. He walked to the door unnaturally erect, not moving his arms pressed against his sides. His beautifully proportioned body was a cruel contradiction to his thickly bandaged right arm, which was much shorter than the other.

"Otto won't play his piano any more. There are no prostheses for that." The one whose legs were amputated very high up grinned crookedly.

Involuntarily, Werter moved his fingers, sensing the painful stiffness in them, then slowly lifted his right hand to his chin below the left jaw where he used to tuck his violin. A hopeless chill went straight through his heart. He felt shame at his earlier words, and he wanted to apologize, but the men looked away.

"Uwe, switch on the radio," a voice came.

After a moment of crackling and humming, a shrill voice cut the silence. "Every German must be proud of his homeland and must be happy and thankful to give his life for his country. Sieg Heil! Sieg Heil!" Then the Horst Wessel song rolled on, brassy and intolerable. "Millions are looking upon the swastika full of hope ..."

"Uwe, switch it off." Someone let out a long, audible breath.

"Well then, to sit in silence like in a grave?" the youth responded with some asperity.

From the knapsack that the medical orderly dumped at his bed, Werter took his mouth harmonica and placed it to his lips. At the sounds of the sweet melody of the *Blue Danube Waltz,* the men turned to him, their eyes lit up gladly. The notes, pure and light, floated in the warm air like the distant voice of something that all of them probably had long forgotten. They sat serenely, sometimes swaying slightly to the music. When the last passages faded away, he saw them smiling at one another as if those unexpected memories were freeing them from the cruel spell of the war. But then, the light in their eyes faded.

In the ensuing silence, Werter did not hear, but rather, felt somebody behind his back. He glanced over his shoulder. In the doorway, the Pianist was standing. He clutched his neck with his beautiful undamaged hand and deep ugly sounds came from his throat as he sobbed.

Werter turned away, unable to restrain his lips from trembling.

The night was well advanced when from the distance a low rumbling came. *Artillery,* Werter thought, half-asleep. *But where? Where is the front?* And then, relieved, he felt himself on a bed with a fresh sheet beneath him. He propped himself on one elbow to listen. A crack came again, closer. The next moment, he saw lightning and the rain thrusting heavy drops at the window glass.

He sat up in his bed and switched on the light. The little lamp shone softly over the bedside table. He took out his mother's last letter and read it again. Then he rummaged in his knapsack for the letter he had started in Stalingrad. It was not there. He continued to feel in the pockets of his trousers and tunic but did not find it.

Den 27. September 1942

> *Meine sehr geliebte Mutti,*
>
> *Only today, I have a chance to return to writing to you again. The letter I started a week ago was lost somewhere on my way from Stalingrad.*
>
> *As I'm writing, I look at your lovely letter, and as I read your lines, I forget what happened to me, and the East, which is still so filled with menace.*
>
> *The hardest battle of my life is behind. God stood next to me thanks to your and Gerdi's prayers. I am in a hospital in East Prussia. So close to you and still so far.*

His mind dwelt on the incidents of the last seven days, living them over and over, feeling the same pain and fear. It was a strangling panic, undefined and threatening, a fear of helplessness and gnawing doubt. *What is this war and the way we wage it—with slave camps, concentration camps, and the mass murder of civilians … and what is my own guilt in it?* The questions he had never dared to answer crowded his inflamed mind. From under his eyebrows, he brushed the sleeping men in the room with his quick glance. *At least they won't go to fight for it again.* For a fraction of a moment, he thought he envied them. *But I can't, I must not write about my doubts to my mother, a proud German mother of a heroic German son*, he thought with bitter irony.

> *Don't worry too much, Mama; it's only a small wound on my left knee. I'm only surprised that up to now I haven't become seriously wounded or ill. I remember how the slightest draughts had sent me to bed with fever! And I remember how you brought me the chicken broth to bed, and I have to confess, I often feigned the illness longer then I actually felt ill.*
>
> *In my thoughts, I am with you, my loved ones. I look forward so much to seeing you soon.*
> *Dein Sohn Werter.*

In Russia, it was winter again.

One morning in late November of 1942, Serafima slowly got up, feeling her joints stiff, her hands and her feet cold. The warmth of the stove from the previous evening had long gone.

She washed her face with icy water, took two bites of rye bread from her day ration and munched slowly. It helped to scare the nausea and usually was enough till the twelve o'clock recess. She changed her baby's swaddling clothes, gave him milk, wrapped him up, and pressing him close to her chest, set off to the factory.

At six in the morning, it was still dark. Outside, it was wet and muddy. Her boots sank in deep and the earth held them fast as though it wanted to drag them off.

At the gatekeeper's office, Semenich hailed her. He motioned her to the side, right under the huge poster with a Red Army soldier poking his finger, asking, WHAT DID YOU DO FOR THE FRONT?

"Well, girl, show me your little one." He peeled back the white sheeting.

The baby sneezed.

"Oh, you, a little snot-nose." His face split into a wide grin then instantly grew serious. "Er … Such a thing, Serafima. You should not have to drag four kilometers every day to the factory. The snow will come soon. How will you—listen, I happen to know that two rooms in the hostel for female workers are vacant, so right now go to the factory management, fill out an application, and I'll see to the rest. I've had a word with—Got it?" He winked cunningly.

"Semenich, oh Semenich, for such a kindness how can I repay you?" She suddenly felt an aching, piercing tenderness, more like a thankfulness for something that must be a norm among people—sympathy—and what she so rarely encountered in her life.

"Don't blabber the nonsense. Go, right now."

As Semenitch had predicted, the next day, the snow came down. After the months of unending drizzle, a virgin white blanketed everything—the ruined houses, the burned trees, the fields, and the mud.

Over the snow-covered ground silence hung, unbroken except for the occasional howl of a wolf deep in the forests that stretched quietly away. A pale red band lay along the horizon. The dim light was coming from snow, which was crisscrossed with the marks of hares' feet.

Serafima adjusted the bundles with her sparse bag and baggage, pressed Vanechka to her chest, and stepped into the deep layer of snow that rasped and cracked under her weight. Each icy breath stabbed her with hundreds of sharp points, all the way down to her empty stomach.

Soon, her hands froze in her thin mittens and the toes of her right foot went numb—it was that boot that had a hole frayed in it.

Cold as the morning was, two hours later, she was sweating. With an aching pain all the way from the small of her back to her shoulders, she had found herself in front of a former stable that was rebuilt into the hostel, its thin coat of paint peeling and blistering from cold. Inside, the timbered partitions divided its expanse. There was no bathroom and two toilets were in the hall and shared by all tenants.

The old boards screeched sonorously underfoot and the snores were heard as she walked along the narrow corridor. The strong odors of people living close together—composed of sweat and smoke and human waste—came to her nose and gave her a feeling of sickness.

The door of room 7 was unlocked. Under the dingy bare window, a small table made of old boards rudely hammered together pressed against the wall. On it sat a soot-covered oil lamp silhouetted against the first uncertain light of the starting winter day. A small iron oven Burzhuika with a flue occupied the middle of the room and a thin pile of firewood lay close to it.

Her eyes were still adjusting. She lowered the child onto a metal spring bed without a mattress and shook her shoulders to free herself from the bundles. In the corner, something else loomed. She bent forward. A hardly perceptible smell of varnish reached her nostrils. She touched a smooth wooden footboard. The thing rocked.

"Sonny, you have your own cradle," she whispered. Reaching further, she felt a cushioned pillow. *Semenich,* went through her mind, and she started crying, though she did not know why.

The first uncertain sun beams touched the melting latticework of the frost on the window—the window of her and Vanechka's new home.

Every day, when the moon gave way to the very first, faint grey tinge of dawn, she hurried to the factory. Aware of the criminal code—arrive late three times in a row and you were a 'saboteur'—people elbowed their way through the gatekeeper's room. Right under the DEATH TO THE ENEMY! banner Semenitch's sister-in-law, the round faced Mashka sat. She checked the workers' names on her list, and then let them rush through the turnstile. "Morning," she would say with a sudden irritation as if disappointed that Serafima had never been late.

One day, in the early spring of 1943, Serafima stopped abruptly in front of the notice board, caught by her own name on it. The huge bold letters announced, FOR CONSTANT OVERFULLFILMENT OF THE PRODUCTION PLAN, SERAFIMA KRIVENKOVA IS AWARDED A PRIZE OF ONE MONTH'S PAY. PROUD OF OUR BEST WORKER!

A pair of shoes for me, or ... She looked down at her old brown skirt, patched in places. *No, no, woolen socks and mittens for Vanechka.* The thoughts chased one another.

A week before, a teaspoon made a knocking sound against Vanechka's gums. Since then, every night, she awoke with aching bones from hours of sitting in her bed, the child curled in exhausted sleep on her lap, or she forwent sleep altogether, walking up and down with her beloved burden to dispel his disquiet. Yet, she often caught herself smiling, living again and again the moments of bliss when she could lie silently gazing at the pale face of her baby sleeping in his little cradle by her side, watching the movements of the frowning brows, and the thin little hands with clenched fingers that rubbed the little eyes and nose. At such moments, she had a sense of perfect peace, and nothing would remind her of what she did not want to remember.

She learned to tell nonsense tales and to sing the melodies of the few revolutionary songs and sometimes, she hummed the only Strauss' waltz she knew into his little ear.

And so weeks went by, and again summer arrived.

On July seventeen of 1943, the weather was perfect, with a soft, almost cooling breeze and the bright sky with the sun setting behind the roofs of the houses. For Serafima, this particular day was different from the other hard and monotonous days.

She carefully cleaned her hands of the sticky, black grease and half-rushed, half-walked from the shop and into the long corridor, past the shop-manager's closet-like room. The door was open.

"Serafima! Wait!" Semenich hailed her.

"What?" She returned and stopped at the doorway.

"I'd like a word with you. Come on in, girl."

Reluctantly she stepped in.

He was sitting at his table, aimlessly shifting things about then bent sidewise and opened the desk drawer door. He drew out a package—something wrapped in the row paper. "For your son."

"Semenich. Do you re—?"

He touched his moustache, as if adjusting it on his face. "Of course I remember. His birthday. Sew something for him. Well, now go. I know where you were tearing off to."

She pressed the package to her chest. On the threshold she turned. "Thank you, Semenich. God bless you."

Some little distance away, there was a sound of feet and voices from the corridor.

Semenich turned his eyes fearfully towards the door. "Shoo. What if the people hear you? With your religious propaganda. Shame on you, a Komsomol member. Now go, go."

To the Kindergarten she sped almost at a run. Less then ten minutes later, she slowed her steps, halted for breath, shoved a heavy lock of her hair under her white cotton headscarf, and pushed open the familiar door.

At the sound of her steps, Vanechka got up on his shaky legs, clutching to the barrier of his crib, then stretched one arm to her without letting a small wooden horse from his hand.

"What is it, my dear one?" Serafima reached out to him.

"My little present for his first birthday." Anna Konstantinovna's tired eyes lit up more intently, glowing with a true, quiet tenderness.

"You are so kind to him, Anna Konstantinovna. We go to my mother to celebrate. I wish you could join us."

"Thank you." She placed her refined hand to her chest. "You know, I have to stay with the children."

Serafima lifted her son from his bed and walked off. "We go to see your grandma, sonny."

And he, as if knowing that something especially wonderful would happen, beamed. Resting in her arms, he pressed his head against her shoulder and was quiet all the way.

The gray road, lined with a growth of prickly thorns, was completely deserted. A warm breeze brought the scent of wormwood to her nostrils. The sun pierced slantingly through the white thin strands of clouds and dropped a fan of clear rays over the field, the pine forest lurking in a distant haze, and her village of two houses spared from fire.

Serafima sniffed as she opened the door. "Mother! What is this smell?"

Glafira's smile brought an immediate softening to her features.

In the middle of the table, a platter of pancakes gave off a faint whiff. "Don't we celebrate my grandson's birthday?" She took Vanechka from Serafima's hands and kept chanting, "Birthday, birthday," while dangling him.

"Mother, you didn't answer. Where did you get so much wheaten flour from?"

"Shoo. Gleaned."

"Is it? What if somebody finds out? What if … You, yourself, have told me they took one of your women to the court for—" She stopped, afraid to pronounce the terrifying word "stealing."

Avoiding Serafima's stare, Glafira waved her arm as though obliterating an insect and said demonstratively, "Oh, grand sonny, how heavy you are." She lowered down on the bench and put Vanechka on the floor, holding him in between her knees. And he, his eyes gleaned to the platter, swayed on his slim slightly bowed legs like a blade of grass by wind and made three steps toward the table.

"Sonny!" "Grand sonny!" they cried out in unison.

He tottered, plopped on the floor, and howled.

Glafira lifted him up. "Now, now, sweetie," she spoke softly and patted his back. He laid his head on her shoulder and let himself be comforted.

As soon as his sobs subsided, he turned his head to the plate on the table again.

"Here it is." Serafima nipped off a petite piece of a pancake and gave it to him. He shoved it in his mouth and stretched his arm to the table.

"There's an appetite for you, grand sonny! Eat, my soul, eat. There is more, don't worry. You'll get your fill."

He gobbled down the second piece as quickly as the first, and then another one. Soon his eyelids became heavy and he passed into sleep.

Glafira lowered him onto her bed. From behind the stove, she took out a half-liter bottle and put it on the table. "What, isn't it a day to celebrate?"

"Moonshine?"

Glafira nodded. She poured the turbid fluid in tumblers and they clinked the glasses together.

"For Vanechka," Serafima said.

"O Lord our God, send Thy guardian angel to protect and keep our Vanechka from all evil. May he live happily and enjoy the best of health." Glafira crossed the sleeping child in a blessing. Then she took a small copper cross from the pocket of her Sunday dress and put it on the child's pillow.

"Don't even dare—" Serafima said.

"Too late."

"What does it mean 'too late'? Do you want to say you—"

"Yes. I did. Father Sergiy, himself, came and christened him and consecrated the cross."

Glafira's cool, detached voice met Serafima's anger. It was like throwing gasoline on a fire.

"But, Mother, I'm a Komsomol member, if they find out my son is—" she shouted.

"And who will tell them? I? Father Sergiy? You?"

Serafima regretted her anger almost immediately. "So, did Father Sergiy pronounce a benediction over him?"

"Not only the benediction. I asked him to pray for Vanechka to have a father. He said, he will."

"Stop it, Mother," she said, though without malice and mentally pronounced, "O Lord, bless my son and keep him and let Thy great beaming countenance shine down upon him and give him peace … and father." She poured herself another glass, felt it burn through her, and suddenly hummed softly,

Dark eyes, burning eyes
Passionate and splendid eyes—

Glafira put a shushing finger to her lips.

"Don't worry, Mother, he likes music. Anna Konstantinovna says he hums perfectly to the melodies she plays on the piano."

Time passed—the leaves withering and blowing away, the snow falling and melting. Another season's summer. Again autumn, again the snowfall.

Somehow Serafima had come to accept herself and the world around her more calmly, and while she still had periods of fear and resentment, they were fewer and less desolately painful than before.

There were rare letters from Victor, short, inflated with enthusiasm as the Soviet offensive grew. They were full of love and confidence in seeing her soon. Her letters were sad and as short as his and full of love, too. In one of his letters, he wrote about Dunyasha's death— their medical train was bombed on her way to the front. The news shook Serafima deeply and still pained like an unhealed wound.

She often thought back of the time since Vanechka's birth and remembered how her son learned to pronounce "Ma" or "Ba-ba," calling for his grandmother, and that to her surprise his first uttered word was "An-na." With a smile, she recalled his first shaky steps, his first teeth, and how she was caught off guard by Anna Konstantinovna's statement one day in the beginning of November of 1944.

She couldn't resist the happiness, the memory of that day two months ago brought her. It was a Friday, and as usual, at eight in the evening, she went to the Kindergarten to take her son. She stopped in front of the inside door, swiped hurriedly some snowflakes from her shawl and the quilted jacket, and entered.

"Ah," Anna Konstantinovna exclaimed and met Serafima's gaze. Her usually calm eyes reflected something new, a kind of anxiety Serafima had never seen in her.

"What?" Serafima's voice cracked. "Did he get sick?" She looked at her son who was sitting on the chair in front of the piano, poking with his little fingers on the creamy ivory keys, and stopping as if in amazement of the sounds that ensued.

"No, no, he's fine. He's just … He's just …" Anna Konstantinovna's eyes seemed to be suffused with an excitement, gleaming fixedly with a moist blueness. "I think he's a wunderkind."

"A wun …? A who?"

"He played piano today. Mozart … A Rondo … Well, he did not play with both hands, but he perfectly picked it out with one finger. Perfectly. Perfectly. Vanechka—" Tears glistened in her eyes.

He, hearing his name, turned his face, and seeing Anna Kostantinovna cry, ran to her, hugged her knees, and burst into tears.

"Vanechka, no, Vanechka." Anna Kostantinovna pressed him to her bosom. You are—" She laughed and squeezed him even tighter.

The next day, Anna Konstantinovna started teaching Vanechka to play piano in earnest.

Den 7. January, 1945

Liebe Mutti,

Your letter and Gerdi's postcard however short tore me away from the mean indifference of the war. As I have written to you before, here, in Southeastern France, in comparison to Russia, is a radiant paradise.

Nothing changed in my position: since there is no hope my leg will allow me to take long marches, the doctors let me alone and I still do paper work in a military chancellery. Now, at last, I can think about my tortured fingers. Oh, how much I want to cradle my violin in my hands, and play, play … It haunts me in the night. My mouth harmonica and Wehrmacht radio help me to escape the unbearable nostalgia. I just heard Bach's D-minor toccata, yesterday—the Beethoven's Spring Sonata.

But of course, my thoughts are tormented that my beautiful city has fallen victim to vile British bomb attacks. But I am so glad you are all right and our house is intact. This is the benefit of living on the outskirts of a big city.

And can you imagine how often I think of home leave? No, not the leave but coming home for good. I'm so tired.

He halted and contemplated if the mentioning of his location and especially his last words would prompt a meticulous pen of a military censor to blacken them or stamp the letter "to be pursued further," which most likely meant his mother would never receive it.

For my first meal, I want chicken in paprika. And of course, your famous honey rolls. Look how selfish I am! I don't even know if you have enough to eat. You have never complained about it.

I know why you have never complained, he thought. He knew why they had never mentioned the abhorrence of their situation—telling the truth had sent many people to concentration lagers.

He shuddered at the comprehension. *Germany is collapsing … Why do we deceive ourselves? Why do we all stubbornly pretend that we believe in the declaration "We will never capitulate"? Because we were educated to stubborn, blind obedience.* He answered himself. *Am I cured by this damned war? Am I?* Involuntary, his eyes moved upward to the portrait of Hitler on the wall. *Do I still believe in my Führer and in the justice of his actions?*

Without tearing his eyes from the painfully familiar and adored by millions face, he said aloud, "Damn him. Not even with death will his guilt be wiped out."

Mama, I hope, no, I feel I'll see you and my dear sister soon. Now, very soon.
Dein Werter.

PART II

THE MERCILESS PEACE

May 1945

"Serafima! You home?"

First, a voice came and then Sashka, their pimply-faced seventeen-year old postmaster poked his head through the door.

"Home. What do you want?" She damped down the wick flame of the primus-stove on which pearl-barley porridge boiled in a pannikin and turned to him.

"A card for you. From Berlin!"

By his cheeks, suddenly spotted red and downcast eyes she guessed he had read it.

She rubbed her hands down her dress and reached out. A hard glossy quadrangle slipped from her fingers and landed on the floor between her and Sashka's equally worn out shoes. Only his were heavily covered with the brown shoe polish and hers were coated with water-thinned tooth powder.

Sashka stared at the card and did not stir.

"Have nothing better to do?" She wanted him out badly.

He raised his eyes, ogling her in silence.

"What's wrong with you?"

"The card. Is it from Vanechka's fa—?"

"You mind your own business," she snapped up. "Out with you."

"Why are you angry? I just asked. I didn't mean it wrong." He shrugged and left.

As if afraid to burn herself, she picked up the card from the floor with two fingers. It was a black and white city street view with the cluster of strange houses clinging to each other and the sharp-pointed churches that dominated the background. She hastily turned the card over and read in the queer, familiar handwriting,

May 9, 1945
Berlin

Serafimushka! It's all over. The Victory is ours. The fate spared me for you.

I am so happy that I soon can press my little girl to my chest that I seem to be walking on air. You are the only one in the world I could ever love and to think that you are mine is wonderful. There couldn't be anyone else for us but each other. It was ordained that we should be together. I have always known it. It's us for the rest of our lives that is going to be the happiest that ever was.

Forever yours,
Victor.

She pressed the card to her chest and for a long moment forgot how to breathe.

Many times, she had imaginary conversations with him, mentally searching for words to explain, to apologize. More over, she felt trapped at the thought, searching for the words and not finding them. *It was not my choice to have my son … Even so, the best thing that life has thus far offered me is Vanechka—and Vitya.*

She re-read his letter. *But of course he'll understand. He loves me.* Smiling to herself, she pictured how he'd approach Vanechka, take him into his arms, and say, "He is your son, so he is my son, too."

Assured she was doing the right thing, she ripped a piece of paper from a notebook.

May 20, 1945

> *Dear Vitya!*
> *I'm holding your lovely postcard in my hand and am so happy that you are returning from the war safely.*
> *I love and adore you. Since the first time I saw you, I had a feeling of absolute security. I knew that whatever happened to me, you'd always be there to help me. But when I needed you the most, you weren't here; you couldn't be. And now, I need you to understand that what happened to me was not my fault.*
> *I know your kind heart and hope you will love my son as much as you love me.*
> *Your Serafima.*

"Oh," she exclaimed, suddenly aware of the burned porridge smell.

May 21, 1945, Germany

It was getting light when Werter reached Berlin. The train passed slowly over patched-up rails, past skeletons of buildings with windows like black eye sockets, splintered telegraph poles, uprooted trees, the angular bodies of burned-out tanks, twisted barricades, and cobblestones torn up by shells. Wherever his eyes could see, there were enormous piles of charred bricks and twisted steel.

From the Berlin Train station, he took the streetcar that drove down a road he no longer recognized.

"Bastards," an old man who was sitting next to him muttered under his nose.

They passed an old cemetery, then a small square with a surprisingly large number of people for such a ruined city.

"What's there?" Werter asked the man.

"The black market." The man turned to Werter and carefully examined his uniform without insignia. "Was a prisoner?" he said after a while.

Werter nodded.

"Under Americans?"

"Under them."

"Lucky you are. Under Soviets it's the worst."

"Why?"

"Beasts. Absolute beasts."

The streetcar stopped.

"All out!" the driver shouted.

People hurried about outside.

"Don't we go any farther?" Werter asked a woman who was elbowing her way to the exit.

"No," she said without turning.

"Why not?"

"Here on Neuss-Strasse, the tracks broke off," a man's voice said.

Werter slung his knapsack over his shoulder and got out.

For an hour, he limped toward Rosenthal. The buildings were guillotined—their roofs gone, sitting in misshapen poses somewhere in nearby backyards. Other buildings were ripped by bombs from top to basement. Everywhere there were the cylinders of German gas masks, flattened by tank tracks ... crumpled helmets bearing the dark signs of eagles ... grey Russian quilted jackets, and the cloying sweet whiff of corpses buried beneath the ruins. At an intersection, a dead horse lay, swarmed over by fat flies.

On the lawn in front of an undamaged private house, there was a knee-high mound marked with four wooden posts painted bright red and topped with white stars. Affixed to them were small handwritten plaques—edged paper under glass. He stopped and read Russian names and the date of their death: May 1, 1945.

From windows of the rare house or building still remotely habitable, the flags hung down—English, American, French, and Russian: a yellow hammer, sickle, and star on the red background.

That was his Berlin. It was quiet, bathed in warm May sunshine. Here and there, miraculously preserved cobblestones, smoothed by centuries of footsteps, looked velvety in the sun.

On a street without a name shield, he broke into an abandoned garden behind the black ruins. It was in full blossom—a wonderful place with short, silky grass, the kind that thrust up so thickly each blade seemed to fight for space. He picked several crocuses. The smells of plant and soil made his head spin.

Exhausted to the verge of nausea by his tramping through the no longer recognizable streets, he collapsed on the grass. He looked up into the transparent blueness with light puffs of spring clouds high above, and already feeling regret for this unplanned resting, for postponing the meeting with his mother and sister, got up.

He hurried, treading unsteadily on the cobblestones, assisting himself with his stick.

At last, he was on Marienstrasse. It still bore the signboard. In front of his house, Werter stopped abruptly and mentally asked himself, *What had I expected? A miracle among all these ruins?*

The house was destroyed. Once it had stood two stories, square and solid. A fragment of wall was supporting the mezzanine, the second floor had one room intact but it was gaping open in front, toward the street. His mother's piano was in the corner of the living room, in its place, dusted, but seemingly untouched, as if saved by a spirit. Above this room, a high, narrow gable reared up, bare, with empty window sockets.

He tried the basement door. It did not give in. Shaking with excitement, he pounded the door with his fists. After a while, he heard noise inside, steps. Finally, the lever of the door shifted and it opened a tiny crack. A woman peered out.

"What are you banging on the door for?" the woman said in a voice harsh and hostile. "Get out of here at once!"

"I lived here before I joined the military."

"Anyone could say that."

"I'm Werter. Werter Lindberg. This is my house. Gisela Lindberg is my mother. Gerda Lindberg is my sister."

The woman stared at him with suspicion then stepped aside. "She's here."

With breakneck speed, he rushed down the stairs. He barely managed to grab hold of the railing in time when his heel caught on the edge of a step. His knees buckled, but he went on, groping his way through, banging into trunks, crates, bundles.

It smelled of unaired closet and burned oil. By the flickering light of a Hindenburg lamp, its wick in tallow encased in cardboard, he could make out people, about a dozen of them, with pasty faces, stubby chins and sunken cheeks, sitting on the cots piled with pillows and quilts or the chairs, which ranged from kitchen stools to brocade armchairs.

He immediately recognized his old teen bed. It was tacked to the wall. On it sat a thin withered woman with gray, disorderly hair, slumped over, motionless, her arms braced. *Mother?* Something in him refused to recognize her. Not his mother as she really was—beautiful, elegant, always immaculately groomed from shoes to collar.

He put down his knapsack. "Mama!" Suddenly, he noticed he had lost his voice.

"Who are you?" She looked at him blankly.

"Your son. Werter. For you."

Her squashed face with its red nose and swollen eyes changed when she took flowers from his hand. "What flowers, what lovely flowers. Bring them to her." Her eyes, circled with blackness, settled somewhere beyond him on the wall.

The people sitting nearby exchanged silent, meaningful glances.

"Mama, where is Gerdi?"

"She is in the garden. There. Behind the chestnut tree. We used our old broom closet … Do you remember that closet? Do you?"

"What closet? Mama, what are you talking about?" His heart threatening to explode from within his chest, he reached with his hand to her, but she wrenched her torso toward the wall and screamed.

Her howls rose up from deep inside her throat—hoarse and guttural. "My daughter! I want my daughter back!" She bellowed out the words over and over.

He stopped breathing each time they came and let her noises tear and scrape through him.

"She is so close. Go … Go to see her …" She stared past him blindly, impassively, threads of saliva dribbling from her open mouth, just like a baby. "Why would they do to her the thing like that? You must know. You are a soldier."

Forcing himself to calm down, he asked slowly and distinctly. "Mama, what happened? Where is Gerdi? What happened to her?"

"My God, my God …" He heard a woman's voice moaning.

Another voice whispered somewhere close to his ear, "Gerdi, poor girl, she couldn't take it any longer. She had been through it several times night after night. There was an entire troop. Each took his turn—"

"God no!" Werter froze then retched but nothing came up. Head in his hands, he wailed openly, wildly, desperately wanting to comprehend something that his consciousness refused to accept.

He could not recall later, how he crawled onto a bare mattress with all his clothes on, slept in fits and starts, uneasy dreams. A strange, frightening feeling of resurrection in his memory of *that* December day of 1941 made his throat squeeze by a tormenting asphyxia. All this came back to him this night—the filthy hut, the curly-headed girl.

The face was very unclear, but it had rebellious blazing eyes and either in a dream or in delirium, he thought of the pain the girl must have felt from the blow of major Schuette's Mauser.

He thought he was sleeping and dreaming, but at the same time, his consciousness seemed to be separated from the state of sleep and his imagination filled in the picture of the first minutes after the girl came to her senses. With merciless obstinacy, he forced himself to imagine the intensity of her suffering. *Shall I ever deserve pardon for that? Can I ever forget?* He ground his teeth to overcome the piercing pain.

An invisible force was crushing him. He could feel its weight, its hypnotic power; it was forcing him to remember—the girl's eyes, rolled back, her patched woolen skirt pulled up, her legs, parted shamelessly and horribly.

We, Germans, raped, looted, murdered ... Now the Russians match atrocity with atrocity.

But is it possible to alter what had happened, what had been fixed forever by Gerdi's death and maybe the girl's, too?

The Russian girl's fate, taking vengeance for his hasty error, had overtaken him and almost four years later raised its avenging hatchet over him and brought it down on his sister.

Somebody opened the door, letting in the warm breeze.

Bathed in sweat, he opened his eyes and drew up a deep breath as if after a struggle. *What time is it?* He strained his eyes and stared at his arm watch, holding it up to the faint glow of the lamp. The glass on the watch swam, but somehow he made out the hands said it was nearly six in the morning.

He creaked his body from the mattress. In the old trunk, he found the gray woolen jacket he wore before the war. It stunk of mothballs.

On the bed, his mother lay huddled up, pressing something to her chest. She looked like a paralyzed animal, her hair in tangles, falling over her face. Her sheet slipped with one of its corners to the floor.

Werter bent over to adjust it and instantly recognized Gerdi's Mittenwald brown violin case in his mother's arms. He stroked her hair away from her forehead. "Mama," he whispered. Suddenly it felt hard to breathe.

He labored from the basement. A bright blue, cloudless sky, the shine of dew on the grass, the twitter of a bird struck him almost physically. *How is it possible it all still exists?*

He stumbled over the untended garden to the chestnut tree, fingered his initials engraved into its bark on the level of his chest, *WL* and *GL* a bit to the right. *How old were we then? Ten? Eleven?* His life before the war was now something he could barely bear to remember—their evenings together, mama's loving arms, Gerdi's laughter—all that remained was a heap of soil. His throat tensed up. *Gerdi, why was it you who died and I who was spared?*

He walked slowly through the town, passed a number of graves. Some were marked with German steel helmets, some with the gaudy red Russian stakes. A bulletin "News for Germans" was posted next to the door of a half-destroyed building.

The entire district seemed to have been scared into hiding. The Russians had the streets entirely to themselves—broad soldiers with peasants' faces and innocent blue eyes, many Asians—swarthy, lean, with a thick jaw and narrow, swollen pitch-black eyes.

Which of you? He was brimming with hate. A hundred horrible thoughts flashed in his mind. He could feel his fists clench, his index finger seeking a trigger. He wanted to be away, far away, someplace where he wouldn't see that uniform, the mere sight of which made his heart lose a beat.

And yet, another thought, another feeling raised a lump in his heart. *We were not much different over there. Was I?*

Limping toward Schönenberg, he saw his reflection in some miraculously preserved shop windows—his tie undone and his black boots unpolished. *Why do I judge myself? I was acting on orders.* He raised his hands to button up his collar, but then it seemed too much trouble, and he dropped his hands again. *But where does complicity begin?*

When he crossed the railroad, he saw German prisoners slaving away—old men in shabby Volkssturm clothes. Unshaven and emaciated, with the gaping eyes of wretched dogs, they reminded him of the Russian POWs he used to see while the fighting in Russia was still on. This, too, was a logical reversal.

He walked on. After about twenty minutes, he realized he no longer knew where he was. He had lost his way among the ruins. They all looked alike and he had a strange feeling that for him, like for these ruins, all was over.

S unday, August 26, 1945

Serafima and Vanechka sat on a wooden bench in Lenin Park. It was patchy with the withered grass. Wide-branching oak trees and shady maples stood as if paralyzed in the windless air, their leafy tops dusty green. The grass and the trampled down ground were littered with cigarette ends and the husks of sunflower-seeds.

The park was alive with movement. Shaded by the canopy, a brass band of five was playing. Vanechka sat on Serafima's lap, his little feet moving with the beat of the music.

On the wooden platform, couples, mostly women, moved and swam amid the slowed-down flow of the music, some walked round in circles, others, barely swayed on the spot. A woman leaned to her dance partner in a faded tank uniform without insignia, looking dreamily in his face, which bore the signs of the old burn scars.

After a fox-trot, the orchestra started the *Blue Danube waltz*. In spite of the stifling heat, Serafima shivered with chill. Her mind kept turning to its tortured thinking. *Two months and two weeks have passed since I wrote to Vitya about my son. He did not come, that means he did not forgive. Maybe he even despises me.* She ran her fingers through Vanechka's hair and he, responding to the tenderness of her touch, leaned back. She kissed the top of his head. "Vanechka."

"Ma-ama."

She pressed him closer to her and listened to his slow breath, aware of a smile spreading over her face.

Incidentally, her eyes rested on a couple, sitting on a bench under the branchy oak. The woman put her arms around the man. The empty sleeves of his discolored tunic were tucked into the belt of his khaki britches. She whispered something in his ear and laughed cheerfully, like a small bell, and he, as if trying to recompense her for his inability to hug her, intertwined her legs with his.

A wave of hurt broke over Serafima. She turned away.

To the right of her, two young women sat, leaning toward one another confidentially, talking in a loud whisper, interrupting each other.

"Natashka's husband brought her two huge suitcases of goods and chattels."

"I saw her on Lenin Street yesterday. Dressed up she was! A silky dress. High heels."

Serafima glanced involuntarily at her tarpaulin shoes ready to break open at the toes. She shed them further under the bench.

"Really? Do tell!"

"What of it? Cow is cow however you dress her."

They giggled.

"I've been trading a pair of silk stockings for half a dozen wheat cakes. Do you need stockings?"

"Oh Liza, I don't know. Kiril brought some from Germany. Do you need silver candle holders?"

Serafima cleared her throat. One of the women glanced at her over her shoulder, and they continued in subdued voices. Caps, dresses, shoes, fabric, boots, leather, brooches, medallions, blouses, buckles, forks, candles, scarves, rings, arm watches, French perfume, a roll of woolen cloth for a lady's coat—they chatted on and on.

Suddenly, the orchestra grinded to a halt. On the dance floor couples uncoupled, turning their faces to a column, crawling like a snake into the broad Dzerzhinsky Street. The gray mass of people, urged on by their escorts, dragged on foot along the road, a whirlwind of dust raised by their passage. Some were old men, judged by their curved spines and abundant wrinkles, some were beardless boys dressed in tattered uniforms, which were far too big for them. These men, emaciated, in a curious conglomerate of worn and discolored German tunics belted with pieces of rope or wire, were mostly shoeless with large rags wrapped around their feet.

Once they had marched as a symbol of German superiority. Now they crawled about, followed by the stares of women, children, and a few men—some faces were frozen in a cold glare, others looked in alarm, yet others muttered curses under their noses.

Serafima took Vanechka's hand and he, bobbing up and down, followed her to the road.

First, in her eyes the prisoners' faces blended into a bleary mass. Then she started to distinguish them one from another. She kept peering into them intently, seeking that particular damned face that was attached to her by the most terrible memory of the war. She could scarcely breathe. A drop of perspiration slowly wended its way down her back. A bitter taste filled her mouth as if it had filled with blood.

"Awww!" Vanechka jerked his hand. "It hurts!"

She released him and felt like running, but at the same time, could not move and stood paralyzed, letting the seconds trickle by, letting the columns of the prisoners pass.

"Mama." Vanechka pulled on her skirt. "Who are these people?

"The accursed ones."

"The accursed ones?" He raised his uncomprehending eyes at her, and his thick lashes fluttered in innocent curiosity.

"They are bad people. They killed our soldiers."

One of the prisoners glanced at Vanechka, and it seemed that tenderness or something very kind and uncharacteristic for such a sad face lit his light gray eyes. "Like my son," he said in a thick accented Russian and tears broke from his eyes.

"Your son! Your son, you say? Three times accursed! Blast you, damned one!" She was shaking, her eyes franticly searching around on the road. She found what she was looking for, and the next moment she grabbed a loose cobblestone and swung her arm to throw.

"Easy, citizen, easy." A hand seized her arm.

She still held that stone when she became aware of a militiaman whistling into her face, and Vanechka's eyes, big in horror. He grabbed her dress, howling at the top of his lungs.

"Shame on you, Mamasha, you scared your own little one." The elderly militiaman shook his head in reproach.

Serafima drew a deep breath and shook her head quickly. She let the stone fall from her hand into the ashen dust.

That night, Serafima fought sleep, for the darkness brought horror. She turned over and over and angrily realized that her memory insistently conjured up fragments of reminiscence: the tak-tak-tak hammering of machine guns; the smoke of the burning houses; a waltz melody, beautiful almost to pain. Like a cloud, the hideous face of the major arose but for some incomprehensible and terrifying reason his features transformed into Vitya's, and then again scraps of war.

She sat up and whispered, "Until I die I shall carry these memories. My whole life has been mutilated, cursed." Almost choking with the poisonous hatred that filled her, she groaned, "Damn you. Damn you."

"Mama?" Vanechka raised himself a little, holding onto the bedpost.

"Sleep my little heart, sleep." She kissed his white brows and stroked his face with her fingers. Lulled with her tender whisper, he fell asleep.

During the night, she went to his bed more than once, straightening his comforter and pillow, caressing him with her eyes—his dear little face pale in the timid light of the moon—and quietly returning to her bed again.

September 16, 1945

Serafima did not pay much attention to the noise from the corridor—the screeching of the entrance door, children's erratic steps and their shouts, shuffling of feet, women quarreling and backbiting among themselves, somebody's exclamation of, "What a handsome one!" and the confident footsteps that stopped at her door. In response to the urging knock, she raised her eyes from Vanechka's much-darned sock.

At the sound of the door opening, she dropped a stitch.

In the silence that ensued, Victor stood on the threshold, not a boy anymore. Grown stronger, he looked even handsomer. He was neat and tidy, his field shirt crisply pressed. His shoulder belt was fastened cross-wise and his high soft black leather boots were irreproachably mirror-like.

The needles clattered to the floor. It seemed forever before she could say, "You."

"Himself in person." His boundlessly happy eyes drank her in. He lowered a suitcase by the door, muttered, "Some gifts for you," then darted to her and snatched her towards him, crushing her in his embrace. "I've been so damned lonely for you."

Her throat tensed up. She buried her face in his breast and wept.

"Now, now. What's that? I'm here, safe and sound. Why are you crying?" He stroked her hair and her back, calming her as no one ever had before. Without letting her from his arms, he took a handkerchief from the pocket of his britches and lifted her face.

Dipping her head slightly, she said, "Don't look at me. I'm not sad. It's only that I've waited for you so long, and now that you are here, it seems so unreal."

"You are my crybaby." He kissed the top of her head. "If I could, I would have been here the next day after the Victory, but I was called up for an important assignment …" For a fleeting moment, his mouth took on an unpleasant twist. "Well, maybe I'll tell you another time."

She did not listen to his explanation. *He forgave me. He really loves me*, hammered in her head. Shame and joy flamed in her cheeks and dried her lips. "I'll be through with crying right away. You mustn't think me hysterical. I'm happy, Viten'ka, I knew you'd understand."

"Understand what? I don't want to understand anything. I only know that we are at last together." His lips brushed against hers as he spoke.

She went limp in his arms and whispered, "Oh, Vitya, how I've missed you!"

"You couldn't miss me more than I missed you." He stroked her hair tenderly.

She put up her hand to touch his cheek, searching his face intently for the answer to the question that tormented her, *why didn't he ask me about my son right away?* and seeing only the light of desire in his beautiful gray eyes.

The pressing despair finally caught up with her, and she no longer wanted to evade it. She wanted clarity. She was ready for it. "Did you receive my last letter in response to your postcard from Berlin?"

"No, my love, I didn't. I sent it the day I left Berlin. It does not matter now. I can't tell you how much I longed for this moment, to feel you in my arms, kiss you, and know I won't let you go from me forever."

"Vitya, I have to tell you something." A wave of hurt broke over her.

"Don't say a word, just let me kiss you." He lifted up her chin and his lips recaptured hers, more demanding this time.

Despite another wave of hurt that swept over her, a tingling of excitement raced through her as he put one arm around her waist and the fingers of his right hand searched for the buttons of her dressing gown.

"Serafimushka, I was dreaming of you all these years, waiting for this moment," he whispered, his breath hot against her ear.

She was conscious of where his tense flesh touched her, sending currents of desire through her. As each wave spent itself and another one gathered, she trembled. When his hand slid down her stomach to the swell of her hips, she moaned softly.

At the sound of the light flapping steps through the corridor, she gasped and recoiled from him.

The door went flying open. "Mama, the other boys—" Vanechka stood in the doorway, pressing a much torn rag ball to his chest and shifting his bare feet covered with fine dust up to his ankles like gray socks. He moved his eyes up at Victor and smiled humbly. Then his gaze froze on Victor's chest with a dazzling row of the medals. Like a bird, he stretched out his thin neck, trying to take a closer look at the slightly jingling decorations, and then took a step forward.

Victor's face contorted, and under his heavy gaze, Vanechka swayed and flopped down on the suitcase.

"What? Did he say 'Mama'?" Victor asked sharply. "Did you adopt the child?"

"I am sorry you didn't receive my letter." She returned her gaze to Vanechka and smiled at him. "No, I didn't adopt him. He is my son."

As though his collar was choking him, Victor loosened it jerkily then extracted a silver cigarette case and a lighter from the pocket of his britches. His hand with two missing fingers trembled so much it took some long moments before he could light the cigarette. He inhaled greedily, expelling the smoke upwards, knots of muscles moving on his cheekbones.

"Well, we-ell! So tha-at's how it is," he said in a drawl, an intake of breath swelling his chest under his field shirt. "Now this was the surprise Dunyasha had written me about. A nice one, I should say." His legs straddled, he was slowly rocking on his heels.

Clutching at the suitcase handle, Vanechka sat very still, watching them.

"Sonny, go to the yard, play something there with the other children."

Vanechka's eyes, filled with moisture, widened and fixed themselves on Victor. He nodded in somehow a hasty way and edged to the door.

Victor followed him out the room and turned from the door, running his bleary eyes over the tangled locks of her untidy hair, her bosom, over her legs, bare under the house gown, taking his revenge on her in the malice of his look.

She wanted involuntarily to stir under his hostile gaze.

"Who's the father, I fancy? A Russian soldier? Somebody local? A shirker? Or—" He sharply broke off and rubbed his throat.

At his words, she shuddered as if from an alien touch or a penetrating chill.

"Or maybe there were many? And you don't know who exactly? Or maybe it was a Fritz?" His pupils suddenly merged with the terrible madness of his eyes, and he shook his head wildly. "Oh no, no, only not that. A fascist's spawn? At the time I was staking my life you were enjoying yourself, banging around like a hussy?"

For a moment, she held her breath then took a swing with her fist at him. "You bastard!"

Instantly, his hand fell with implacable insane speed to his holster.

Straining to remain externally calm, she did not drop her eyes.

Their gazes collapsed.

His handsome face was repugnantly stiff.

From the corridor, a child's scream intruded upon the silence in the room. "Kill the fascist, kill the fascist, tak-tak-tak-tak."

"Tak-tak-tak-tak," another boy shouted boldly. The thumping of their trotting feet broke off abruptly after the smack of the entrance door.

Victor thrust his pistol into the crackling holster with a gesture from which the fire had gone, as though this movement had released the rage pent up in his breast. "You call *me* a bastard?" He smiled crookedly. "Love?" He leaned forward, hissing his words at her. "You trampled it. Trust? All that kept me struggling to survive?"

He paced the room then halted in front of the child's picture on the wall. "What is his name?"

Gripped by the fire of resistance, she said, "Vanechka."

His nostrils flared angrily. "The name of my father. Eh? Why?"

"Dunyasha wanted it."

"You ..." His mouth twisted into a threat. "So now you put all the blame on Dunyasha, now that she can't retort. She, on the front, sacrificed her life for you and this whoreson, who knows whose bastard—" He contemplated something for a moment. "But why, *you* must know whose he is."

He started to the door with a rolling gait, opened it with his fist, stepped out, then turned to seize his suitcase, and swaying, hit the doorframe with his shoulder. As he slammed the door, he cursed.

A stifling silence fell in the room—she heard only the cautious scratching of the mice in the old cupboard. The silence pressed physically on her shoulders, on her chest, on the skin of her face. *Already tried and found guilty, in fact*, she thought.

Her legs gave way, buckling at the knees, and she fell forward on the bed, her face in the pillow, whispering in a fit of feverish, choking despair, "Damned, damned major, may he find no peace, neither in this world nor in the next." His eyes bleary with frenzy and the blow had not left her memory. She involuntarily stroked the scar on her temple. *How to make peace of all these torturing memories with Vanechka's existence in my life?*

She made hard ugly noises because she hated herself for crying, yet couldn't help it, and had to wait a long time until the waves of hurt stopped breaking over her.

Then she pulled herself to her feet and paced across the room, the old boards screeching sonorously underfoot. As she passed by the mirror, she saw her face. She did not recognize it. It was the face of someone else. She turned away.

Behind the window, the Indian summer day was sunny and mild—the balmy sky with light puffs of clouds, and a lonely maple tree bright with red and yellow foliage.

A big green fly buzzed in the corner of the window frame. She opened the vent to release it and let fresh air and a landrail's single screeching call rush in. She leaned her temple against the window-jamb. It was warm from the sun and smelled of old paint.

The children's high screaming voices came from somewhere behind the nearest tenement. Vanechka sat on the worn boards' bench alone. As if feeling her stare, he lifted his eyes and beamed. "Mama!"

Some seconds later, he rushed in out of breath and buried his face into the hem of her skirt. She stood very still, holding her hand lightly on his blond-haired head. She loved him and wanted to forget all else in her silent happiness, behind which stood the shadow of the man she had loved, making her feelings to this little creature only deeper, more essential to her very being.

On November 6, 1945, a day before the twenty-seventh anniversary of the Great October Revolution, Victor was summoned up to the head of the regional NKVD.

He knocked and entered, bringing his hand up in a prescribed salute. "Present!"

General Glubov looked quickly at him, and his ear glued to the receiver, continued listening closely to whoever was on the other end of the phone.

With a bang of envy, which he would not admit even to himself, Victor ran his eyes over the hall-like room paneled two-thirds of the way to the ceiling with golden oak and the large writing desk with its monstrously solid ink-stand.

A huge portrait of Stalin hung on the wall, right over and behind the general's head.

Glubov was a stout and broad-chested man, with a thick growth of close-cropped gray hair on his square head and a scar on his notably fat face.

Victor liked him … He had always admired him. He was elated every time he went to his meetings and could imbibe and charge himself with the general's all-embracing willpower and energy. Afterwards, he would cheerfully feel like carrying out his instructions in time for the next meeting, whether it involved uncovering a new group of enemy of the people or a theft of scrap metal from the local military plant. However, this time, for some reason, he felt no upsurge of enthusiasm.

"Yes, Comrade First Secretary, we have a few minor problems, but those will be ironed out." Glubov's voice was filled with awe and respect yet an almost imperceptible, momentary look of anger crossed his face. He carefully put down the receiver, mopped up the perspiration from his forehead with his handkerchief then transferred his eyes to Victor.

"May I report to You, Comrade General?" Victor drew himself up and fixed his gaze on Glubov.

"At ease."

The General got up, walked to the window, and stood there with his back to him, his arms stiffly hanging a little away from his sides, his big fists clenched. "So how is it going, Comrade Kholodov?" he said, pronouncing each syllable in full. He turned and fixed his gaze on him. "Take a seat."

"After you, Comrade General." Victor seated himself on the very edge of the chair, up straight, without using its back for support. A cold knot formed in his stomach. The muscles of his forearms hardened beneath the sleeves. *Why is he so official with me today?* His heart thumping, he tried to recall what he had said wrong or to whom he had spoken.

The general returned to his table, opened the drawer and took out a thick folder. "I have made myself acquainted with your report." Suddenly all trace of severity disappeared from his face, and he broke into a half smile, the other half remaining rigid.

Victor unclenched his fists under the table.

"Your informers did a good job. I think we can make arrests, and I know you will get the scum to talk."

Yes, Victor's specialty was obtaining confessions. Tens, hundreds, broke before him. He found a weakness of each person. On some, there was use of brutality, on others, starvation. Some broke from the lack of sleep, others quickly succumbed to terror. There were days that brought former colleagues to him to confess. Eventually he got them all. Except for those two—*the German colonel*—involuntarily Victor's hand touched the silver cigarette-case that served him well, *and that intellectual, a former teacher at the Leningrad University.* He clenched his teeth at the unpleasant recollection.

For a long moment, the general's gaze caressed Victor's neatly pressed field shirt laden with medals and two Orders of the Red Banner. "I recommended you for continuing education, Victor, and the comrades from the Regional party committee endorsed your candidature. NKVD needs people like you. After you finish … ultimately … Yes, who could be a better successor to me than you?"

"Fyodor Timofeievich, too early for you to talk about retiring. Without your wise leadership how can we—"

"Stop singing praises to me, Victor." He pushed a black and green hard cigarette pack toward him. "Help yourself." He took one for himself and briskly raised it to his nose. "Gertsegovina Flor. First grade!"

In silence, they smoked for some time.

Victor drew hard on the cigarette. NKVD higher education would open doors for his career. One scene after another rushed through his mind—the grandiose building of Lubianka prison in Moscow and himself in an office there. And even if not in Moscow, to succeed the old man Glubov was not a bad opportunity as well.

Automatically it would bring with it a higher salary, an access to the special stores, an apartment in a pristine concrete building, a Pobeda car at public cost, everything, everything. The images intoxicated, taking his breath away as if he was standing on a high ledge with vertigo. Yet something unvoiced was in the general's eyes and Victor waited uneasily.

The general rubbed the scar on his face with the back of his hand, and looking hard at Victor said with a silken thread of warning in his voice, "You'd better think over how you decide to handle your scandalous family situation."

The words fell on Victor like steel girders. "What family situation, Fyodor Timofeievich?"

"I mean your little one. What a lovely boy and so musically talented, just after you. People still haven't forgotten what a great singer you were …

Dark eyes, burning eyes
Passionate and splendid eyes

he crooned under his breath, moving his head a bit in rhythm with the words. "Ah, how lovely you sang this song." His eyes warmed. "What's going on between you and Serafima? Why can't you both come to your senses? Everybody knows what a big love you had before the war. She waited for you. She did not marry."

Victor's hands locked into fists again.

"The little boy grows up without his father." Suddenly, the Glubov's voice had a metallic ring again.

"The boy is not mine," Victor said jerkily in a barely audible voice. "You don't know everything, Fyodor Timofeievich, not—everything." He looked up at the clean-shaven fold of flesh beneath the general's chin.

"Hm, not yours … And I say, Victor," his brows were drawn together with mockery, merging over the bridge of his nose, "you know there were no secrets from the military censorship." He gave him a roguish wink.

Victor grinned back.

"In your position you have to be not only a perfect communist, you have to have an unblemished reputation. Now go and manage the situation with Serafima. She's a good girl, a good worker," he said, slow and steady, as if to imprint his words on Victor's brow. "Forward march!"

A girder, larger then the previous one came crashing down. "Yes, Comrade General!" Stifling his anger with a slight smile, he got up to his feet and saluted in the prescribed manner.

It does not matter what you think so long as you obey. He recalled the slogan. He saw it written in Gothic on the wall of a half-destroyed Hitler Youth school in Berlin and remembered how he liked it then. Now was his time to obey. He would happily obey if only without that particular price.

He exited the NKVD building, paused to light a cigarette and sucked on it twice. It tasted bitter on his tongue. He flung it to the ground and stepped on it.

Serafima. A thought lashed him as a razor. *I won't let this lucky chance slip from my hands even ...* Instantly, he knew what he had to do—be gentle with her, teach her to trust him again. He would restore her faith in love and in him. She only had to succumb to one of his terms.

Suddenly, feeling much easier, as if a noose on his squeezed throat slackened, he went around the corner and entered a small food shop. It was warm and dimly lit inside. A yellow bulb overhead flickered. At the bang of the entrance door, a female's voice shouted, "Whoever's there is the last. We are closing."

The smell of alcohol merged with the sweaty sourness of half a dozen men and the fierce rosewater most likely coming from the sales woman. His eyes adjusted to the semidarkness and over the heads of the people in front of him he could see her blonde hair tucked under a coquettish, starched white headband.

One after another, the men silently handed to her their Rubles and hurried to the exit, slipping the craved half-liter vodka bottle into the bosom of their faded military-cut greatcoats or drab padded jackets.

The woman bent down and with an exhausted "O-oh" lifted a wooden box with more vodka bottles on the counter. *Clink, clink* the bottles rattled against each other.

She pulled herself up and eyed him from his waist to the three silver stars on the gold-blue striped epaulettes of his greatcoat of fine fabric to the peaked cap. Her lascivious lips parted, revealing white even teeth.

He returned her insolent gaze. In a rapid glance, he scanned her figure that beamed with health—an ugly gray-blue overall could not hide the voluptuous roundness of her shoulders and broad hips, a white smoothness of her strong neck and the large hands without an engagement ring.

"A pack of Gertsegovina Flor and a half-liter vodka bottle," he said.

"Huh, you, Comrade Officer, don't find Gertsegovina Flor in a hole-in-the-wall like this, but vodka, that's easy." She wrapped a bottle in a coarse brownish paper, and her hand lingered longer than necessary before she handed it to him.

How was it that nobody had snatched such a ripe, tempting berry yet, the quick thought run through his mind. He lay money on the counter and turned to go.

"Hey, Officer, come tomorrow." She leaned forward over the counter and lowered her voice. "I'll get you Gertsegovina Flor."

"Zinaida, stop flirting with customers." A man, sitting all the time at the small desk in the corner knocking on his abacus, lifted his head. He squinted at Victor and at the recognition of what kind of uniform the customer wore, his eyes assumed a shifty expression. He instantly dropped his gaze.

Zinaida's big slightly protruding eyes widened with false innocence.

Victor turned sharply and exited into the freezing evening to find the grey blur of the pre-winter daylight vanished.

"Serafima!" Victor's voice entered the room at the same time as a loud knock at the door. "May I come in?" Without awaiting her consent, he stepped in.

He was holding something, bundled in the coarse paper.

The silence continued for several seconds while he surveyed her from head to foot, as if a completely unfamiliar person. "There is something we must straighten out."

She tried to keep her heart cold and still, yet a wave of apprehension swept through her.

He put a vodka bottle on the table. "Have glasses?"

She took a thick, faded and overly scratched tumbler from a wall shelf and lowered it on the table with a bang. "What do you want … t-to straighten out?"

He poured the crystal-clear liquid into the glass until it splashed over, and tossing his head back, drained it in a draught. "Why are you on your feet? Sit down."

"Thank you. I shall find it more convenient to stand," she retorted, not yet prepared inwardly for a conversation. *But what can it be that must be straightened out between us? What?*

He topped off the glass with more vodka. "Drink it down."

"What for?" she said, lashed by a stubborn refusal to submit.

"Drink it down. Drink to this damnable life of ours, or to the fact that we are alive—but drink it. Today, we have to talk." He tabled the glass before her, spilling some onto the table.

"All right, whatever," she said more temperately. A tide of alcoholic fire flowed across her tongue and burned its way down her throat. After the burn came a fiercely warm afterglow. While she recovered from the sensation, he refilled the glass and drank it greedily. Then he filled the glass once more and drank about half of it.

"This is to us." He pushed the glass toward her.

Us? Her lips mouthed air, then dropped open, slack with shock, and nothing came out.

He approached her and put his hands on the sides of her face. "Serafima, look at me." He stared unblinkingly into her eyes. "Who am I?" he asked, and the color of his eyes was like the stormy clouds.

"You are Victor," she said.

"Yes, I'm *your* Vitya and I *love* you." He slipped his arms around her shoulders. "I'm Vitya," he said again. "I'm not that brute who dishonored you and left you with the child."

"Don't!" she screamed and tried to pull away from him.

But he held her tightly against him, and with his undamaged hand, he rubbed the small of her back and then ruffled the locks on the neck. "I love you, darling."

He released her for a moment to step to the door to latch it. When he turned to her, his gaze was as soft as a caress. "After that evening—" He reached to her and pushed a wet forelock from her face. "I've thought a lot about what … Never mind. It's forgotten." He looked searchingly into her face.

A thrill of anticipation touched her spine and she quivered. *He was angry then … but he loves me. He has forgiven me.* And suddenly, she realized her own driving need for his love, the protectiveness of his arms, but most of all she wanted a father for her son.

He stood so close she could feel the heat from his body. Her mind told her to resist, but her body refused, aching for his touch.

And he, as though sensing it in her, crushed her in his embrace, hurting her through the coarse woolen dress. He kissed her, his mouth heavy and wet and merciless. His hand slid down her stomach to the swell of her hips.

She wrenched herself away. "No, Vitya."

For a moment, he stared fixedly and sternly over her head, and she noticed a rash on his neck. "So it is. So it is … I understand. You insist on following the custom. Well, if you want, I'll go to your mother for an approval to marry you. I'll buy you a beautiful wedding dress—"

"No, not that at—"

He cut her off in a rushing voice. "All right, so be it, Serafima. I'll do for you whatever it is you want." His mouth stiffened, the cheek muscles contracting on the right side of his nervous face. He pulled a cigarette case from the pocket of his khaki trousers, clicked a lighter abruptly and lit up. Breathing out smoke through his nostrils, he choked. He looked around, and finding a metal jar lid on the kitchen table, quickly extinguished the cigarette in it. "There is more to it, my darling. Soon, I'm leaving for Moscow for a two-year course at the Academy. I'll take you with me. Imagine what a good life you'll have—a concrete building with an elevator, an apartment with electricity and indoor bathroom. The windows as broad as this entire wall—" He shifted his eyes around the room. "A phone. A car at our disposal. I won't allow you to work. I'll give you whatever it is you need—new shoes, dresses of fine fabric you've never had before, maybe even haven't seen. No matter what, we still have our life in front of us." He injected an ingratiating softness into his voice. "Don't you understand that I love you? I'll take care of you, be with you forever. I would do anything for you."

"Vitya," she said several times, and then her voice cracked. "What about Vane—"

He cut her off. "I have thought about it. We'll leave your … him to live with his grandmother, and when he's ten, we'll enlist him in a military school so he won't be in our way."

The torment, the dreary emptiness lashed through her head. But then it passed as if exhausted at the bottom of her heart. For a long moment, she studied his face, mentally separating herself from him forever.

"I think it's better that you say nothing more and go. It was ridiculous of me to think even for a second that you might—" She pressed her fist against her mouth to steady herself.

His face turned ashen, perceptibly losing its healthy color, and again the muscles of his right cheek worked.

"So it is … Why then do you spread rumors your bastard is my son? What is your plan? What's the purpose?" he said in a deep, unnatural voice.

"I've never … Dunyasha, she … read your letters to me. She decided …"

"Again Dunyasha! I offer you a big favor, you and your bastard who would never become more than a tractor operator or a plumber. And you, however good you work, won't have anything more, maybe one more decoration."

Fury almost choked her. "Get out!"

He kicked the easy chair with his feet, sending it flying and the glass following to the floor. "All right, so be it! You will be sorry about that." His unrecognizable voice lashed her with a ringing shot. "But mark my words. You'll weep tears of blood. You and your bastard!"

She lifted her palms toward his face as though warding off a blow.

He moved to the door with a rolling gate, hit it with his mutilated fist, staggering a bit as he stepped out and slammed the door so hard the kerosene lamp flame swayed.

Conscious of searing shame and sharp hostility towards him, she thought, *No, I should not be sorry. Forget, sweep away everything that recalled him and my love for him.*

She snatched her overcoat, wrapped her head in a shawl, and ran outside. The blood gushed through her temples, mixing and pulling apart her thoughts as she rushed to her old house, first leaving the suburbs of the town behind and then following the familiar road.

The sky was filled with lowering clouds, which threatened the first snow of autumn. At intervals, the icy north wind blew in gusts. From somewhere, late-departing cranes called to one another with voices like little silver bells. The fields were dotted with haycocks and the grass along the road had a volatile, deathly smell.

In the setting dusk, she saw a shaggy, brown wolf swiftly crossing the road with his body close to the ground. The wolf stopped. She stopped too, and for a fleeting moment, Victor's face rose up in her mind. She screamed and looked around for a stone or a stick. With a springy stride, the wolf made for the wood.

As she reached the house, the short day dimmed to a grey murk. She opened the door with her key and slipped inside.

"Who's there? Serafima, you? What's happened? What time is it?" Glafira asked, yawning into her hand.

"Mother, how is he?"

"For heaven's sake," Glafira interrupted her in a whisper. "Talk more quietly. Thanks God, he's better today. What the devil brought you here in the night?"

Is it worth telling her? Instantly, she refused the idea.

She unwound her headscarf and hung her overcoat on a hook in the wall. "I'll stay over the night with you. I was worried and missed him so much." She tiptoed to the bed on which her son lay in adorable unkemptness, curled. He wriggled, distressed by the noise, and turned over.

In an impulsive gesture, Serafima seized him, cradled him in her arms, shaking off a blanket clutched in the small fist. He began to whimper, softly repeating with weak cries, "Ma-ama, ma-ama," stretching his tiny arms covered with the dots of chickenpox. She whispered a soft mist of words, her breath coming into contact with the warmth of her son's uneven, scarcely-drawn breath. "No one can separate us," she muttered into the little ear.

"Serafima, Serafima." Her mother tugged at her. "Aren't you late for work?"

With a start, she came to and sat up on the bed, her mind turning sharply to the night before. "Oo," she muttered, recalling again every detail of her conversation with Victor and the acutely painful sensations caused by his accusations. Noticing a glimmer of light peering in beside the curtain, she dropped her feet on the cold floor. Her teeth made little biting sounds. "Sure, I have to go," she said, realizing that her bitterness spilled over into her voice.

She went to the anteroom, her mother following in her steps. As she splashed her face with cold water from the washing-stand, she winced.

"Are you sulking or something?" Glafira said.

"I'm all right."

"You're lying. I have got eyes to see."

"Well, and what can you see?"

"You are not like yourself. Is it because of Victor? I've heard he returned."

"What of it?" Serafima's voice grew harsh.

"Have you seen him?"

"I don't want to talk about it."

"So did you—?"

Serafima's voice notched up higher as she repeated, "I don't want to talk about it."

"Letters he had written, 'my one and only, my dearest—'"

"Mother!"

"You'll be the only woman I'll ever—"

"Sto-oop!"

And with this hysterical outburst, everything seemed to come together within her as though this scream released the last uncertainty in her breast. A sudden feeling of liberation from something oppressive, an intense pleasure of freedom engulfed her.

With a long, exhausted sigh, Glafira moved off on tiptoe, and after lingering for a moment on the threshold, disappeared behind the inner door.

 onths crept on, blanketed with monotony and perpetual hunger. Another brutal winter, another unfriendly, windy spring, and the only joy—her son growing.

From a besmeared *Old Russian Fairytales* book she borrowed from a library, Serafima read to him about *Father Frost* and *Sister Alenushka, Brother Ivanushka, The Frog Princess* and *The White Duck*. From her son, she learned the new names: Beethoven and Paganini, Listz and Mozart … That was in the evenings.

In the mornings, she rushed to the factory—to the discordant symphony of clatter and saw-edged whines of the turning lathes and grinding machines, and the smell of the warmed up metal and lubricants.

July six of nineteen forty-seven began like every other day. She entered the vastness of the shop, pulled on her overalls bleached to an undistinguishable color by washing, grabbed her soiled gloves and with her usual confident step approached her lathe.

At once, through the noise, she discerned Semenitch's artificial leg stamping and creaking, *nothing unusual*, and yet there was something odd in it.

"Serafima," his labored breathing reached her ears. "Don't turn on the lathe, don't."

"What is it? There's something wrong, Semenich, I can tell by your voice."

"Your mother. They called from the hospital."

What could it be? Nothing serious I guess. She soothed herself. A week ago, when Glafira was in the city on some Kolkhoz' mission, she visited them and was perfectly fine. *Was she?* Now Serafima was not sure, remembering how her mother's face wrinkled in pain and how her hands returned constantly to her belly, and how at her question, "Are you feeling well?" she angrily dismissed it with a wave of her hand.

"Don't stay here like a monument, for God's sake. Go!" Semenich's voice tore her from her reverie.

Fifteen minutes later, she found herself in a queue to the hospital reception.

"Next!"

"Krivenkova Glafira," she said into the opening in the transparent wall.

The old man dragged his forefinger down the lined page, his lips moving with every name. "Nope," he mumbled to himself then spat on his forefinger, rubbed it against his thumb, and flipped over the page. "Krivenkova … Krivenkova … Nope. Next!"

"But how is it possible? I was told somebody had called and said she's here."

The man looked at her with the impatience of a person who had to deal with strangers' misery every day. "Go to the head nurse, she may know. Next!"

"Where is it?" Serafima pushed off a woman who elbowed her from the window.

"Just go straight on past the laboratory and the room to the right is where you find her. Next!"

She half-ran along the corridor. Through an open door, she saw two nurses sorting through the bandages. "I am looking for Krivenkova, I was told she is not on the patients' list."

"Do you know who she is?" The older woman stifled a yawn with her hand.

"That may be the one with the ruptured appendicitis." The younger woman continued arranging the bandages, not bothering to look at Serafima. "She still must be in ward sixteen."

Still? Trying to suppress a feeling of chilling cold in her chest, Serafima looked from one nurse to another. At last, the younger one turned her head. "Sixteen. What, didn't you hear it?"

Serafima bolted ahead. Doors lined the narrow corridor on both sides. They were half-open, giving away the acrid smell of medicine of some kind, the undistinguished hum of voices and moans.

In front of the door with a plaque that read sixteen, she stopped and lingered before entering into a lifeless silence. Through the bare window, the sun blinded her for a moment.

She slid her eyes fearfully over the beds. There Glafira was, on the bed closest to the window with the sheet drown up. Serafima approached her.

"Mother?" She drew her breath in. "Mother?" With trembling fingers, she lifted the gray sheet a bit.

Glafira wore a baby blue hospital shirt. Her face was pale, calm, remote, and mysteriously young, as if ten years were stolen from her. Her ugly, deep nasal wrinkles were gone. It seemed all the pain and grief and worry had left her face.

Serafima noticed for the first time how finely arched her mother's eyebrows were and how beautiful her golden hair was. Loose, it lay in heavy waves on the pillow.

She wanted to call to her, but she was not master of her voice. The spasm of inner pain passed over her lips, and she sank to her knees. She touched her mother's forehead with fingers that fluttered. Something was stifling her, stuck in her throat. A terrifying realization that she did not love her mother came upon her with crushing clarity. She stretched out her arms in front of her, across her mother's body, and dropped her head.

For a moment, all the memories of her childhood came flooding back to her. "You have never embraced me, Mama, never stroked my head, never …," she whispered. "Was it my fault being born a bastard? But you loved Vanechka."

She recalled that even in the summer time, she could not so much as open a door in the house that would not worry her mother. A memory brought back Glafira's voice, saying, "He might catch a cold." "Shoo, don't wake him up." "Did he have enough to eat today?" When it thundered at night, she would go to his bed, fix his blanket, and whisper that he mustn't be afraid, that she was there.

All of a sudden, it dawned on her that her mother's love for Vanechka—that unconditional acceptance of his coming into her life—was her way of confessing to

Serafima her guilt, her love she did not know how to express.

Serafima felt tears that had frozen together in her throat in a solid lump were growing ... growing. "Mama, sorry, forgive me, forgive me," she pleaded as if scorching herself, and the tears came. She wept long and silently, and with these tears, her bitter offence against her mother was forgiven.

In July of 1948, a year after her mother passed away and just days before Vanechka turned six, Serafima stopped to catch her breath in front of the *Kindergarten* door, mentally still seeing herself in the factory's assembly hall and hearing the director's announcement, "According to the Order, Serafima Petrovna Krivenkova is appointed a foreman." Her heart sang with gladness and pride.

Tap, tap, tap, sounded from behind the slightly ajar door. "Settle it under your chin this way, yes, yes, good." Anna Konstantinovna's voice reached her. "Keep your thumb farther back."

Serafima pushed the door open.

Anna Konstantinovna and Vanechka turned to her and exclaimed simultaneously, "Mama!" "Serafima!" both staring at her wide-eyed, like thieves caught in the act.

"I'm earlier today—"

Anna Konstantinovna rose from the piano, and supporting herself with her hand on the instrument, said solemnly as if declaring something inevitable, something she could have no power over, "He is ready."

A stony silence ensued. Serafima swept her hand through her hair slowly, tucked a loose strand behind her ear, all the while looking at Anna Konstantinovna. "Ready? For—"

"Mama, Mama, please." Vanechka looked up at her, hiding something behind his back, and smiling beseechingly, his head cocked slightly on one shoulder.

"Ready for what?" she repeated.

"Serafima." Anna Konstantinovna took her elbow and moved her to the wooden music stool in front of the grand piano, pushing her down slightly. She was silent for a moment and then spoke without a pause as though the words had been long in her mind. "It has been clear for some time that your son possesses an exceptional musical ability. Do you remember he was two years old when I noticed he would hear a melody and then pick it out with one finger on the piano? You probably thought it was just the child's curiosity many children have in the early ages and there was no talent behind it. But his progress in piano playing shows he is a really extraordinarily gifted child. It would be unforgivable—"

Serafima stared at her, baffled, and Anna Konstantinovna, as though sensing her confusion, added in a rushing voice, "He has particularly facile fingers. The fingers of a violinist."

"Violinist?" Now, Serafima noticed a tiny instrument in Vanechka's hand. "But I can't pay for this thing, I can't pay for his lessons, and what does he need it for in his life? His future is a tractor operator or in the best scenario a plumber," she responded with some asperity.

"No!" A choked sound came from Anna Konstantinovna's throat. "He is in this world to play violin. If you decide he is not going to learn to play violin, you will kill him, if not physically, then certainly emotionally and spiritually."

"Kill? Spiritually?"

"This is his fiddle and I'll teach him. You only have to allow his unusual gift to develop."

Tears sprung to Serafima's eyes, hot, unexpected. Her heart felt full and tender, and she did not see that she had any choice. "I will allow it."

Anna Konstantinovna's face relaxed. "Of course, he has to devote a considerable amount of time and seriousness to his study." She peered intently at Vanechka who shook his head "yes, yes," his eyes sparkling. "If you don't mind, I'll take him after Kindergarten to my place and you'll pick him up after your shift. Every day."

"Every day?

Anna Konstantinovna turned to Vanechka again. "Every day?"

He nodded.

"Do you know the cow-house structure?"

"Of course I do," Serafima said.

"On the neighboring street, Tchernishevskogo, twenty-one. The very last house. That's where I live."

The sun was still up over the serrated outline of the fir wood looming behind the huts that formed the outer edge of the settlement when the next day, Serafima went to Anna Konstantinovna. It was a short walk, about ten minutes or so from the factory.

On her way, she scared off a group of sparrows that bathed themselves in dust on the road and chirped loudly at each other. A lazy warm wind carried a warm smell of withering grass and dung from a cow house nearby.

On the small plot to the right of a little hut, a woman weeded between the pale green of potato plants, her stooped back turned to the street.

"Is it twenty-one?" Serafima called upon her.

The woman continued her work.

Serafima halted in confusion. "Is it twenty-one?" she shouted.

It was not right away that the woman straightened herself up, lifted her battered aluminum bucket with the grass thrusting out of it, and turned. She noticed Serafima, smiled, and moving her swollen legs with difficulty, approached the wicket. "Who are you looking for?" She raised her hand to her ear.

"Is it the house number twenty-one?"

The woman let the bucket drop from her hand. Continuing to smile with her toothless broad mouth, she extended her left arm with the rheumatically contorted fingers and moved her other arm as if playing violin.

Serafima nodded and returned her smile.

"Annushka Konstantinovna said you'd come. I'm Matrona. It's my house." She tucked a gray strand under her floral three-cornered kerchief, picked up the bucket, and after tumbling it down onto the dusty grass at the side of the road, returned to ravaging her weeds.

Through an open, small window with a white guipure curtain, Serafima saw Vanechka in front of a music stand and Anna Kosntantinovna adjusting the violin under his chin. She placed the stick into his arm. "Keep the bow this way. Don't hit it on the string. Go on."

Suddenly, an awful screech hit Serafima's ears. Involuntarily, her hands flew to cover her ears.

"Easy, sonny, easy. Let me show you how."

Sonny? Serafima stopped mid-stride. An undistinguished feeling pierced her. Through her confusion, Anna Konstantinovna's tender voice reached her again. "Let's try this way, my lovely one."

Serafima lowered down on the wooden bench earthed right at the wall under the window, scarcely aware of tightness in her jaw. *My lovely one? How is it that I have never called him such tender names?*

She continued listening closely. Another wretched sound came.

"That's better, Vanechka."

Better? Serafima shook her head.

"No, Anna Konstantinovna, I can't."

"Yes, you can, my dear."

And then, a beautiful, pure sound ensued. *Of course, he can!*

Through the open window a chiming of a clock came.

"Enough for today, Vanechka. Let's have your cup of milk and a cookie, and we'll go to look for your little mommy."

Little mommy? Serafima shook her head in embarrassment. "I'm here," she said loudly and got up from the bench.

"Serafima, come in, dear."

She went round the corner, entered and passed a low-ceilinged anteroom with a kitchen table and easy chairs, and opened the inner door into another room. The last rays of the setting sun spread its glowing shine over a narrow bed with white coverlet, a wardrobe with a full height mirror, and a boxy commode of dark wood.

At the round table in the middle, Vanechka sat on a chair with a thick pillow tucked under him, licking a little rim of milk from his top lip. He opened his hand up, showing to her a gnawed piece of a cookie. "My favorite, Korovka!"

"Anna Konstantinovna, you mustn't spoil him." She screwed her eyes at the table then met Anna Konstantinovna's reproachful gaze.

"Do you want some?"

"No, I dined at the factory." She felt a blush creep up her face and burn the shell of her ears at the lie and stepped to the commode. Two framed photographs set on it. Her gaze stopped on a middle-aged man in the naval uniform. The confident set of his shoulders and firm features suggested power and strength.

Anna Konstantinovna followed her gaze. "My husband … He … I know nothing about him since the war began." She shifted her sad eyes to the picture on which a boy in his teens stood on the stage, a violin tucked under his chin. The picture was snapped from a prospective of a hall, over the heads of the spectators. "This is my Kostik, my son. He … From typhus … On our way to evacuation from Leningrad."

Serafima stepped up to Anna Konstantinovna and took her in an embrace, feeling her shoulders vibrate in suppressed sobs.

When in September of 1949 Vanechka went to school, Anna Konstantinovna had arranged with the director that volleyball and other "dangerous" physical activities were curtailed because of the risk of hurting his hands.

In months to come, Vanechka continued practicing with Anna Konstantinovna for two-three hours every evening. Saturdays and Sundays were not an exception. He talked the language Serafima could not understand— bowings, fingerings, articulation, shifting, vibrato, arpeggios, spiccato, and all the other words that with time stopped clicking in her ear as foreign. Names like Bach, Mozart, Beethoven, Kobalevsky, Shostakovich, Tchaikovsky, Kreisler, Dvorak, Bartok, Wieniawski, Bruch, Haydn, Mendelssohn, Vivaldi, Chopin flew from Vanechka's tongue with remarkable ease.

A faded black and white lithograph of Paganini, the Italian virtuoso, which Semenich framed rather elegantly with birch laths, adorned the wall right above Vanechka's bed.

"Rhythm is in the left hand—not in the bow, Anna Konstantinovna says." "My tone, dynamics, and intonation are all much improved, Anna Konstantinovna said." "The pizzicatos. I still have a problem with them," he would announce with assured certainty.

Music was all he wanted to talk about. It was always the same, but December 24 of 1949 happened to be a day that she would never forget.

Vanechka placed his violin on the table in front of him and the music score nearby. "Did you know sound control depends on bow speed, sounding point, and weight? Let me show it to you."

She broke into laughter at his impersonation of Anna Konstantinovna's tone of voice. "Hold on. What about your school home work? Did you do that?" She raised her eyes at him from his sock she was mending.

"Uh-huh. I did. I have to work on vibrato. Listen."

Encouragement and approval are the vital ingredients. You have to support him in every possible way. She smiled at the memory of Anna Konstantinovna's advise, and she had taught herself to say it every time: "That was a really beautiful sound." But today, it was too late for that.

"No, sonny. You'll wake up Aunty Anfisa."

"Tuk, tuk tuk." He moved his little fist as though tapping an imaginary wall. "What a shame! In the middle of the night. Hooliganism." He imitated their neighbor in a loud whisper, mimicking her brows drawn together in an angry frown.

She raised a shushing finger to her lips, and their shoulders rose in a half laugh simultaneously.

With his eyes glowing, he threw his arms around her neck and whispered into her ear, "Mama, I love you. You are the best mama in the world."

Long after the hostel was quiet with sleep, she lay awake, staring into the darkness. Big warm tears rolled down her cheeks and onto the pillow. For the first time in her life, those were happy tears.

June of 1950 arrived and Serafima made up her mind to go on the first journey of her life. She was thrilled to see Moscow but kept fretting over parting with Vanechka. *You can't expect never to be parted*, she remembered Anna Konstantinovna's words, and they gave Serafima courage.

The day was rainy. Water rippled off the roof of the station building. Oily puddles between the tracks reflected the gray unfriendly sky. Clouds floated northward, towards the capital. Serafima stood very still, watching with sinking heart her white rag shoes becoming wet, changing the color to muddy dark stains.

At last, the faraway sounds were a roar and the train came straight toward the platform. One by one, the passengers got down.

"Bo'o-aard!" A shout came to her.

Why do I go there? What for? Go back, she thought in sudden panic.

The train started off and she still was on the platform. "Jump!" somebody yelled. And she jumped.

Soon the train moved with a soothing motion, lulling her anxieties and fears, bringing her thoughts back to three weeks before. On the solemn conference dedicated to the Victory Day over the fascist Germany, Semenich presented her with a Certificate of Recognition and a travel permit that was almost impossible in those days to obtain. "Here, Serafima, a ticket to Moscow. You deserve it. Go, see how people live in the capital of our great country, come back and tell us all about it. I'm so very glad for you." After a short pause, he added, "That's not all, comrades. In the Party meeting, we decided to delegate comrade Krivenkova to continuing education. We need homegrown engineers."

The train sped on, leaving behind a scarf of smoke.

She slid down the window and watched the fields without end and the occasional villages slide past, the fir woods looming blackly on the horizon. The earth exhaled moisture. She took off her kerchief and let the wind blow back the strands of her hair. It stroked her forehead, like tender hands.

Little by little, the rain stopped. The sun cut through the melting layer of clouds, its rays stretching from the sky, down to the ground. More fields, villages, and soon the suburbs, factory stacks, monstrous cranes, multi-story buildings.

The train jerked and her forehead bumped hard against the windowpane.

"Moscow!" called the conductor. "Kievskiy Train Station!"

Oh dear, she thought, rubbing her forehead. She smoothed her skirt and adjusted the blouse. When the train came to a halt, she was one of the last off.

First, the stream of cars that rushed along an impossibly broad road impatiently throwing scraps of petrol fog on the gray asphalt frightened her. She halted and stared in amazement at the mechanical winking of traffic lights at the intersections, abruptly halting and releasing the pent-up crowds of cars into the canyon of streets.

The air was scented with the smell of warm asphalt, burned gasoline, the indefinite aroma of perfumes, and the myriad other odors strange to her sense of smell. Moscow folk, going about their business, filled the pavements and bulked in shifting crowds at the crossing points and bus stops.

Walking along the Gorky Street, she stole furtive glances at the beautifully dressed women, and looking at her own reflection in the shining shop windows, thought, *They are many worlds away from me.*

She asked her way to the Red Square and for a long time, wandered its cobble-stoned vastness overwhelmed by the beauty of the red-bricked, crenellated Kremlin walls and towers, the brightly colored St. Basil's Cathedral, and the Historical Museum brick structure the color of clotted blood. The modesty of Lenin's tomb disappointed her a bit.

The next site she resolved to see was Bolshoi Theatre. Not even looking at the grandiose eight-columned construction, the hordes of Muscovites streamed by and into Petrovka Street. On the right side of it, there was a seven-story building of breathtaking beauty. Over the broad windows of the ground floor *Central Department Store* read. She lingered, hesitating to enter, but a cramming crowd took her inside as though she had no choice about it.

She sauntered slowly, jostling through queues, pausing to look at half-empty shelves. A man, keeping pace with her, turned his head to look at her. Automatically, she pressed her hand to her chest where she'd hid her money tucked into her bra. To get rid of his attention, she stopped in front of the *Hats* section.

"I'll try that one." She pulled off her white cotton kerchief and poked her finger at the jade-green hat that looked out of place among the scanty assortment of black berets and men's caps.

"It's a new shade," a sales girl said and exchanged quick glances with an older woman who stepped closer. "The color will bring the rosiness of your cheeks." She set the hat straight at Serafima's brow and almost strangled her with the aroma she had on.

With an impatient flick of her hand, Serafima jerked the hat from her head. "It's too small." She took her kerchief from her canvas bag and retied it.

"It'll keep the wind off your head better than a hat," the girl smirked.

"Milkmaid," Serafima heard them giggling as she strode briskly in the opposite direction towards the section of *Shoes*.

Several people stopped to look at the rows of identical black galoshes, which reflected the abundance of sunlight streaming through the broad windows.

"Do you have size thirty six?" a young woman asked but all of a sudden was interrupted by a girl's voice that came from behind Serafima's back. "Zoya, Zoya, they are putting out summer dresses. I'm in the queue, but hurry, please hurry."

The Zoya ran headlong after her friend. Not knowing why, Serafima hastened after her and without thinking about it, crammed herself into a mob of women in front of the section *Women's Dresses*.

"You didn't stay here." "Where do you push your ass?" "Don't elbow me, I was here before you even woke up today." "Push off." The women quarreled and backbit among themselves.

"What kind of dresses?" Serafima asked a short woman in front of her.

"I don't know, maybe summer dresses. You can exchange it to what you really need later if it's of no need for you."

"How much?"

"I've heard forty-seven Rubles."

Serafima turned to step out of the line then halted. She made a quick calculation and decided that she'd still have enough left for the train ticket back and a lunch.

In about forty minutes, when only one woman was in front of her, she, bending forward and shielding herself with her shoulders snatched a roll of Rubles from under her shirt. As it was her turn, somebody pressed her hard to the counter from behind.

"Size?" the sales person asked angrily.

"Aa—"

After a quick glance at Serafima, she muttered, "Thirty six," and handed her a folded dress wrapped in the coarse brownish paper, counted Rubles, and said with annoyance, "Ne-ext."

Happy to have a full breath again, Serafima sided to a full-size mirror. She unfolded the wrapping and mentally aahed. The fitted at the waist and flared at the bottom dress was of dark green sateen with big yellow polka dots, short ruffled sleeves, a turned down small round collar of green silk and four tiny buttons covered with the same fabric.

Holding the dress close to her bosom, she couldn't tear her eyes from the mirror. Not in a sweetest dream could she imagine having such a treasure. The kerchief slipped from her head and her unruly locks scattered upon her shoulders.

"Tsk, tsk." She heard a voice behind her back and instantly noticed a reflection of a man ogling her openly. "It sets off your beautiful eyes," he said. He opened his mouth to say something else, but she, crumpling the dress and pushing it inside her canvas bag, hurried off to be swallowed up by the throng of people.

Suddenly, above all the noise and hum of the crowd, a child's scream arose. All heads turned on the howl. "Do-olly, I want that do-olly."

In front of the *Toys* section, a young woman stooped over a girl of about five, her face burning with either embarrassment or annoyance. "Which one exactly do you want?"

"That dolly." With her little forefinger, the child pointed out the doll in a heavenly blue silk dress and the matching hat and shoes. It had blonde braided hair and big blue eyes with long coarse eyelashes.

"Imported item. Closes and opens her eyes. We have got only one. Two hundred five Rubles fifty Kopeks," the salesperson said, smiling sugary at the girl. "What is your name, little one?"

Not tearing her stare from the doll, the girl took no notice of the woman's words.

"Tanechka, let's find some other toy, darling, this doll is too expensive. Besides, you have your Malvina."

Immediately, the intractable Tanechka threw herself on the floor and beat against it with her feet in hysterics.

"Well, I'll pay." The young mother bent to lift the girl from the dirty floor then opened her elegant purse.

With her gaze, Serafima followed the happy child who was pressing the doll to her chest. Like a miracle, her tears disappeared from her small round face.

What kind of mother am I? She startled. *A small wooden horse, which Anna Kostantinovna gave Vanechka for his first anniversary and a rag ball I handmade for him from an old blanket, that's all he ever had.*

She tore her gaze from the gorgeous doll. The multicolored striped metal tops, kaleidoscopes, big and small cube-shaped blocks with letters on their sides, plastic baby dolls, tin soldiers, trumpets floated in front of her eye.

She counted out for the ticket back home and for a lunch in a cantina, and pressing twenty-five Rubles in her sweaty hand, ran her eyes over the toys again.

Relaxed and determined to justify herself for the luxury of the dress purchase, she put her hand on the edge of the counter's polished surface, liking the way it felt, and waited for a long time before the sales girl with rosy cheeks deigned to attend to her. "Show me those tin soldiers," Serafima said with confidence.

"One hundred."

"Ah so. Actually, I like that trumpet more. How much?"

"Eighty Rubles and thirty Kopeks."

"Do you have a similar one but in a blue color?"

"Only red ones, Citizen, do you want it?"

"Yes, yes, but I need a blue one."

The girl turned to a man who elbowed Serafima a bit away, and pointing to the tin soldiers, asked the sales girl to wrap them.

Serafima felt how her cheeks flared. Suddenly, she noticed a simple small plush brown bear with lustrous button eyes sitting askance in the corner of a glass window almost hidden behind a gray rag-hare with drooping ears.

"How much does this toy cost?" she almost yelled at the girl.

"This one?" The girl put her finger at the hare.

"No, no, how you don't understand? The bear, that bear with button eyes!"

"Thirty five."

"Thirty five? Did you say, 'Thirty five?'"

I still have my biscuit and there is a hot water shed in the train, ran through her mind and she quickly dipped her hand into her blouse.

"I'll take it." Serafima counted out the Rubles and pressed the bear to her chest exactly like the capricious girl had pressed her two-hundred-five-Rubles-fifty-Kopeks doll. Holding herself proudly erect, she exited the store.

She sauntered about, not knowing what else to do in this hurry-scurry city.

She was thirsty. On every street corner, as though teasing her, the kiosks painted light blue were selling fizzy water with syrup. Resisting the temptation, she licked her lips and walked by.

Her feet ached. Yet in this monstrous congestion of the buildings, she could not find a single bench. In front of a beautiful, massive building on Gorky Street, she rested against a huge concrete flowerpot with nasturtiums and looked around.

From a door, a strapping blonde-haired woman in an elegant hat and high-heeled white shoes stepped out. She looked up at the sunny sky then to the right and to the left and knit her brows. Instantly, a gray Pobeda screeched to a stop and a young soldier-chauffeur sprung out and opened the door for the woman. She went to the car, her heeled shining shoes clicking over the asphalt. Before lowering herself inside and still frowning, she said, "My husband won't be happy with your ..." Serafima could not make out the end of her sentence.

The young man lowered his head, and without retorting, closed the car door after her carefully.

Serafima watched the car speed away up the broad street. In her mind an inner voice spoke, *That's how it could be with me. That's where I could live. With Victor.*

I loved him so much once—and sometimes I think I still do. But he … Instantly, her fists clenched and her eyes burned with remembered rage. *What am I doing here? I should be home, with Vanechka.*

Walking the busy streets, she remembered her son's voice, his smile, and the touch of his small lovely hands. *That's what matters*, she told herself, losing the last signs of interest in these fancy glass windows, the impressive buildings, the beautiful dresses and shoes of the Moscow women. Already longing intolerably for her shabby room, her darling Vanechka—and imagining in a flash the sweetness of her return—the hours spent in Moscow seemed like the eternity to her.

With a mass of men and women and children, she was swallowed by a subway entrance at the corner of Marx Street and thirty minutes later, in the Kievsky Railroad Station, with pleasant anticipation, let the conductor punch her ticket.

The train plunged headlong into the space that separated her from Moscow. Through the rhythmic clatter of the wheels, through the scrape of the car and the ring of the rails she wondered how the Muscovites could live without the scent of the wormwood, the sunflower blossoms and perfume of rain-washed apple-trees in the air? She recalled her old withered poplar, their she-goat Zor'ka and the scent of its milk on her hands, the haystacks, the sweet aroma of the young grass and a damp-smelling earth turned over by a ploughshare, a cock crowing from a yard.

Holding the soft, velvety toy in her lap, she gave herself up to delicious thoughts of her reunion with her son.

She startled at the conductor calling the name of her station. "Get ready! Who exits, get ready!"

Five minutes later, the train reduced speed and finally stopped.

All the way to Anna Konstantinovna's she ran. Darkness seeped into everything, erasing edges. One window of the house was lit up. In the shadow of the porch, she did not see her son.

He recognized her and with an excited cry, "Mamochka!" ran to meet her.

Her heart beating violently, she pressed him to her bosom and couldn't stop inhaling the smell of his hair. She took the toy from her bag and stretched it to him.

His eyes went big and his hands trembled. He pressed the teddy bear to his chest exactly like the capricious girl had pressed her doll.

November of 1950 was more than half-gone when Serafima received the confirmation of acceptance to the preparatory courses to a technical institute.

Will I, five years from now, be an engineer? she thought, absentmindedly stroking a thin stack of Vanechka's exercise books. She chose the *Mathematics* one, opened it, and ran her eyes over the short columns of figures. *Well, it's easy. That I remember.*

She startled at the chime of the wall clock. It was time to go to Anna Konstantinovna to pick up Vanechka. She reached for her padded woolen coat but stopped, recognizing Semenich's artificial leg creaking and stamping through the corridor. *It can't be him. Why? Or maybe something's wrong in the factory? Then why would not they send somebody else?*

After a knock on the door and her, "Come in," he paused a moment in the doorway then stepped in. His eyes had an oblique, shiny expression that alarmed her. "Something's wrong?"

"Er ... Serafima, I came to ask a personal question," he said in a subdued and timid tone.

"About what, Semenich?"

"Semenich, Semenich," he mimicked with a quiver in his voice. "Did anybody ever ask me how my parents christened me? Vasily is my name, and you, Serafimushka, I beg you, call me Vasily."

What's the matter with him? "Take a seat." She motioned with her head and lowered on the chair too.

During an uncomfortable pause, never taking his tawny shade of brown eyes off Serafima, he seemed to ponder, touching his moustache as though adjusting it, but all at once, his face took on an expression of determination. "A year and a half has passed since my wife—"

"God rest her soul."

"And your mother ..."

"Yes, three years since."

"A good person she was, your mother. Er ... helped you a lot with your son."

"Yes, she did."

"How do you manage without her, I'm surprised."

"I do. Besides, Anna Konstantinovna spends a lot of time with Vanechka."

"I see, I see. And yet, it's not good for a boy to grow up without a man in the house."

His words made her uncomfortable. *What does he want?*

"I have been waiting ... now it's time when it's no longer disrespectful to the dead to speak out. I could not go on living without deciding the question, would you or would you not be—"

"Be what?"

"You don't interrupt me, Serafima," and he made haste to speak. "Too many nights, I've spent thinking of how I can tell you what's on my mind ... Er, in my heart. I feel I could not be at peace seeing you struggle alone, raising your son without a man. You must stop waiting for him. Since your heroic Victor still hasn't claimed his fatherhood, he never will."

His words caught her off guard, and during the seconds that followed, the humiliating scenes of her last conversations with Victor flashed through her mind.

Semenich fidgeted on his chair. "And that's the truth, how could he now, since he's married and who knows maybe sooner or later they will have a child together? Hmm, what does he care about Vanechka? And that's what I'm asking you, what good is it for a boy to grow up without a man in the house?"

There was a struggle in her heart between the desire to tell him it was not his business and the consciousness that it would be base to do so.

"I am in a position to take care of you and your son. Besides, with my director's salary and your foreman's one we'll have a decent life."

Mentally suffering and already comprehending what was coming, she tried several times to interrupt him, but could not.

"Look at me, I'm still strong." He stretched out his muscular arms. "I can do most of the work in the household. My house is big enough for three of us. Vanechka will have his own room, and there he can play his violin as much as he wants … Though I'm twenty-four years older than you, I'm still …" He reddened up to his ears. "Need I be saying I love you?'

Tell him to stop it, she thought, conscious of her throbbing heart. *Put an end to his own humiliation.* And the more she tried to compose herself, the more uncertain she felt.

"But it's up to you. If you don't learn to love me, I won't force you. I can wait as long as ..." His eyes like deep wells of light were fixed on her.

I must tell him that's impossible. I must. I must. She was utterly sorry for him. *But what should I do? It can't be*, she thought. *Away with weakness.*

"Vasily."

He glanced at her with gratitude and moved to take her hand, but she drew back from him.

"It's so complicated, much more complicated than you think. There is nobody like you. You are good, you are generous." Her voice cracked. "That cannot be ... no ... no."

He gave her a long, silent, sad look. "It was bound to be so," he said.

"You have been so kind to Vanechka and to me, and I used your kindness. I have just taken and taken and taken." There was a catch in her breath as she watched his tortured, suffering face. "I feel so bad."

He seemed to be pulling himself together for a few seconds, as though he did not know what to do next, and then, getting up rapidly, he tottered, and clung to the back of the chair to support himself. "I can be a father to you, a brother. I'll be the one you can lean on. Let me come and check on you—to make sure you're all right."

"I am lucky that you ... I am really lucky." She was stabbed by the soft sadness on his darkened face as he turned around on the threshold to look at her before walking out.

The first frosts struck to the end of November. By New Years Eve, temperature settled in below fifteen Celsius. With the fierce winds blowing from the north, 1950 became 1951.

The streets were lined on either side with peaked, white piles of snow pushed there, out of the way of traffic and pedestrians by the sharp-nosed snowplows. Serafima shifted her feet, trying to keep them closer to each other as if it could help to shield the annoying hole. The right shoe had sprung a leak at the beginning of the winter. She kept putting a wad of cotton in there and every morning she changed it. Of course, it would be better to get a new pair of shoes altogether, or maybe felt boots, but first she had to manage a new pair of shoes for Vanechka, and maybe—if only she knew how—a new pair of pants.

But this afternoon of January eleventh, she stood on the tram station among the jostling pack of people, stamping about to get themselves warm. When the squealing of metal against metal announced the tram's approach, the crowd swayed, and she was lifted with the rest of the mob of passengers over the step and into a suffocating closeness with stinking commuters. "C'mon citizens, push up!" they cheered each other up.

Serafima was wedged against a steel pole on one side and on the other against a man in a dark wool coat. His bright, clear blue eyes considered her for a long moment. She pointedly looked away. *Intellectual*, she thought, yet automatically pressed her oilcloth bag with the wallet to her side—pickpockets worked the trams, so it was best to be careful.

She gazed through the window between the heads. The fragments of the town slid by—one and two-story houses with dim lights on in some windows, solitary leafless trees, rare pedestrians, wrapped tightly in their coats with pulled up collars.

The tram screeched to a stop at the corner of the massive building of the local State Security Committee. A black Pobeda stopped in front of its brightly lit entrance. The chauffeur hopped from the car and opened the passenger door for a man in the senior officer's uniform, stout, with the air of importance in his moves.

Vitya. A soft gasp escaped her and immediately she was vexed with herself for this fleeting surge of tenderness she had believed to be buried. *Can't I forget? Is it stronger than me?* And with an agonizing pang of humiliation, a dream-like memory flashed before her eyes—his face, distorted by rage and his voice falling on her like steel girders, "You'll weep tears of blood, you and your bastard." Impulsively, her hands clenched into fists and the knuckles cracked.

The tram moved. A calm voice came through her reverie, "Are you getting down at the Institute?"

"I am," she snapped out.

The door opened, welcoming the cool, refreshing air into the dampness of the car. Moving his shoulders and elbows, the *intellectual* created just enough space for her to force her way behind him to the exit door before it closed.

Then he jumped out and offered her his hand. Ignoring it, she stepped down and walked away without looking back. She felt him falling in step after her. *A student, like me*, a quick thought came.

In the entrance hall of the brightly lighted two-story building of the Technical Institute, it smelled of the freshly shaved wood of the new floors overpowered by the fumes of a new paint. She hardly glanced at the placard in blood-red lettering LONG LIVE OUR GLORIOUS COMMUNIST PARTY pasted on the wall and made her way upstairs, following a group of people. At the top of the staircase, a large alabaster Stalin grinned fatherly at her from under his stone whiskers.

In the circular lecture theater, she took a seat on the farthest bench. Most of the students, about thirty of them, were men in patched old uniforms without insignias, with rows of ribbons pinned to their faded jackets.

Serafima's eyes traveled around. More people were coming in. A young woman and a man walked in and stopped at the blackboard. She talked and he listened, his head inclined to her slightly. She was tall and slender, with a face of a fairytale Alenushka. A dark blonde braid lay heavily on her shoulder and down her chest. She wore a gray skirt suit that accentuated her graceful figure.

Serafima's gaze stopped on the woman's nice black laced ankle boots. She sighed and shifted her feet deeper under the bench.

Two male lowered voices cut through her musing.

"Tsk, tsk."

"The dean's daughter. Not your field's berry."

"Ha, you'll see, I'll have her in my bed in no time."

"Comrade students, attention!" the young woman said in a firm voice, creating immediate silence. She turned to her interlocutor and made a slight gesture with her left hand. "This is your teacher, Yakov Antonovich Melnikov. He is the son of the famous mathematician, professor Melnikov, from Leningrad. At fifteen, he entered the university and started teaching there at aged twenty."

There was a hum of respect from the audience.

"He will instruct you in algebra and geometry."

Serafima recognized the *intellectual* from the tram. He looked painfully thin without his heavy winter coat, and the gray stubble on his head made him seem older than she had originally thought.

"Thank you, Larisa Leonidovna," he said.

She leaned to him and said something into his ear.

He nodded and waited till the door closed after her. "Let's start with basics, comrade students." He half-turned to the blackboard and reaching out for a piece of chalk stopped when a male voice came from the front row. "Were you at the front?"

With his shoulders suddenly hunched, it seemed the teacher contemplated an answer before he turned and nodded.

"What action?"

"The South front, fifty seventh Army."

"Which was your unit?"

The teacher looked aside as if considering his answer. "Three hundred thirty fifth."

"Wha-at? We were close at hand! I was in the three hundred thirty seventh. Encircled in nineteen forty-two?" The same brisk voice rang out with more deference now.

As if to work free of the pictures called up by the question, the teacher rubbed his hand over his chest and gave the man a long, silent, sad look.

All faces turned to the sound of the door opening. Larisa Leonidovna entered, carrying a tea glass in a metal holder and put it on the teacher's desk. He thanked her with a smile and the nod of his head then stepped to the blackboard again.

Serafima found his style of speaking unusually attractive—the way he stopped if he thought someone wanted to interrupt with a question and answering it with a staid calmness of his friendly, interested voice.

Enjoying his tone of voice, she could not help but acknowledge to herself that she didn't understand a bit of what he was saying. She was about to get up and leave, wishing she was home. But when she looked around and saw that most of the students had the same confused, dull look on their faces, her despair lessened. *I'll recall it. We had it in school.*

During the first two weeks, Yakov hardly had an opportunity to look at the girl he first met in the tram. Even if he had had a chance to study her face, he would have felt too uncomfortable to do so. But every time he entered the lecture theater and noticed her, always in the farthest row, he was troubled with a long forgotten, agitating feeling.

One evening, after the lecture, he quickly detached himself from a group of students who delayed him in the class and ran down the steps to catch up with her.

Outside, the gray blur of the winter daylight had long vanished. The tram had just left. Its taillights blinked and disappeared around the corner.

"Comrade Krivenkova!"

She turned back to him with some query. She waited for an answer, her head slightly tilted, her eyes bent on him, her hand tidying a thick black lock of hair that had fallen below her gray-brown woolen shawl.

But he did not catch her question. He stopped, gripped by a pleasantly painful feeling. He knew it well—he had experienced its stab at another important turn in his life. Now, he felt it again as he stared in the bottomless depths of her black eyes. The lines of her mouth were strong, yet childishly tender. The wind whipped color into her cheeks. She stood before him, with her beautiful, arched brows quivering. She looked ethereal in the dim light. A wave of rapture and heavy joy carried him away. "Sorry, what did you say?"

"Are you taking a tram?" Her smile made her appear more simple, approachable, and earthy.

"I don't think one will come soon. Which way do you go? Where do you live?" he asked.

"Krasnogvardeiskaya."

Suddenly fobbed of breath by a jolt of his heart, he asked after a brief hesitation, "May I accompany you?" He looked her in the face and in her lovely eyes—he fancied—flashed an expression, suppressed by the smile that resembled confusion.

Her lips parted, sending his senses spinning. At the base of his throat, a pulse beat and swelled as though his heart had risen from its usual place. With an inner effort, he forced himself to throw off the veil of sweet delusion of his secret fantasy and extracted a pack of Belomorkanal from his coat pocket. "A cigarette?"

"No." She jerked her head.

He lit a cigarette, greedily took two whiffs at it, and expelled the smoke while turning his head away from her. "Sorry. It's difficult without … so long."

They turned off the central street and kept trudging in silence along empty, nocturnal alleys swept from end to end by an icy wind.

She gave him a sidelong glance. "Your family might be waiting for you."

"I have no family. Do *you* have a family?" Then, overcoming his momentary confusion, he added, "a loving husband?"

Her eyes widened and ran, surprised, over his face. "I have a son."

Something soft and defenseless that came out in her gaze and especially in her voice touched him with a bemused feeling of tenderness towards her. Impelled by his overwhelming need to protect her from what he did not know yet himself, he felt how his arms ached to reach over her to press her closer.

"I don't have a—" and without finishing the sentence, she added hurriedly, "I'm almost home, comrade teacher, it's around the corner."

"Yakov, my name is Yakov."

She quickened her steps. "There … That window."

He instantly noticed a silhouette of a child, dark against the lamplight.

"Four evenings a week he's glued to the window, since I started school," she said as if she blamed him for it and took a hurried step toward the house.

"Wait!" He looked straight at her for several seconds. "You have a nice face," he said, "especially your eyes. You have beautiful eyes."

Before he had time to notice her expression she turned around and was running to the entrance.

He watched the door slam behind her and suddenly realized all his terrible loneliness.

That night when Serafima brushed her teeth, and in the morning the next day, she examined her face in the mirror. She had never spent much time on her face, had disparaged rather than admired it, and she couldn't say that she found it particularly attractive.

Then, for a long moment, she stood in front of the wardrobe, deciding which of two wool dresses to put on, though both were threadbare. She regarded her face once more in the mirror and said aloud, "How stupid! What do I care?"

During the day shift, despite the astonishing news about her being awarded the Labor Order of the Red Banner and congratulations from her colleagues who could barely contain their envy, she caught herself sneaking glances at the big wall clock. *But why time drags today?*

She tried to concentrate on her work, but her reveries of Yakov distracted her—his high forehead, his grown back gray hair, his firm, almost hard profile that contrasted strangely with the tentative sweetness of his expression and the delicate elegance of his manners. *But why do I think he … if there is Larisa Leonidovna—* the dean's daughter—so beautiful, so elegant, with pale slender hands that did not know hard work, with her immutable glass of tea exactly a minute before he would start his lecture, and their shared smile.

To free herself from this obsessive thinking, she went to the window. The muddy clouds rushed low in the sky washing everything in gray and something like a shadow was gathering in the east. The lonely leafless aspen stood gray, dull, dead from the frost.

"Comrade Krivenkova …" Yakov cleared his throat. "Your test … well … maybe you need help? I would suggest—"

"Sorry, comrade teacher, I was really, really very busy. I—was busy," she said, feeling how her face flamed under his gaze.

"I see. I've read the article in *Proletariat Avant-garde,* today. Congratulations. It called you an engineer in the nearest future. But you have to study hard to make it happen. By the way, comrades, Serafima Krivenkova was awarded the Labor Order of the Red Banner." He picked up a newspaper from his desk and read, "For distinguished service in connection with increasing the production of arms and munitions during the war."

A scanty applause came.

She waved her hand in the air, almost unconsciously, to dismiss the unwanted attention.

"Well, our heroine and comrade Azarov—" The teacher searched for the oldest student in their group, a tank man with the burned face, "are welcome to stay after the class. I'll be more than happy to go over the material with you once more." He turned to her again and the look of longing on his face was so naked she thought everyone else was bound to notice it. She dropped her eyes under his gaze in fear he might detect the aching joy that filled her from inside, and she felt her cheeks redden.

Suddenly, the door went ajar. Larisa Leonidovna half-stepped over the threshold and waived her hand. "Yakov Antonovich, may I ask you for a second? Sorry, comrade students." As always, her appearance provoked an agitated whispering among the male students.

He got up and went to her, the door closing behind their backs, and the *second* lasted much longer.

The joy of staying with him after school instantly changed to irritation. *I spend so little time with Vanechka.*

After the lecture, she excused herself and hurried to the door.

Something troubled her, and it wasn't that she spent little time with her son. Against her will, hope she had believed to be buried, rose up and stirred within her heart. She startled at her own admission—she wanted to be loved, needed to be loved.

No, no, she gave herself a mental shake—she had no right to hope for that, her past wouldn't let her. *If something springs up, eventually, he'd ask me about Vanechka.*

What should she tell the man who fought on the front? That her son's father was a German? Or would she tell him what she had told her son when one day he came home and asked her, "Where is my father?" Her memory seized that image—his curious face and weakness in her knees, and her inability to speak. Luckily, he prompted the answer himself. "Was he killed by fascists on the front?" It looked like all he needed from her was her flabbergasted, "Y-yes."

She dreaded the breaking up of the inward peace she had gained with such effort. *No, I don't want. I am happy. All I need in my life is my son.*

Yet she felt awkward in Yakov's presence, and as though in revenge she was exaggeratedly cool in her manner.

A few days later Vanechka had a cold, and since on Fridays she did not have her classes, she looked forward with joy to spending the entire evening with her son. At work, the day, as long as it usually was, went by quickly.

Despite the merciless storm of the early March evening that ate through her coat and drove biting icy needles into her face, her heart sang with delight when she hurried home.

From afar, she saw her window aglow and Vanechka's silhouette, his nose and hands squashed to the glass.

She was not especially pleased when, at the entrance door, she found Yakov, waiting for her, hugging his shoulders and stamping about to get himself warm.

He noticed her and came lunging her way, his face brightening. "Comrade Krivenkova, I have two tickets for *Meeting on the Elba*."

She regarded him with somber curiosity. "Yakov Antonovich, I should—My son—"

In the expression of his face, there passed a shade of dismay.

"Serafima, I would like … Couldn't we go to the cinema some other time? That is to say, if you, some day, don't have anything else to do."

"I don't know," she replied sharply and let the door bang behind her back.

It's all nonsense. I don't need it. But when she awoke the next morning and went to the factory, she smiled and without realizing why, recalled, *Today is a happy day. But why? Oh, classes.*

As the days went on, she discovered that she was looking forward to the lectures and so the weeks went, and spring arrived and then June. The last days before vacation were filled with joy in anticipation of it, and at the same time somewhere, in the depths of her consciousness the thought tormented her of something only just understood and broken off, disturbed and incomplete. She had previously caught herself with this shifting sensation, which struck her with the dim familiarity of a brief moment, on more than one occasion: that was how it was or something like it … *Where? When?* And she shivered in the recognition. *Victor, before he went to the war.*

She looked forward to the school year's last class, and feared it. She hardly knew what it was she feared, and what she hoped for. And when this day came, she said to herself, "I can't cheat myself any longer. I'm afraid of not seeing Yakov till September."

Today is the day, was the first thing that rose to Yakov's mind when he woke up with a jolt.

In the anxious mood, he left his home one hour earlier then usual and went to a local market. Meat, eggs, milk, butter, and all kinds of greenery were laid out on the rows of rough-hewn plank counters. The peasants from the neighboring villages followed the rare buyers with beseeching eyes and marketing their tenfold priced goods offered tenderly, demandingly, and enticingly, "The freshest." "Just milked." "Slaughtered this morning, still warm, warm." "Come on closer, see, the best in the market." "You won't find it of a better quality."

He looked around for flowers. From the small aluminum bucket that stood at a young woman's feet, a bunch of yellow jonquils and white and red tulips erected their heads.

"Do you have roses?"

"Roses? At this time of year? Come in July or August, I'll bring you roses," the woman said joyfully and winked at him.

"Give me tulips, the red ones. Eleven. Oh, no, no, give me all."

The woman picked up the bunch and let the water drip off. She wrapped the flowers in a newspaper.

Yakov paid for the flowers, and while taking them from the woman's hand, he realized his fingers twitched nervously. Feeling the hard, hurtful beating of his heart, he asked himself silently, in panic, *What if I deceive myself?*

"The lucky one, your girl. She'll like the flowers."

He almost startled at the woman's voice. "Yes, yes, thank you," he said and immediately was swept up by the recollection of Serafima's charming little curled head and the expression of her eyes, like deep wells of blazing light, strong and sad, and humble at the same time.

He was afraid of giving way to this delirium. Suddenly, he realized he was in front of the Institute and pulled himself together. Before entering, he unwrapped the bouquet. In doing so, he saw that the front page had a picture of a group of people, open-mouthed, with their fists thrust over their heads, and he read the headline: ANNIHILATING ENEMIES OF THE PEOPLE, CLOSING OUR RANKS AROUND THE BOLSHEVIC PARTY AND OUR GREAT STALIN, THE SOVIET COUNTRY MAKES RAPID STRIDES TO COMMUNISM.

He crumpled up the paper and threw it away in disgust.

Walking along the school corridors, he felt uncomfortable with the flowers in his hand. Everyone seemed to be staring at him. *Be quiet*, he conjured his heart, and the more he tried to compose himself, the more breathless he felt. Students and teachers greeted him, and he forced himself to do what was expected of him, that is, to nod, to shake hands, to answer questions, even to smile.

Conscious of his racing pulse, he entered the lecture theater and went directly to his desk.

Mechanically, he congratulated the students on their accomplishment, handed the mark books to them one by one, not for one second losing sight of Serafima. She was fascinating in her simple summer dress, fascinating were the straying little willful tendrils of her curly hair, which she tried to put up under her three-cornered kerchief now and again. He noticed with joy that she was conscious of his stare. For a single instant, there was a flash of something in her eyes, and he was happy for this moment. He watched her growing thoughtful and bending her head lower and lower as less and less students remained in the class until she was the last one.

In the silence that ensued, swift light steps sounded from the corridor. The next moment, Larisa Leonidovna half opened the door and looked in, without entering. "Yakov, we—" Her glance swept over the flowers on the table, and a joyous light flashed into her eyes. Noticing he was not alone in the room, she seemed to make an effort to control herself, to try not to show these signs of delight, but they came out on her face. "Yakov Antonovich, the comrades are waiting for you in the dean's office."

"Soon, we are almost done, Larisa Leonidovna. Please start without me," he said.

Before walking away, she threw another look at the flowers, and he recognized the shy smile that always trembled over her lips when she talked to him. He again experienced tightness in his chest as a grown up person may feel while hiding deliberately a desired toy from a small child.

Instantly forgetting the fleeting sensation of disturbing consciousness, he stretched the mark book to Serafima. She moved closer to his desk. The ends of their fingers touched, and he lingered for a moment at this delicious contact. "Good job."

"Thank you." She headed to the door.

"Serafima."

Her steps slowed and she turned a frightened but eager face towards him.

"May I see you tomorrow?" And since she was silent, he added in a quivering voice, "Or after tomorrow, I mean to say … when you will have time?" He felt that all the muscles of his face were quivering too.

She brushed aside a loose tendril of hair that fell over her brow and bowed her head. Her deep, blazing eyes faltered and turned away from his. "Well." It took her several seconds to continue. "People say mushrooms are good this year. Want to join me for picking mushrooms?"

In his emotion, he did not at first understand her invitation and pushed the flowers to the other end of the desk. Then, it occurred to him that he ought to give them to her.

She blushed and seemed not to know what to do with them. At first, she held the bouquet with blossoms downward then clamped them under her arm. Flushing even deeper, she said, with embarrassment in her voice,

"On Sunday, at ten in the morning, wait for me at the last bus station toward Grinevka."

The door closed after her.

Mentally hearing the sound of her voice, and only distinguishing the words, "Sunday, wait for me," he could not restrain the smile of rapture, totally forgetting about the faculty meeting.

If it was off beam to be this excited, Serafima wanted to be off beam all the rest of her life. On Sunday, all she felt was an overwhelming, grateful sense of expectation and her eyes kept returning to the wall clock. Its hands seemed frozen.

She rummaged on the upper shelf of her wardrobe and pulled out a package of coarse brownish paper. She unwrapped it with jerking fingers, and holding the dress close to her bosom, studied herself in the mirror.

"Oh." Vanechka's eyes widened. "Is it the one you bought in Moscow when you brought me Teddy?" He turned his head and looked with loving eyes at the bear toy that sat askance on his bed.

"Yes," she said.

After she carefully ironed the dress and slipped it on, she examined herself in the mirror as if a stranger— her face, her figure, her legs. With joy, she noticed that it was one of her good days. She decided not to wear a kerchief and knotted her hair, letting the little tendrils break free about her neck and temples.

With a fluttery, empty feeling in her stomach, she stepped into the street. Trees, houses, little orchards were all bathed in the pellucid summer light. A white dove, with a whir of her wings, darted away from the roof, flashing in the sun.

Either feeling her anxiety or just happy to have his violin class, Vanechka scampered in front of her, raising with his feet small clouds of ash-colored dust, chasing after the butterflies and scaring the sparrows from the roadside.

"Serafima, you look so beautiful today." Anna Konstantinovna surveyed her kindly and then turned to Vanechka. "Doesn't she?"

"My mom is always beautiful," he said matter-of-factly.

"Yes, yes, of course." Anna Konstantinovna's smile widened in approval. "You know, dear, this dark green with yellow is so becoming to your hair. Are you going to a concert or what?"

Serafima blushed, angry with herself for blushing. "Actually, I'm going to look for mushrooms."

"Ah, mushrooms—" Overcoming her momentary confusion, Anna Konstantinovna added, "That's right, that's right, good weather for it."

"When do I have to pick up Vanechka?"

"No rush. We have a lot to do." Anna Konstantinovna put her hand on his head and bowed a bit to look into his face. "We'll practice playing to the bridge and to the fingerboard so that you can feel a difference in speed that the bow needs. Ready?"

He nodded agreeably.

Serafima turned to go, and the last impression she carried away with her was the smiling, happy face of her son holding his teacher by her hand.

Conscious of her throbbing heart, she half ran half walked to the bus station.

Seeing Yakov from afar, she slowed her steps deliberately. She had always seen him in his formal dark blue suit of good cut and ever-white shirt with a tie. Now, in a light blue, short-sleeved polo shirt and gray, linen trousers, he looked different, more approachable.

He also noticed her and darted up to her but stopped short. For a few seconds, he seemed to be pulling himself together, as though he did not know what he next had to do. "You are so—Aren't we going to—"

"Y-yes, we go to pick mushrooms, why?" she said, looking resolutely into his eyes but feeling hot all over from the burning flush on her cheeks.

From her hand, he took a wicker basket into which she squeezed a smaller one, and they walked toward the mass of dark green. Sunlight came in flickers as the road snaked through the forest—young-green from the oak, slashed with white birch here and there, with their hanging twigs, and their buds swollen almost to bursting.

The soft breeze carried a smell of decomposition, resin, and warm earth, of dead leaves and moldering wood. Tiny birds twittered, and now and then fluttered from tree to tree. A cuckoo uttered once her usual cuckoo-call, then gave a hoarse, hurried sound and broke up.

"Only one year?" Serafima muttered.

Yakov's eyes traveled inquiringly over her face.

"The cuckoo counts how many years are left to live," she said.

"Do you believe in such superstitions?" In the expression of his face there passed a shade of embarrassment as if he was trying to reassure her in what he himself believed.

She shrugged and looked around.

A patterned carpet of modest greenery that stretched up through rotten pine needles and last year's foliage covered the ground.

"Find a thin branch and use it to hold back the grass and the leaves so you can spot a mushroom more easily," she said. "Look for pale pink heads or dirty white, more like gray."

He followed her about as though chained to her. She felt his eyes fixed on her and turned round. "Don't fall on my steps, you, a wretched mushroom hunter."

He drifted away, treading down the grass and leaving an undulating track behind him. "Hurrah!" A cry came and he darted to her, holding a pale fungus in his triumphantly thrown up arm. "I have found one! The first mushroom in my life."

"Yakov, drop it, drop it immediately, and clean your hands with grass." She put up a hand to stop the laugh that came to her lips.

"Why that?"

"Because the first mushroom in your life is a toadstool." She put a huge, slender-stalked agaric in his basket, and noticing the flash of glad and alarmed

259

excitement that overspread his face, she felt her own face blushing. "Let this be the first mushroom of your life."

"I'm going to pick by myself, or else my efforts will make no show," he said and went into the heart of the forest.

In the glowing light of the slanting sunbeams, she watched his figure walking lightly by the trunk of an old birch-tree and a softened feeling came over her. Then he squatted.

Seeing her approaching him, he did not get up and did not change his position, only looked up at her with his eyes that were smiling. "Is it a toadstool? That one, near the twig?" He pointed to a little mushroom split in half across its cap by the dry grass from under which it thrust itself.

"This is the best mushroom I have ever seen in my life," she said.

He stared at her with eyes that asked whether she was laughing at him, but she had no notion of making fun of him.

"It is a perfect orange-cap boletus."

He picked the mushroom, and they moved still further into the middle of the wood. Flying cobwebs tickled their faces, and they swept at them now and again.

Not taking her eyes off Yakov, she pondered. *Something magical has happened to me, like a dream, when you are frightened, panic-stricken, and all of a sudden you wake up and all the horrors are no more.*

"What's there?" He pointed to the clearing. "It looks like a dugout."

The walls were about to cave in. She stared at the square hole of the dark doorway.

"Why are you frowning?" He touched her hand lightly, bending down to her. "What's about this place?"

All the thoughts she had suppressed before rushed swarming into her brain. The other love had ended in blackness. *Victor does not exist for me. I will never see him again,* she told herself.

"Let's go away from here." Yakov's caring voice switched her mind back, and suddenly, she felt a surge of happiness.

"It's nothing, nothing." She made haste to lower down on a fallen birch, and he sat down beside her.

A breeze was blowing quietly as though fanned from the wings of invisible passing birds. From afar, a distant sound of a blast reached their ears.

"What was it?" Yakov said.

She detected a fleeting expression of alarm in his voice.

"It's from the Rogovka mine. They quarry sandstone there."

Another blast came.

The light died away in his eyes. "It reminds me of war ... actually, I can't even claim I was fighting. The war I experienced was on the other side of the high-wired fence: first in Germany, then—" He pressed his hand over his neck convulsively.

She laid her hand on his shoulder and said as though completing the conversation they had left unfinished, "Of course, Yakov, tell me, tell me."

Nervously, he pulled a cigarette pack from his pocket, lighted one up with trembling fingers, inhaled, and blew a long thin stream of smoke out upwards, toward the branches overhead.

"After the crash course, I was sent to the South front and a week later, in May of forty-two, our army was encircled by Kharkov. I was taken prisoner.

"In Germany, at the Krupps Works, we worked like galley-slaves, producing bombs for Wehrmacht, from five in the morning till six in the evening on a thin gruel that was served us three times a day. After an attempt to escape, I was sent to a concentration lager.

"We were not men and women, only swine, dung-beetles, harlots. Our tormenters had been given a free hand to indulge their lust of power and cruelty, and they made full use of the opportunity. In the camp, we were at the point of starvation: a half-liter of thin beet soup and a handful of sauerkraut to put in it, but we had the sauerkraut only every other day. It did not take us long to discover that birch bark and particular kinds of grass that grew along the nine-foot fence of barbed wire were quite palatable. It dulled the pangs of hunger.

"We had an Allied prisoners of war camp behind the wired fence. They were mostly the English and the Norwegians. Out of kindness, they threw our men handouts over the fence. We jumped on them like a pack of dogs on a bone."

"Why would they do that?" she asked.

"They were inundated by the International Red Cross with parcels from home. They didn't even bother to line up for the German rations."

He lighted up another cigarette.

"The biggest treasure were cigarettes. But that was not a present of every day. Some of us got accustomed to smoking manure.

"Those three years in Germany … Even now, all these years afterwards, I am sometimes so oppressed by memories I still dream about it. About their tidy cities and villages, their luxurious little gardens at every house. And the camp.

"Only desire to return home, to my family, made me survive. A lot turned out differently. Terribly." He studied the burning end of the cigarette. "My parents and my wife … she was pregnant with our first child … all died of hunger, in Leningrad. I didn't know anything about them till recently. I learned it from a letter of my aunt that she wrote four years before. She was the only one of my family who survived."

She saw his eyes narrow in the expression of pain. "I understand why you have sad eyes, yes, I understand. Give me your pain, Yakov, if you can, give it to me."

"In the mornings, I'm so filled with bitterness that I don't know what to do with myself and only the thought that I'll see you in the evening … I wish it would happen every evening."

In a surge of compassion, she slid her hand toward his.

He grasped it fervently. "What cold hands! Are you ill or worried?" he said, not letting go her hands and bending over her.

"For some reason I'm often cold."

He breathed on her fingers, rubbing them with careful tenderness in his palms, comforting her with rapid words—"Everything will be fine now."

But all at once he stopped. The reflection of troubled uncertainty passed over his face. He dropped her hands, took out his cigarettes again and shakily tapped a filter tip out of the pack. "Serafima, perhaps I have no right to even think of impinging upon your life. There is something shameful, disgracing in my life that may raise feeling of disgust in you. Perhaps you will despise me if I tell you—but I have to."

"Tell me. W-what is it?" A cold knot formed in her stomach.

His expression darkened with an unreadable emotion. "I am a criminal, a traitor of the Motherland. I was sentenced for ten years, just recently dismissed from a labor camp. Seven months ago, some character had come to our camp and distributed Gulag registration cards. The most important question on it was 'Trade or Profession.' I wrote 'teacher.' They probably were short of teachers. That's why I'm here."

Suddenly, she felt an aching, piercing tenderness, like a pain. "Yakov," she said, "Oh, Yakov." Not knowing how to unburden him of his pain, and feeling a cutting spring plunged into her chest, she touched his face with trembling fingers. "It's nothing. It does not matter."

She looked at him long and attentively. *And now, after his confession, do I have to tell him the truth about myself? But how can he not despise me after that, after what he suffered in the hands of Germans? A bastard is better than a damned fascist bastard,* she recalled her mother screaming into her face once.

The long suppressed feeling of guilt and shame aroused in her the desire to break off, forget Yakov's caring hands that just brought so much warmth into her heart. To end all this and bring back her former state when she did not need anybody in her life except her son. But at the same time, she was gripped by an almost inexplicable sensation of fear, the terror of not seeing him again. I'll tell him, but *not now … Some other time.*

He drew her to him and she yielded. She felt his arms around her and suddenly everything dissolved. She wanted him and she did not want him to let her go.

He was smiling at her. He changed completely when he smiled. It was as though all the windows in a dark house had suddenly opened. "You are the sense of my life," he said.

The sensation of the happy expectation of something new, something that had not yet been accomplished in her life, the agonizing readiness for what had been not yet experienced sprang up in her with incomprehensible force.

"Serafima, let's—" His exclamation ended on a vague questioning note. "I have tea and ring-shaped crackers. We'll just sit, drink tea, and talk," he said in an unfamiliar voice.

"T-talk and ring-shaped crackers … y-yes," she said and slipped her hand into his.

They walked on. The sunset became stronger and deeper. It touched their faces tenderly.

The little private house on the end of Communisticheskaya Street was not lit. Yakov's room was in the attic. It had a strange, secluded peacefulness. She swept her eyes over the narrow bed crafted from white birch and the armchair that squared one corner of the room, the red velvet curtains drawn across the window, and a bookshelf sagging under volumes.

"Serafima."

"Yes?" With an impulsive movement, she raised her head and her heart lurched madly.

He cupped her chin in his warm hand. She closed her eyes. He kissed her gently, as if he were afraid to hurt her. And she, with a slight groan of relief, with a kind of decided, expiring feeling in her heart let her head fall on his shoulder. Her breath almost stopped. She felt his body pressing close, his arms around her neck. She was conscious of his terrifying nearness, of the imminence of that dangerous thing that happened to her nine years ago through violence and which she herself desired now.

Jerkily, she began to unbutton her dress, and then turned to him, trembling convulsively and sobbing through the chattering of her teeth. Her hands fluttered feebly to protect her nipples from his stare.

"I love you," he said.

"Yakov," she whispered. "Yakov." She dropped her eyes and was silent.

His hands slipped up her arms, bringing her closer.

She leaned away from him, tugging her dress into place and then, overcoming agonizing embarrassment, said at last, "I must tell you something about Vanechka."

He stretched out his hand, almost touching her lips. "Not now, later, later."

"No, no, I want to tell you. You have to know," she said hurriedly. "I didn't want my son at first. I wanted to die when I found out that I ... and I tried to hang myself in the barn, but the balk broke, and when he was born, I wanted him to die."

He leaned against the wall, white faced. "But why? Why?"

"Vanechka's father is a German. He ... I hate him!" She felt as if a hand had closed around her throat.

He took her hands in both of his, bringing them up to his lips, soothing her with rapid, decisive words. "Everything will be fine now, all those terrible days gone by. We both have to forget what we have seen and how the war has hurt us, otherwise it will crush us. We will help each other to forget."

Suddenly, a flood of feeling swept away the damp of restraint. She madly kissed his face, his neck, his arms, the curly graying hair on his chest, and while gathering her breath, whispered, "I'm not afraid of anything anymore. Yakov, oh, Yakov." And then, "I love you."

He took her in his hands and carefully lowered her on his bed and the ceiling was suddenly very high, and became a sky, and she felt him come down on her, and she did not resist him.

She did not know how long she had been away. She was coming back from a great distance. The warm air of the room seemed doubly warm. She quieted in the curve of his arm and felt safe, protected from the menacing world.

They lay for a time in silence. Biting her lips, not wanting to pronounce these words, she said, "I must go, Yakov, to pick up my son from his music teacher."

"We go together to pick up Vanechka from his music teacher," he said with quiet emphasis.

Victor stood by the large window of what used to be General Glubov's oversized room—now his room—letting his eyes rove over the walls paneled two-thirds of the way to the ceiling with golden oak, the large writing desk with its monstrously solid ink-stand, and a huge portrait of Stalin in the Generalissimo full dress in a heavy gilded frame. He would gladly exchange this pompous office for a more austere room on Lubianka in Moscow. *But how? What can I do to make it happen?* He turned and pressed his forehead against the windowpane filmed with the blue mist of rain, following the lazy slide of the drops with his half-closed eyes.

The shrill of the phone interrupted his thoughts. He returned to the desk, picked it up. "Yes." The ebonite receiver felt cool and heavy in his hand.

A moment later, a young officer entered, saluted in the prescribed fashion, put a thin stack of folders on the desk, and went off.

He scanned them quickly, one after another, and opened the one with THE GERMAN DELEGATION typed on the cover page. ARRIVAL JANUARY 11, 1952. *Not urgent. In four months.* He slid the folder into the top drawer of his desk and returned to the case that bothered him lately.

One of their student-informers from the Technical Institute reported the names of the books that were changing hands, and those were exactly the names banned from the official circulation. *Who is that person?*

Or maybe there is a whole group? He pushed the papers aside with tired disgust. *I'll make somebody confess.*

The massive floor clock announced two p.m., his usual lunchtime. Somehow, today he did not feel hungry. He dialed his home to say he was not coming, but it was not answered. He slammed the receiver into place with a furious crash. Where was Zinaida? She was out of control recently. He had to fasten the screws. *She doesn't understand that changing clothes every day, at the time when other women can hardly find means to dress their children … She compromises me … Is it what's oppressing me?*

At work, it was all as good as it could be. His recent star on the epaulettes automatically raised his salary, but he did not want to rot in this little town to the end of his life. He knew he was capable of more. His thoughts kept returning to that grandiose, terror-awaking building of the Lubianka prison in Moscow.

He liked the look of terror on vile creatures' faces. All those enemies of the people, their eyes, which translated nothing more than would the eyes of an animal facing mortal danger. He had experienced on more than one occasion the exciting sensation of his hands pressing on the throat with an iron hoop and his feeling of triumph at the sight of one's servile helplessness.

Zinaida, though capricious, knew her place in his life, was submissive whenever he wanted her to be. He felt one corner of his mouth twisting upward.

Women, girls … They paraded in front of his mental eye. They were many—all subservient—they fawned upon him like pussy-cats. *Katen'ka* ... she was the most beautiful—looked like a doll with her round face, big blue eyes, and full lips. A curved voluptuous body, soft without being fat, and the hips that swiveled provocatively. And how one day she cowered before him, trying to catch his eye, imploring, "Just don't shoot me." But he sent her away, where she belonged—*a German doormat.*

Serafima. She was the one who had never yielded to his will. The thought struck him as a slap in his face.

He shook his head as if trying to shoo her image away, but memories of her flashed into his mind with sudden brutality, like apparitions—she, weightless, in his arms, the semidarkness of the dugout, a pile of the flattened straw at the wall. He shuddered. Sensations, which he had thought he would never feel again, immediately revived. For a moment, it seemed he could even smell the sodden pinecones and the long-lying straw rotting. He dilated his nostrils and closed his eyes, and instantly a vision danced in his mind of how she hurriedly removed a small cross from her neck, slipping the string over his neck, and praying, "Wear this, Vitya. Defend him and save him, Lord; cover him with Thy wings. He is all I have in the world ..." and how he unfastened her hands from his neck and ran, only to catch a moment of unguarded sadness on her face as he glanced across his shoulder one more time.

He could feel his throat thicken, and all the emotions he had buried with so much difficulty crashed upon him. *Could it be possible?* But it had always been possible—how could he doubt it? He suddenly admitted to himself the full weight of his despair, how absolutely he could not expel her from under his skin.

Involuntarily, his hand curled into a fist, crumpling a document. *Who is her son's father?* The thought was consuming, paralyzing. *Stop thinking about it*, he commanded himself. To break off this obsession, he pulled the drawer open and lifted the folder with the names of the delegation members from the German Democratic Republic. *Mother f ... now we are friends with them.*

His eyes glided professionally from name to name: six metalworkers, all formerly members of the German Communist Party, now the leaders of the local branches of the Socialist Unity Party of Germany, five of them survivors of Nazi concentration camps. Two couples announced coming with their children. *That's smart, children always make people more trusting.*

He quickly skimmed the information attached to their names. One mineworker, 25 y.o.

Neither of the men served in Wehrmacht.

Werter Lindberg, 32 y.o., a teacher at Berlin Conservatory. Eastern front, 1941-42. Western front, France, 1943-45, junior Lieutenant then Lieutenant in Wehrmacht. SED member since 1948. Opposite the name, he wrote, *Where exactly on the Eastern front?*

A long moment later, he caught himself pressing on the page with his crippled hand. *Relax. They are all our Comrades.* He smirked. *We'll find out how comradely this Lindberg was on the Eastern front.*

He took a cigarette from his silver case, clicked the lighter, and lit up, breathing out smoke through his nostrils. Suddenly, he felt how the surroundings oppressed him, and quickly extinguishing the cigarette in the ashtray, got up.

Through a long corridor he strode, returning the salutes of the sentinels on his move, down the broad staircase, uttering at the bottom, "Lunch" to a lieutenant at the gatepost before he exited to the misty street.

He did not notice how his legs brought him to Serafima's house. How many times he had told himself to forget, to stop coming here and staring at her window and suffering … tormented by being unable to crush her in his embrace.

From afar, he spied her in a conversation with a man. Partially hidden in the shadows of the tree, he towered over her. *Who is she talking to? What is he to her? A lover? A fellow worker?* He ducked out of sight and continued his observation from behind a bush. He did not hear what they were talking about, but he saw her throw her head back in a hearty laugh. *What did he tell her to make her happy?*

They conversed a bit longer, and then shook hands, but the man stood there as if stoned, waiting until the door closed behind her.

I have to find out who this son of a bitch is.

After each such meeting—unknown to her—he was seized with yearnings for her that would go only if he poured out his wrath on Zinaida or his subordinates.

Zinaida, rosy after a bath, in a silky nightgown that did not cover her heavy legs, moved languidly to the bed. "Viten'ka, hubby, dear, did you miss your pussy cat?" She puckered kittenishly to receive her kiss, and not getting it, pressed her voluptuous bosom to him, her thighs sliding toward him, scorching him with her hot flesh. Her tongue glided playfully over his jowls.

He shivered at the tickle, repulsed by the musky scent of her skin. "Exhausted am I, Zinaida. Let me alone." With difficulty, he repressed a sudden urge to strike her.

Leaning over him, smiling and revealing her white even teeth, she kissed each of his eyebrows. "Don't you love your pussy cat anymore?" she whispered, running her fingertips over his bare chest.

He tore himself away from her with a shudder.

"Why have you moved away? Do I disgust you?"

"Nonsense. Just tired." He exhaled his breath sharply.

Zinaida wrapped herself around him and soon quieted down.

He tried to sleep, but his thoughts drove all sleep away. *Who is that man?*

With renewed pain, he resurrected his feelings for Serafima, which in the excitement of the first year of his marriage, he had dismissed. He thought he could forget her, but she refused to be forgotten, and the wound bled at the memory. Only now he realized that despite nursing his pain and hatred in his soul, he loved her with a devastating, hateful love. "Serafima," he moaned.

In sleep, Zinaida sighed deeply and turned to her back, spreading out her milky well-fed body over the bed sheets.

Serafima, my love, my dear, I would rather you be here, beside me, not this infertile cow. He moved away from his wife. *Serafima, so thin you are.* Suddenly his mood swung sharply. *Idiot, why did you do that? You could have all you wanted—a big apartment, clothes, shoes, you would eat caviar from a silver plate.*

Again, Zinaida turned and her soft hand upon his nakedness brought a shudder of revulsion. He pushed her arm away, got up, and went barefoot over to the kitchen. He lit a cigarette. The fumes of *Gertsegovina Flor* filled his lungs, calming him a bit while he smoked three cigarettes in succession.

At times, when he got maudlin, he would take Serafima's small cross from its hiding place as he did now. For a long moment, he held it in his painfully pressed fist then pushed it back under the wooden panel behind the cupboard.

He moved to the window and cranked it open. The night air entered the room and cooled his face. It was so still outside he could hear himself breathing. Resting his head against the cool windowpane, he looked out at the dark night. A lone light winked in the distance.

"Serafima," he said, before realizing he had said it aloud.

Yakov took a seat in the first row. Watching the people entering the committee room one by one, he wished to be somewhere else. Somewhere else was where Serafima was. Thinking that because of this unexpected meeting he would not see her, brought pain into his chest.

He saw Larisa Leonidovna entering and peering around the room and raised a little, waving his hand to attract her attention. She noticed him and stopped as if in hesitation then headed to him, nodding to the people as she moved. He glanced towards the seat to his right. Before sitting down, she silently searched his face. He could not bear the touching, helpless look in her dark blue eyes and hastened to say, "Do you have any idea what this is all about?"

"Yes, we are going to host—"

"Comrades!" Gavrilov, the second secretary of the Komsomol group of the Technical Institute, jumped to his feet from the long table covered with a green felt on the stage. "Comrade Communists and Komsomol members! Comrade teachers!" He rattled a pencil at the jar with water. "The meeting is called to order. Quiet, please!"

When he secured attention, he said deliberately, "We gathered you for a very important announcement. Let me introduce to you Comrade Victor Ivanovich Kholodov." He bowed slightly to a man to his right whose sharp eyes scanned the attendees.

Where did I see this man? Yakov thought.

Kholodov rose. His military bearing was recognizable despite a perfectly fitting civilian suit. Strong, large-boned, with immaculately trimmed pale blond hair, there was something commanding about him. "Comrades! Our Party pays us high honor to be in the avant-garde of those who will build friendship between the Soviet and German folks."

A wrathful mutter came from the audience.

Kholodov's gray eyes became flat and as unreadable as stone. He waited until the howl of voices died down then said sternly, "The wounds of war are not healed yet. I understand. But there were other Germans, Ernst Tellman—" he looked at a piece of paper in front of him, "Otto Grotewohl, the common German communists who shoulder to shoulder fought with the other antifascists against Hitler." He stamped the words out.

The tone of the man's voice—the cool authority and a silken thread of warning—sent a ripple of awareness through Yakov. *Where did I hear this speaker?*

Kholodov's timbre interrupted his thought. "In nineteen forty-nine, the German-Soviet Society was founded. Our German comrades ... Let me read it, 'The new Germany, the working people of the German Democratic Republic consider the Soviet Union as their friend, the liberator from Fascism and slavery. Today, all democratic minds of Germany realize that the close and friendly cooperation between the German Democratic Republic and the Soviet Union answers the interests of both countries and to a great extent serves a cause of peace in the whole world."

An insistent buzz of anger rose from the people. "Fascists are fascists," a shout came from the audience. "They killed my entire family," a woman's high pitch from the back row cut the ears.

Tap, tap, tap went Kholodov's fingers.

"Silence!" The second secretary held up his hand for quiet.

The hum of voices died away.

The momentary look of annoyance on Kholodov's face had already disappeared. "Comrades, I call your attention to the fact that this is a Party order. We are honored, I want to make it clear, to lay a solid foundation stone of friendship and co-operation between our countries. I call to your party-mindedness."

Kholodov's glance coincided increasingly frequently with Yakov's, beginning somehow a little irritatingly to disturb him. It seemed as though covertly from the others, Kholodov was studying in detail his suit, his tie, or his face. As if he were a subject of a long and wearisome interrogation, Yakov wanted to stir under his gaze, to change his position.

"Yakov Antonovich, you …" His eyes bored into Yakov's face.

How does he know my name so well?

"And you, Larisa Leonidovna." Kholodov's face lost its severity. "Please take care of the schools. Find what they can offer. For instance, school pupils reading verses, patriotic of course, maybe some in German, dancing, singing, playing musical instruments. Well, you'll come up with the program and we'll discuss it at the meeting. We'll see what we can approve."

They killed my family, my life, my future, and now I have to take care of a concert to their honor? Yakov thought, conscious of a stab of hatred and a kind of inner constraint.

He felt Kholodov's fixed, questing gaze on him again and shuddered as if from an alien touch or a penetrating chill. Against his will, he glanced at Kholodov and saw his face close-up, before there was time for it to change, to hide behind the cigarette smoke. His gauging glance, mixed with revulsion, reminded Yakov painfully, obscurely and elusively of something. *What does it remind me of? What?*

Suddenly, all the memories of that year came flooding back.

On a lovely May day in 1945, their concentration lager was liberated by Americans. The Yankees arrived on tanks and broke down the gates.

He was thin as a rail and could scarcely move from exhaustion. But there was freedom, and he looked at the sun and the grass with tears in his eyes—he was alive and the damned war was over.

Together with a group of other Russian prisoners, he dragged himself along the road, past the neat houses with tiled roofs glowing a cheerful red, engulfed by a white blanket of flowering apple orchards and smiled at the spring day and peaceful smell of warmed stone like a happy madman. He was on the way to his family and soon would walk along Kamennoostrovsky in Leningrad.

In the morning of the third day, they reached a small town. In the cool air, there was a dense scent of early lilac, which was hanging pink, purple, or blue, luxuriant and heavy, over the iron fences. This intoxicating smell mixed with the smoke of field kitchens and the petrol fumes of vehicles, dozens of field guns, and the sight of hordes of Soviet soldiers.

But there was no shared happiness in their liberation. Their compatriots glowered at them even more grimly than at the Germans. As soon as they crossed the front lines, they were arrested and transported to a special "filtration camp" in the Soviet Occupation Zone of Germany.

The men in blue and red peaked caps came to the train, read off the names, and those who were called stepped out and were loaded onto another train. It was almost prosaic.

After eight days in the overcrowded goods car, he was in his Motherland that embraced him with the festooning coils of razor wire.

Then there was a room, a young SMERSH officer behind a plain desk. The Order of the Red Banner fitted neatly to his perfectly ironed field shirt. He was shaved to his shining cheekbones and was almost revoltingly good-looking with his clear, gray eyes and carefully combed pale blond hair.

The examination lasted for five hours and Yakov had to tell everything about himself and his family and how he became a prisoner. The first day, the interrogator was polite, squinting sleepily at Yakov's nose, his gaze bored, not objecting by a single word.

On the night of the second day, Yakov had another examination when he was asked exactly the same questions, only in a different way. It continued with that the next night, and in the end he was on the edge of a nervous breakdown and so confused, he began contradicting himself. He had no feelings anymore. To sleep, that was all he wanted.

"Pack of lies! You, fascist scum! At the time we shed our blood defending our country, you collaborated with lager administration in exposing the Soviet Army officers among the prisoners. Betrayer of your Motherland! Hound!" His voice raised several pitches and his fist with two missing fingers crashed atop the desk, making it bounce under his fury. "You scumbag, I'll put nine grams of lead in your skull!" He was foaming at the mouth.

And then, Yakov, with dozens of other former prisoners was taken before a court. In his record, it said he committed treason: "Surrendered to the enemy with the intention of betraying his country." He was sentenced to ten years hard labor.

Shortly after this, he and about two hundred others were driven late in the night to the railway station and loaded into a goods-train. They were let out in Tobolsk. The labor camp there had nothing to learn from the Nazis' terror camps.

Tearing himself from the memory, Yakov intended tactfully to refuse, pleading pressure of work, but conscious of a stab of hatred and a kind of inner constraint, he said with a cutting voice, "I won't do it. I—" His hands were trembling.

Everyone turned instantly towards him, molecules of fear hanging about in the stuffy air. The room had grown very quiet to the extent that it was hard to believe there were fifty or so breathing humans in it.

The knotted muscles on Kholodov's cheekbones bulged. He took a cigarette, lit it carefully then said unnaturally, too calmly, "Well, you seem to want to tell us why?"

"Yakov Antonovich." He heard Larisa Leonidovna's whisper and felt a hand seizing him by the elbow.

Feeling his throat clutched by a shortness of breath from the pounding of his heart, he gently parted her fingers, pulling his sleeve and rose with a jerk. Controlling himself with an inconceivable effort of will, he said, "I'm not going to explain myself. I just won't do it." Without making eye contact with Kholodov, he walked out. The last impression he carried with him from the oppressing atmosphere of the room were Larisa Leonidovna's eyes widened with horror.

What am I doing? What will happen next? How will this end? He felt himself growing hot. *Why am I afraid? I have already had all the fears there are. I have no place left for new ones … But I have. When you love someone, there are many new fears you didn't know about at all before.*

Serafima. With sweet pain, he recalled her burying her forehead in his shoulder, as if for defense, and her arms round his neck, her whispered, "I'm not afraid of anything anymore. I have you." And he, accusing himself for what he had just committed, was at the same time conscious of an intolerably joyful and sharp torment of the recollection of her arms covered with goose pimples, her little breasts, the smooth skin of her thigh, her disheveled dark locks on the whiteness of his pillow when she had lain beside him, and how later, under the vast dark sky adorned with stars, by the entrance door of her housing, she turned and said in an expiring whisper, "I love you, Yakov, I'm yours forever."

Yakov staggered between dream and waking, seeing everything through a veil, yet somehow with excessive clarity, as if he were unconscious and also overly aware. *"Fall in! Form up! Forward march!" The dogs on their chains howled at their favorite command, at the excitement of the moment. The convoy guards marched ahead in their sheepskin coats and the doomed prisoners in their summer clothes trudged through the deep snow on a totally untraveled road somewhere into the dark Siberian forest, nary a light ahead. "Down on your knees!" A gunstock blew on his back.*

He woke in the depth of the night with a feeling of horror and half-raised his head, listening to the lifeless silence of the house, utterly without sound. With unbelieving fingers, he touched the bed sheets. Yes, it was linen on the bed, and the soothingly soft pillow, not the bumpy ridges of the bunk heads knocked together from boards.

He put his bare feet down on the cold floor and went to the window. The night was deathly still. There were no watchtowers, no pointed poles with barbed wire, no clear, hostile searchlight beams. Above the roofs hung the moon, flooding the city with its cool soothing light.

And then, Yakov, his mind put at rest, again fell asleep.

It was already dawn when he was jerked into wakefulness by a strange sound somewhere nearby. He opened his eyes with a sharp jolting in his heart. He was conscious of the terror, trying and failing to control the chattering of his teeth. Behind the window, a jack hammer rattled furiously.

Now … what will happen now? he thought, wrapped in drowsiness, in a kind of physical devastation, failing to find a clear logic that could explain with rational precision how everything had happened. Why? Why now, when he lived his life deeply and passionately as never before, did he not hold himself in check? To comply, to do what they expect from him. *What now? Back to a camp?* And the "daily sermon" of the camp escort hammered in his mind: "A step to right or left will be considered an attempt at escape, and the escort will open fire without warning!"

With a chilling emptiness in his chest, he recalled Kholodov—his eyes, his voice, his hand with an amenable ugly gap where two fingers were missing.

He recognized me. What a cruel fate. Out of, probably, thousands he interrogated, his path crossed with mine.

At the sound of steps coming upstairs, he rose from his bed as if propelled by an explosive force and stood frozen, silently waiting. His landlady's voice came from behind the door, "Yakov Antonovich, tea is on the table."

He exhaled with relief. "Coming down, Vera Petrovna."

Tormented by headache and a pain in his chest, he washed hurriedly and went down to the small kitchen where on the oilcloth-covered table, a cup of tea and a small dish with homemade wild strawberry jam was placed. On a plate, three thick pieces of white bread heaped up.

He took one piece and covered it thinly with jam.

Six ounces of bread. The vision flashed through his mind and cast-iron, sick misery squeezed him in a vice.

He remembered how he dreaded daybreaks in the camp. Yet, there was something so desirable in every morning—a piece of unrisen wet bread, with its swamplike sogginess of texture, made half with potato flour. It tasted so good to nibble off those little bits and turn them over on your tongue. It was the main event of the starting day.

At lunch, they had flour mixed with water, or rarely, the oatmeal mush. There was no fat in it—just water and oats, and still, those oats were more filling; that was all that counted. They cared more for this bowlful than freedom.

He wanted to wipe those years from his life, bury them deep, as though they had never been, yet there was no escaping the visions, and he knew he would wear the burn scars of that time as long as he lived.

A sound of trickling of water brought him back. "No, thank you, Vera Petrovna, I won't have any more tea."

"Have you slept badly? What, what is the matter with you?" She was sitting sideways, with one elbow on the table, propping her head and looking at him with her motherly eyes. No doubt, she sensed instantly with a special woman's instinct that something was wrong.

"All is fine, fine, Vera Petrovna," he said, and conscious of doing a rude thing, but incapable of keeping up the conversation and to get away from the inquiring attention of her kind eyes, he rose hurriedly and left the house.

Gray clouds covered the skies. Wind drove icy needles into Yakov's face. Cold ate through his coat; it curdled the blood and petrified his bones so much that the freezing temperature felt like a biting pain in all his nerves.

Now, what? Do I tell Serafima what happened? he thought in panic. *It's out of the question. But can I pretend nothing happened?*

He walked aimlessly, but the stroll did not distract him from his thoughts, nor did the lectures at the institute. The long hours of the day seemed never to come to an end. When at eight he at last saw Serafima's happy face at the factory keeper's gate and a moment later her eyes, burning with strange light, he felt more frightened than ever. *There has to be some way out*, he thought, his fingers rubbing against his shirt just over his heart.

Serafima looked sidewise at Vanechka who was swinging back and forth on his chair, staring into a textbook propped against the jar of wild strawberry preserves. *So the concert is tomorrow. To the honor of …* She ended mentally, *the damned Germans.*

"Mom?"

"What?"

"What do I need these mathematic exercises for?" He put his forefinger into the jar, licked it clean, and screwed up his eyes in pleasure.

She slapped his hand teasingly. "Take a spoon."

"Ma-am, you did not answer." His finger dipped into the syrupy, ruby-colored mass again.

"Well, everybody needs to know how to count and … I could not become a mechanical engineer without mathematics at all."

"Aaa." He drooled. "But I'm not going to be an engineer."

"And what are you going to become?"

"I'll be Paganini!"

She was about to burst out laughing while moving her eyes to the picture of an ugly long-nosed man above his bed yet her mood swung sharply when her gaze fall on Vanechka's pioneer uniform. It hung neatly on the back of a chair, cleaned and carefully ironed, ready for the concert.

She recalled that day when he, like a wind, burst into the room and from the threshold, with a note of ecstasy in his voice, announced, "Mama! I'll perform at the concert. Some Germans are coming. Anna Konstantinovna said I am playing *Spring Sonata* by Beethoven. It's a difficult piece." And how she asked in shock, "Germans?" and was stunned at how long she did not recall the painful past.

Later, she could not keep the terror from staining her night. She turned over and over, angrily realizing that she was wide-awake. Her memory insistently conjured up fragments of reminiscence: the faces of those two Germans who billeted in their house; the echoes of gun cannonades; the melody of the mouth harmonica—beautiful almost to pain; the young man's white hands with long refined fingers. *What was his name?* She tried to recall it and could not.

By midnight, her agitation reached a pitch that felt something like an inner scream. "Damn them! Damn them! Not even with death will their guilt be wiped out," she whispered.

Almost choking with hatred, she sat on the bed, squeezing the nightgown in her hands, pressing, pressing them hard against her chest till it hurt. She gulped for air and gagged, and deep ugly sounds came from her throat as she sobbed.

As if sensing her unrest, Vanechka turned, emitted a drawn-out, "Ma-ama," and quieted again.

She got up to straighten his blanket, kissed his lovely fair-locked temple, and could not keep her eyes off him. *How is it possible that I love him so much and at the same time can't forgive the evil that brought him into my life?*

She shook her head, shooing the images away, returning from her reminiscences into the warm room lighted mildly with a table lamp.

"Are you scared, sonny?"

"About what?" He tilted his brow.

"Well, the concert."

"Why? Not a big deal." Without altering his indifferent expression, he moved his hand dismissively.

She smiled to herself. The memory prompted that day when Anna Konstantinovna astonished her with the news that Vanechka had an extraordinary talent, and how uncomprehending and unreal it was to her.

"Mom, tell me the story about my first concert." Seated with his elbows on the table, his face raised between both hands, he looked at her with his lovely gray eyes filled with innocent mischief.

"But you know everything."

"Did you tell me everything? All to the last, to the littlest detail?"

"Well …" She kept her face serious. "It was on May ninth, five years ago, more actually. In our hospital, a concert was held for the soldiers who were recovering from their wounds. Children sang, danced, Anna Konstantinovna accompanied them on piano."

"I know, I know about that. What then?"

"Then … you played piano. You know who nailed together a box for you, and they placed it on the music chair."

"Semenich did. He is good. He gives me candies all the time." He cocked his head to one side and his face wrinkled into a big smile.

"I have told you a thousand times that candies are bad for—"

"I know, I know, Mom, you better tell me about the concert."

"I remember it as if it was yesterday. I sat in the first row and beside me, a soldier. He had no legs. Two orderlies brought him there. When you played piano, he leaned to me and whispered, 'What a little one! Attaboy!'"

No longer rocking, Vanechka listened with his whole body, leaning forward as though he were about to jump out of his chair.

"And what, did you say I was your son?"

"Of course I did. I was so proud of you."

"What was it I was playing?"

"Er …"

"Mom, how can it be that you never remember? Ode to Joy by Beethoven." He gave her a roguish look.

"Right." She could not help but smirk.

"And what about Anna Konstantinovna?"

"What about Anna Konstantinovna? She was sitting beside you turning the pages."

"And what, was she crying?"

"She had tears in her eyes."

"Was she proud of me?"

"Proud? Of course she was."

Glowing joyfully to his ears, he jumped to his feet and threw his arms around her neck.

"When you finished, there was so much noise—applause, acclamations, cheers, cries of 'bravo'—that you ran from the stage tear-stricken." She smiled.

He didn't smile back. Pouting, he released his embrace. "But of course. I was three and a half years old then. I was just a little boy." He sniffed and wiped his nose with the sleeve of his shirt.

"Yes, yes, my big man." She gently ran her hand through his hair, but her thoughts immediately returned to the damned concert.

The floor clock struck midnight. Victor lifted his head from the desk that was sparsely lit by the green glass shade table lamp. The corners of the room lurked in the darkness. The window came into focus. In the coal-black sky, the full moon hung like an enormous porcelain plate with remnants of gray gravy. He covered his burning eyes. By now, he could be home, in his bed warmed by Zinaida's hot body.

He buttoned his tunic, got up, heavily, like an old man, pushing on the desk with both hands then fell back on the chair. A persistent, uneasy thought troubled him, vague but torturous. He knew it would be another sleepless night if he did not solve the dilemma connected to the arrival of those *damned* Germans.

Tap, tap, tap. He caught himself drumming his fingers on the desktop. Among the stacks of files, he found the one he wanted. CONFIDENTIAL. REQUESTED FOR THE EYES' ONLY USE OF OBERST V.I.KHOLODOV.

He'd been pondering the content of this file for weeks now. Before jerking it open, he again felt the tension in his neck.

MEMORANDUM

WERTER LINDBERG, DOB: July 1, 1918, Berlin, a teacher at Berlin Conservatory; Eastern front, 1941-1942; Stalingrad-wounded; Western front, France, 1943-1945; Lieutenant in Wehrmacht. Membership in a political party-SED since 1948. *Never a member of the Nazi party?* —his handwritten remark on the margin.

Mother, Brigitte Lindberg, born Karstens, DOB: November 10, 1896, deceased 1945, a pianist; membership in a political party—unknown.

Father, Claus Lindberg, DOB: December 24, 1890, a pediatrician, deceased 1921, cause of death unknown; membership in a political party—unknown.

Sister, Gerda Lindberg, DOB: July 1, 1918, Berlin, a student at Berlin Conservatory, deceased 1945; cause of death—suicide; membership in a political party—unknown.

He skimmed over this already familiar information. As though magnetized, he peered at the previous day's dispatch clipped to the page, *40ᵗʰ Motorized Corp., 9ᵗʰ battalion, quartered in Rogovka, Moscow region, November 7-December 2, 1941.*

Rogovka, Serafima's village. Kholodov caught himself biting his fingernails, the habit he recently developed. He spat out and felt a kind of nausea in his throat as a subtle uneasiness seeped onto his consciousness.

Her son, her son, when was he born? He shuffled through the pages impatiently. *Here, July 17, 1942.* His eyes shot from *November 7-December 2* and back to her son's date of birth. The pieces slowly fit together. He broke into a cold sweat. *Lindberg?*

From a half-empty pack of Gertsegovina Flor he removed a cigarette, put it in his mouth, and clicked the lighter several times. It was dead. He flung it away, rummaged in the upper drawer for a box of matches and lighted the cigarette. Before even drawing on it, he instantly crushed it against the bottom of the ashtray.

With a battering influx of blood in his temples, he pulled another folder from the file.

SERAFIMA NIKOLAEVNA KRIVENKOVA, DOB: January 19, 1924.

Mother—Glafira Nikolaevna Krivenkova, DOB: June 10, 1894, kolkhoz worker, deceased June 13, 1948, cause of death—peritonitis.

Father—Vasile Dzhalakayev, DOB: August 2, 1890, a gipsy; current whereabouts unknown.

Son—Ivan Victorovich Krivenkov, DOB: July 17, 1942.

His hand curled into a fist. *I think I already know who fathered her son.* Now, he had to figure out how to get rid of *her bastard*, once and for all. Then an even more terrifying realization washed over him. *A German easy woman or worse? My relation to her in the past may cast a dark shadow on me. I run the risk of losing everything.* On Serafima's folder he wrote in a tired and shaky hand, *Recruited? Cover?*

He took a sip of cold tea from the thick glass tumbler then put it down with a bang and hastily turned over the page.

MEMORANDUM

YAKOV ANTONOVICH MELNIKOV

DOB: February 19, 1918, graduated from the Leningrad University, faculty of physics and mathematics, a teacher at the same university 1938-1941; had an exemption from military service; enlisted as a volunteer in January 1942 …

Did he have the treachery in mind while volunteering? Or maybe he was already recruited by Abweher by then? Victor's eyes glided down, ... the crash officers' training course, military rank—junior lieutenant; the South Front, 57th Army, Unit 335; surrendered to the Germans in May 1942; 1942-1945 worked at Krupps Works first and then imprisoned in a concentration lager in Germany (according to the interrogation in May 1945); freed by Americans in May 1945. *Why did not he defect then? Since he did not ... Americans or Germans? A double agent? ...* 1945 tried and sentenced to ten years, Article 58-1a; released on November 11, 1950; currently a teacher at the Technical Institute.

"Such a nit! He managed to escape from the Gulag, the place he belonged. He should be rotting there to the end of his days," he said through his teeth. *If only I ...* There was the first creeping realization of his own error.

He did not remember questioning Melnikov—there were thousands back then—but his signature under the interrogation report undoubtedly indicated he did.

He once more re-read the report he had ordered from the Archives and that was enough to make his heart start pounding again. The terror of previous days returned in full force. *Why did I not press him on admission of being recruited by a foreign intelligent service?* Just one little letter, *b* instead of *a* in the Article code would have bestowed a military execution on him. He undid the top button of his shirt. *I could have shot him down in cold blood and no one would have even asked why. How easy it was then.* His hand darted to that place where the holster leaned comfortably against his thigh. *Dammit, I was probably too exhausted.* For a fraction of a moment, the image of a hue-like mass of hundreds of faces flashed through his mind.

In case he confesses to espionage now, they will look more carefully into my interrogating him back then in 1945. Staring at the page and as though seeing Yakov in front of him, he said, "You, brute, you don't know how your emerging here endangers me." *What a cruel fate! Out of thousands I interrogated, my path crossed with this scum.* He shivered at the thought that all the luxury of his life, even his life entirely, may break off, end, disappear as it did for the perpetrators he himself grilled. Some of them were his former colleagues. So he was not immune.

Again, he felt his heart beating faster and faster, his body bathed in a cold, sticky sweat. *Is it what they feel when I …?*

He closed the file with a bang, got up, and pulled an open package of Gertsegovina Flor out of his tunic pocket. He lighted a cigarette and drew the smoke deep into his lungs, but today, it was bitterer then ever and it did not relieve him.

He crossed the room from one corner to the other then went to the window and there, looking at a lonely dark figure that crept along the opposite building, he started, as though from a bite.

Hurriedly he returned to his desk, jerked the file open and wrote, *24 hour surveillance* on both Werter and Yakov's case folders.

The clock's persistent *tick-tick-tick* punctuated the silence. By the time dawn dimmed the stars and in the east the mistily gray heaven looked as though splashed from below with blood, he knew what he'd do. He locked the files in the safe and made for the door.

It was very early in the morning when they crossed the border into the unwelcoming Russia they once wanted to conquer. The train rolled on, its wheels singing the never-ending song of the rails.

Werter stood at the window in the narrow corridor and watched empty expanses and fields flecked with snow under which the uneven black furrows were visible. The landscape suddenly spoke. It came from all sides with its dark forests of pine and firs alternating with the whiteness of birches.

The biting icy wind of those two unforgettable Russian winters lashing his face wandered into his reverie, and he thought he could feel his fingers stiffen with cold.

Now and then, the villages slipped past. Some of them were just foundation walls still standing, lonely chimneys, and heaps of old ruins blanketed by snow. In his mind's eye, huts burned, the smoke swirling through the air and then another fire, glowing. He could suddenly hear crackling and spitting in the big, whitewashed Russian stove, and with the familiar pertinacity, kept envisioning the conflagration of the Russian girl's black eyes, the flutter of her eyelashes, and the strong yet tender lines of her mouth. These recollections mingled with the painful image of the girl's eyes, rolled back, a dark bruise of unshed blood on her left temple, her patched woolen skirt pulled up.

The girl's features did not fade or darken with the passing of time, and through the vitality of his re-creation of her, his torment was intensified tenfold. For all his blunders, he had to find his way back to the man he had been before the outbreak of war. And he knew, there was no other way than to come back to where he had lost himself.

Another day, the train trundled through the white winter land. Minsk, Smolensk, Bryansk, and at last the point of his destination—a small town about 80 miles from Moscow.

Vanechka had been taking himself to his school this last year, but today, to the concert in the Technical Institute, Serafima wanted to walk him right to the door, and watch him go inside.

She pulled her cotton-padded coat with the rabbit-skin collar on over her house gown and they wrapped themselves up in scarves, gloves, and fur caps with earflaps.

Vanechka pressed his violin case tightly to his chest.

They took the route behind and between the apartment buildings. On the paths, the snow crunch-crunched under their feet. With every step, Vanechka's face contorted painfully, but he endured with courage the benefit of wearing new boots.

"Mom, why? Go with me. Don't you want to see me play?"

She felt momentary panic as her mind jumped to the prospect of confronting anyone or anything that would remind her of her past. Especially now. "I have to study a lot. My teacher … Yakov Antonovich is not quite happy with my progress."

"A-a, Yakov Antonovich, but he won't reprimand you," he said matter-of-factly.

The corners of her lips twitched, stifling a smile.

They crossed the street to the institute building. Here the sidewalks were swept, and they joined an increasing traffic of other people trudging along.

"Sonny—" She bent to him.

"Anna Konstantinovna!" He darted to his teacher who was walking through the glass door before Serafima could kiss him.

Werter let his eyes play everywhere—the banner above the stage read in fresh blood-red lettering THE SOVIET UNION IS THE FRIEND OF THE GERMAN WORKING PEOPLE! To the right, on the wall, the one they brought with them proclaimed NEW GERMANY MARCHES TO PEACE WITH OUR SOVIET BROTHERS!

He looked about him at the people, their care-worn and severe faces, and remembered the lean, pale throng treading through the roads of Russia, those faces sweating with hungry anxiety, people wandering along the streets covered with muddy snow, trying to escape the advancing German troops. And from time to time, out of the throng, a living glance—a flash of hate and despair—amid the thousands of dull glances that followed German soldiers crossing the road in their hobnailed boots.

Around him now were the same faces. It looked like they recalled the same events he did. When his glance coincided with one person or another, he saw them darken suddenly with a shadow of revulsion. *The girl, she had the same expression in her eyes when she looked at Major Schuette.* Now, he boldly searched for those black, strong eyes.

Only children, all in matching school uniforms, looked at his people with an astonished curiosity.

A very beautiful young woman in a gray skirt suit that accentuated her graceful figure and with a dark blonde braid lying heavily on her shoulder and down her chest greeted the German delegation.

Werter listened half-ear, only fragments of sentences reaching his mind—"brotherly greetings, faces of new friends …" A murmur of approval came from the members of the German delegation.

The speech of the head of their delegation was indeed greeted with frozen silence.

Then, a wisp of a girl, in a black skirt and a white shirt with the red neckerchief of the Young Pioneer slipped onto the center of the stage. "Our friends from German Democratic Republic will show their … will sing a song. A German song—" She glanced about for help, her chin trembling.

"Lorelei," a loud whisper came from somewhere.

"Lorelei." With a crimson blush, the girl retreated.

Spontaneous laughter came from the audience when Hildegaard and Ulrich stepped out from behind the curtain. She was dressed in a white blouse with sleeves shirred at the shoulders and a long black and blue streaked skirt with a white apron over it. He was in a lederhosen costume and olive green hat with a field pheasant feather.

"Look at them," a male voice came.

"See what leather pants he has." A woman giggled.

"And a feather on his head."

"Shhh, you blockheads, that's their Fritzes' folk costumes."

"What? Is that how they walk about streets?"

His compatriots sang the song sadly, and after they finished they made a grand bow, like opera singers, evoking more laughter than applause from the audience.

The girl with the pigtail braids appeared again. "A Folk-dance by Greta and Fritz!"

The children's dance was met with hardly more enthusiasm.

From the first row, a man got up to his feet with parade-ground abruptness and turned facing the audience. Beneath the softness of a few extra pounds, his military bearing was striking to the eye. He held up his clasping hands over his head in the move of encouragement—two fingers were missing from one of them. *Surely he was also fighting at the front. He may have been the one who shot at me. He may have been the one who killed Schuette*, Werter thought, yet simultaneously chasing the images of the war away.

For an instant, their eyes met. Werter shuddered as if from an alien touch or a penetrating chill.

Meanwhile, on the stage, local kids created a human pyramid, then a small chorus yelled a Soviet Pioneer song, then a middle-aged accordionist came and took a seat on an easy chair. The familiar sounds of the "Einheitsfront," the march of the German Communists, reached Werter's consciousness and he joined the delegation members who rose as one to sing.

Drum links …

After they finished, and the three-tiered accordion scattered, drooped, and fell, they rewarded themselves with an enthusiastic applause supported only by the man without two fingers and some scattered clapping from the audience.

The same girl came forth and with her ardent voice announced, "And now, Vanechka Krivenkov will play *Spring Sonata* by Beethoven, for violin and piano, Anna Konstantinovna Troyanovskaya accompanying."

A boy in new shining shoes and a threadbare school uniform, his pants and sleeves already too short for his lanky figure, stepped onto the stage. He carried a quarter-size fiddle in one hand, and a bow in the other. He took an assured stance between the piano and the music stand, fitted the violin into the hollow of his shoulder, and moved his head to the left before adjusting it onto the chin rest.

Werter noticed that the boy already bore the violinist's stigmata—a raised red patch just below the left jaw line where the instrument tucked under the chin.

The boy moved the fiddlestick over the body of the instrument and inhaled deeply. Then he made an almost unnoticeable nod to the beautiful, elegantly dressed middle-aged woman at the piano who looked at him with loving eyes, and the first powerful sounds came.

This boy will have no problem being heard with an orchestra. Werter was smiling to himself while swaying slightly to the rhythm of music. *He plays with such spontaneity and such musical insight … But he should rather have a full-size bow than the three-quarter size he's using.*

He could not take his eyes off the boy, trying to absorb everything about him all at once. *Who does he remind me of? Who had this way of swooping down-bows from high off the string, slashing strokes on the double-stops?* he thought.

Suddenly, his hand flew to his chest. *Gerdi?* He shook his head. *No, it can't be. I'm dreaming. Just a coincidence.*

Taken by the beauty of the melody and his pounding heart, almost subconsciously, he took his violin from the case and got up. He fitted the instrument into the hollow of his shoulder, caught up the tune without even being aware of the four steps he had to pass before he found himself side by side with the boy.

The boy's gray eyes widened and ran, surprised, over his face, but he stubbornly kept playing.

As the last vibrating notes faded into the air, Werter started *Blue Kerchief.* The lady at the piano and the boy joined in.

An ecstatic groan of "Oh!" welled up out of the great mass of listeners. Then a restrained hum arose, then a sob, then another, and some voices joined. From somewhere, the accordionist appeared, and the words about love and a soldier who during the battles remembered a simple blue kerchief that covered the dear shoulders of his beloved seemed to shake the hall.

When the song ended, Werter leaned to the boy and whispered into his ear, "'Katyusha?'"

The boy nodded. They simultaneously started the melody.

A strained voice from the audience began to sing, then another one, and soon, more and more took it up. It was a song about a girl who waited for her beloved, a soldier serving on the border of the Motherland far away and whose letters she treasured and kept.

Barely had the last words stopped sounding when applause broke like a rain of artillery. Never before had Werter confronted so emotionally charged an audience.

He stretched his hand to the boy for a shake. "I'm proud of you," he said in Russian.

The boy's face broke into a happy smile.

"'Blue Kerchief!'" someone shouted from somewhere in the rear. "'Katyusha!'" another voice cried. The roar of approving shouts rose to an extraordinary pitch. The audience leaped to its feet, cheering, applauding.

They bowed. Werter wrapped his arm heartily around the boy's shoulder, carrying him behind the curtains.

The chant rose to a new height. "Dugout! Dugout! Dugout!"

"Do you know 'In the Dugout'?" the boy whispered.

"Give me a tune ... Yes, I know."

The clapping and the shouting continued.

Concealed behind the curtains, they started the melody. The noise subsided and then, as a thunder, the hall resounded with the massed voices singing.

Werter could distinguish only some words, "a tear ... your eyes ... the sadness ... lost happiness."

The power of the voices from the audience muffled the sound of the violins. People continued singing, and when Werter and Vanechka were on the steps leading to the ground floor, they heard the thunderous applause.

"It's amazing how easily you can catch up a tune of our songs," the boy said, wrapping his antediluvian violin case carefully into the woolen scarf.

"I know these songs. I first have heard them in nineteen forty-five. Russian soldiers used to sing them. Anyway, it was in the concert program that I would perform 'Blue Kerchief.'"

They took their overcoats from the old woman at the cloakroom and stepped into the breezy evening. The street was poorly lit and quiet with only the occasional bus steaming away with a belch of black exhaust, or the screech of a tram, or a lonely pedestrian hurrying by.

"The 'Spring Sonata' is not an easy composition to play. Your timing was excellent. It sounded so strong," Werter said.

"Did you like it? Do you think it was good?" The boy lit up and smiled from ear to ear.

"You are a big talent, young man."

"So they say. But actually, I just like playing violin. No, I am always happy when I play. My mother says one must like doing something very much and then no talent is needed."

Werter burst out laughing. "Your mother is not quite right ... but maybe she is." He continued smiling without taking his eyes from the boy. "For music, the talent won't harm. I learned to play 'Spring Sonata' when I was a freshman at the conservatory. By the way, how old are you?"

"Eight. Eight and a half, already," he said hurriedly. "And you. You studied at the conservatory? It must be cool. Which conservatory?"

"Stern conservatory."

"Where is it?"

"In Berlin."

They trudged off on foot, speaking without stopping, passionately, of the magic of cadenzas, double harmonics, and chords, bow and vibrato exercises. As he listened to the boy, looking into his sparkling gray eyes, he could hardly restrain himself from stretching his arm to brush the lock of fair hair falling over his brow, to embrace him in rapture. He was somehow unable to entertain the thought or to agree that they should part, that the boy should go to his parents who may be worried about their son now, while he should go back to meet the members of the delegation who, as well, may be concerned of his absence.

Suddenly, gripped by a misty disquiet, he glanced back. Two dark shadows flattened to a wall of a two-story house. *Is somebody on my tail? Stuff and nonsense.* The metallically sharp feeling of danger instantly disappeared as the boy's voice brought him back to reality.

"You know …" A small hand seized his sleeve, the boy's face sweaty and excited, and the collar of his battered coat open. "Anna Konstantinovna is going to take me to Moscow next summer. She has a friend there, a professor at the most important conservatory in our country. He said I might come to take exams. He may be my professor … If he accepts me." He raised his shoulders and inhaled deeply.

"That's great. I am almost sure he will. Anna Konstantivovna, is that the lady who accompanied you on the piano?"

"Yes, she's my music teacher … My second mom."

"And who is your first mom?" He took a calming breath. "Is her name Serafima?"

"How do you know?" The boy raised his eyes at him in awed surprise.

"I met her during the war," he said softly, letting his eyes rove over the boy's face.

"During the war? Were you a f-fascist?"

"I was a soldier."

"Did you shoot at our soldiers?" The boy looked up at him with eyes full of terror.

"I did. But I regret it."

The boy stopped mid-stride. His eyes widened and he backed up. "I have to run. Mom will scold me. Here is my house." He motioned to a shabby structure.

Then, she lived in a small village. Yes, indeed, we burned the huts. More than ten years ago. The unmerciful agony of the winter of 1941. A pathetic hut with the stove that was bliss. A girl with dark curls and strong blazing eyes. Then horrible days … weeks … months … Stalingrad. All this flashed through his mind like a filmstrip at a mad speed.

"So will your parents allow me to stop in?"

"Parents? No, I have only my mom … My father was killed in the war, but maybe I soon will have another father." A sly smile lighted the boy's face.

The night wind cried outside the window. The frosted glass kerosene lamp lit the room weakly and fitfully. The corners were shrouded in darkness. Serafima stared down into the textbook until its letters jumped before her eyes, her hands frozen in place, holding the book's open wings. *How is Vanechka there?* She drove away the disturbing thought, but for a moment, her mood veered sharply to anger. *Why did I agree to let him perform at that concert? Why did I allow him ever to go there?*

Like muck stirred up from the bottom of a pond to stain the clean water above, things she had never wanted to resurrect drifted up from the depths, rising up into her mind. She was freezing. The woolen shawl thrown over her shoulders did not warm her.

She got up and boiled tea. It soothed. She went to the mirror, staring at her face, looking for the first mottles. *Soon my life will change.* Her heart warmed within her. Clutching at her belly, she smiled a dreamy smile like that of a blind man listening to the noise of life, feeling over and over again the incident of the day before, reliving the same excitement. *Yakov*! With him, she would have a future full of tenderness she had never known.

A dream-like recollection of their last conversation flashed in her mind. They stood at the window in his room, silently watching the setting sun. In the west, the misty blue heaven looked as though splashed from below with blood.

He pressed her head against his shoulder, and she inhaled the pleasant scent of his hair and felt the tickling of his breath on her ear.

"Why are you so quiet? What's the matter?" he asked.

She detached herself from his embrace and watched down through the window at a little child carried by his mother over the street.

"I waited … I didn't believe it at first. Now I know. In six months, maybe even less, I shall be the mother … of your child," she said, expectantly raising her eyes to his.

There was a spark of some indefinable emotion in his gaze. He stroked her shoulder, but she did not reply to the caress, terrified by his reaction.

The silence was torturous. She did not know what to do with her hands, adjusting her collar, fingering the buttons of her blouse.

"There is only one thing you can do—"

She swayed. As she awaited the end of the sentence, she clenched her hands until her nails entered her palms.

"Marry me." And as if sensing her next question, he hastened to add, "I'll adopt Vanechka. I will love him. But, of course, what am I saying! I love him, love him like my own son … But why! Of course he *is* my son."

He seized her hand and began kissing her fingers in a frenzy of tenderness, repeating, "I can no longer think of life without you, and now that we'll have a child! Oh Serafima, I'm so happy."

She sagged against him with an expanding feeling in her chest.

And now, like the day before, with tears welling up behind her eyelids, she smiled to herself, listening to the stirring of the new life within her. *I will tell Vanechka about the child today. About a sister or a brother he will have soon.*

Instantly she heard her son's voice at the door. He was talking to some one. *Yakov!* She straightened slightly from a feeling of suffocating joy, and from the beating of her heart, in order to draw more air into her lungs.

The door opened.

"Mama, Mama! We played 'Spring Sonata' together, and 'Katyusha,' and 'Blue Kerchief,' and 'In the Dugout'! People applauded like crazy! They did not want let us go." Unconcealed triumph sounded in his voice. "It is Werter. He is a teacher at Berlin Conservatory." He turned to somebody. "Come in, will you?"

From the gloom of the corridor emerged a tall man in an elegant dark blue, fine wool coat. In one hand, he was holding a pair of woolen gloves and a violin-case was in the other, the knuckles of his fingers were white. He bowed politely, apparently asking permission to enter.

"Mom, he is a go-o-od German!" Vanechka stopped abruptly as if struck by the expression of her face.

There was a long moment of silence, which seemed to last forever.

She already knew, even while she was inducing doubts in herself, she could not be mistaken, could not deceive her memory of what she wanted to reject, forget, what she kept forcing out of her mind through all these years.

"Do you remember me?" There was a faint tremor in the man's voice, his heavy accent noticeable.

She raised her eyes at him, appalled at and not believing what memory prompted, comparing the adult refinement of the good-looking man in front of her with that face of a young German who, with the other damned Fritzes, came to her village to burn their houses. Involuntarily, she fingered the scar on her temple and its hardly bulging surface scorched her with a stifling wave, just as on that impossibly far-off December afternoon of wartime.

"I don't remember you," she answered so calmly, lied so resolutely that she again felt her throat clench in suffocation, by a shortness of breath both from the pounding of her heart and from his stunned silence.

He approached her with a slight limp, and his eyes came down as if studying her thoughtfully. There was an almost imperceptible expression of pleading in his face. From his pocket, he pulled an old mouth harmonica and laid it down on the table in front of her. "I saved it through the war. I knew you were fond of it." He unbuttoned his coat, reached into his breast pocket, and removed a folded yellowed paper on which the ink had run. "Your letter. I could not know then how important this letter may be for you … and for the other person, Vitya. I am very sorry."

She stared at him not understanding. *My letter? Vitya?*

In the silence that ensued, especially long by the measured ticking of the wall clock, it seemed to her that he intended to say something, something serious and important to him, which she could not know, could not even imagine. "Well, you seem to want to tell me something," she said unnaturally calmly.

"Yes, I do … Every time I recalled … I was sickened by what happened then. When I finally decided that my inability to come to terms with it was going to chip away at my mental and emotional strength, I had to accept the fact that it happened. I filed the issue away in a dark corner of my mind … Till I returned home, to my family … to what was left of my family."

What is he talking about? she thought, gripped by a misty and hot disquiet.

He put on the table, in front of her, a picture of a young girl in a white dress with a violin at her chin. "My twin sister. Her name was Gerdi."

What do I have to do with his sister?

"In May of forty-five … the Russian soldiers raped her … She hanged herself."

"God no!" Serafima pressed her palms over her lips.

"I hate the damned war. I was brought up—we all were—in unquestioning obedience. War was an order. But I can't escape my share of guilt … the horrible thing I have done to you."

"The horrible thing?"

He turned his head to Vanechka who still stood at the door, frozen, pressing the violin to his chest.

She shifted her eyes from him to her son and then back to him. The resemblance came suddenly, a flare of recognition that called up the father in the son. The likeness caught her off guard, and during the seconds that followed, she felt a pain in her gut that rose into her chest and lungs and seemed to choke off her breath.

"So it was not that damned—" her voice trailed off. She moved her eyes at him then turned her gaze away, and a feeling of troubled uncertainty passed over her mind. *That kindhearted youth?* Who, consciously or not, protected her from the major. Who secretly gave them chocolates and other food and medicine for her mother. Who did not give them away when he found the pitchfork and the hatchet they hid? The one she mentally excluded from the accursed intruders. *How was it possible? Goodness and evil, how can they coexist in the same person?*

"I am the only one to blame." His words were measured as though he had recited them many times. His voice, lowered, scorched her with a stifling wave. "Schuette paid for my crime. He was killed that very day."

He stood erect, downcast. She waited for him to say more. After a long pause, he looked up at her, then at Vanechka, and said, "I know I hurt you."

She watched him stiffen to fight off a shudder and mentally asked herself, "What do I feel towards him now? Anger? Disgust? Hatred?" and experienced the dark, dull blows inside her head as it had been then, that day, in December of 1941. Suddenly, she wanted to pummel him with her fists and shout at him, that he had twisted up her entire life, had stolen her youth, her love, had deprived her of happiness. That he had to reverse the time and bring all that she'd missed to life. These were insane thoughts, and she knew just how unhinged they were as she stood in front of him and realized that he was feeling guilty and wanted everything to be different from now on. She saw his face distorted by suffering and pain.

"Did you come to ask for forgiveness?" she said distantly.

After a long silence, he said in a firm voice, "Yes, I had to come here again, to find you. Yes, I could not live a normal life. I went down again and again, into the past, its pull so strong. Do you know what it's like to have your life unravel because of something you did under false pretension to be strong, under pressure of authority? Order. It is rooted deep inside us Germans. We do as we are told. I was not different. I did that to you to demonstrate the 'man' in myself, to demonstrate it to my superior. It haunts me like nothing else."

The ticking of the clock became audible.

She remembered that sensation of the end of her life when she comprehended she was pregnant. Pregnant with a child of an evil. *Was it he who did that evil to me? Is Vanechka evil?*

He turned his face to her, his eyes large with pain, and all at once, there was a liberation from the hatred that had been nauseating and stifling her all these years.

She reached out to touch his elbow. "You gave me the best I could ever have in my life. My son is—" But she did not finish the sentence. She clearly heard the outer door opening with a screech and then the echoing rumble of many distant footsteps over the corridor floor. They were still far away, but something told her they were coming for her. Something with scorching, jagged edges twisted in her chest. At the sound of a sharp knock and the door flying open, she lifted her eyes and felt her mouth move suddenly, and a small involuntary cry came from her. "Vitya!"

August 13, 1952

A leading article in the newspaper *Proletariat Avant-garde.*

A picture of a group of people, open-mouthed, with their fists thrust over their heads.

From the unanimous resolutions of the meetings of the workers at the Mechanical Factory and the students and teachers of the Technical Institute.

SPIES! TRAITORS! FASCIST HIRELINGS! AGENTS!

Our glorious Chekists have exposed a gang of vile enemies of the Soviet people, a German spy and his Russian collaborationists.

These rascals dreamed about the downfall of the Soviet Union. They continued their attempts to destroy our Socialist country, the great achievements attained under the wise guidance of the Communist Party and personally our great comrade Stalin.

For many years, Serafima Krivenkova concealed her true beast face. She deceived us all. Behind the mask of a shock worker was hidden a sworn enemy of the people, an adept spy, working for a foreign country, who managed to penetrate to the very heart of our State military industry.

Yakov Melnikov, who took advantage of the benevolent nature of our judicial power that pardoned his treachery of his Motherland and entrusted him to teach our Soviet youth, abused the confidence of the Soviet people. But our Chekists who are always on alert, defending our workers and peasants' state and the triumph of socialist ideas exposed him.

Some aggressive imperialist states do not want to give up their attempts to destroy our happy life. It seems like nothing would stop their attempts to restore the capitalism in our country and spread the influence of the western ideology. They constantly send the mercenaries of their secret services under the appearance of our friends.

Despicable creatures, who have sold themselves to our enemies, were caught in the very act of committing a crime while new instructions for their treacherous actions were changing hands.

For their crimes against the Soviet folk, they were proved guilty and the just Soviet People's Court bestowed a severe sentence on these enemies of the Soviet power.

The deeds of these human degenerates evokes profound indignation in the heart of every faithful Soviet citizen. The ignoble vermin, the traitors of our Motherland must be, and they will be, eradicated.

The enemies of our country must know that we are powerful, that our glorious Chekists are vigilant, and our court is unmerciful to its enemies.

Every worker, every honest Soviet citizen must be even more protective of our happy life from the capitalist hirelings.

Glory to the leader of the Soviet people, comrade Stalin!

Glory to our great Communist Party!

Glory to our Chekists who exposed the enemies!

The article was silent on the point that in the meeting at the factory, Semenich got up and left the room. Larisa Leonidovna pleaded to illness and did not attend the meeting at the Institute.

Epilogue

The Great Patriotic War was over; however, the explosive waves of Article 58 of the Soviet Penal Code—regarding counter-revolutionary activity—kept rolling over the country in an all-encompassing embrace.

As hundreds of thousands of other "traitors," "spies," and "agitators" against the Soviet Union were punished by the wide sweeping Article 58, Serafima, Yakov, and Werter were sentenced.

SERAFIMA got eight years of imprisonment with property confiscation. YAKOV and WERTER each got ten. All were sent to internal exile.

As a result of the *Enemy case*, VICTOR achieved his goal. He was awarded the Lenin Order and transferred to work on Lubianka, in Moscow.

After petitioning for eleven months, ANNA KONSTANTINOVNA was granted permission to take Vanechka from a shelter for the children of the enemy of the people.

Serafima's newborn child did not survive her first winter.

After Stalin's death on March 5, 1953, many cases were re-tried.

SERAFIMA was acquitted, and in August of 1956, returned from Kamyshlag Corrective Labor Camp to her small town where she lived for many years with Vanechka and Anna Konstantinovna.

WERTER, after spending three years in Soviet detention in a labor camp in the Irkutsk region, was allowed to return to the German Democratic Republic and continued teaching at the Berlin Conservatory.

Not until 1987, after Perestroika broke out in the Soviet Union, did Serafima receive a response to her numerous requests about Yakov's whereabouts. A one-fourth of a piece of paper said, *Died of cardiac insufficiency in 1952 while in Tomsk transit prison. Place of burial unknown.*

Until his death in 1991, VICTOR worked in Moscow, covering prominent posts in the State Security organs MVD-KGB. He was buried in the most famous Moscow cemetery, Novodevichy, with full military honors.

In 1992, after the final break-up of the Soviet Union, Werter went to Russia to find Serafima. Because of the love he felt for her and the sincere remorse he carried through all those years he won Serafima's forgiveness and her heart. In 1994, they married. They settled down in the small town of Beelitz near Potsdam, about 30 miles from Berlin. When Vanechka, his wife Lena and his children Anna and Kostya came to visit them in Germany, he and Werter played violin together.

Serafima died in December of 2006. Werter followed her four months later.

Still, some people living on Trebbiner Straße in Beelitz may remember a tall, slightly stooping old man and a tiny woman with snow-white, wild locks and amazing black eyes that blazed when she raised them at the man. He would never let her hand go.

Glossary

Chekist—A member of Cheka, the first Soviet secret police organization

Commissar—Soviet Communist Party official, responsible for political education and organization

German Democratic Republic—East Germany, a state in the Eastern Bloc from 1949 to 1990

Iron Cross—A military decoration during the Franco-Prussia War, World War I, and World War II

Kilometer—Is equal to 0.621371 mile

Kolkhoz—Collective farm

Lubianka prison in Moscow—The headquarters of the Soviet secret police after the October Revolution

Mauser—A German-made pistol

MVD, KGB, NKVD—Abbreviations of the Soviet secret police agencies at different periods of the Soviet history

October Revolution—The revolution in October 1917 in Russia that overthrew the czar and brought a Communist Party to power

Sieg Heil!—Salute of the Nazis or so called Hitler salute

SMERSH—Acronym of "death to spies" was an umbrella organization for three independent Soviet counter-intelligence agencies

Sovinformbureau—Soviet Information Bureau

The Great Patriotic War—The term is used in Russia to describe the conflict fought during the period from June 22, 1941 to May 9, 1945 along the many fronts of the Eastern Front of World War II

Acknowledgements

For the basics and the honing of my writing craft, I am very grateful to all my writing teachers and especially Richard Goodman, the author of *The Soul of Creative Writing* whose books, lectures, and workshops were and still are an indispensable source of inspiration and instruction to me.

I owe a debt of gratitude to Judy Roth who is a dream of an editor for challenging me to do better and for cheering me on the last stretch of the book. Her insights, tactful suggestions, and comments were always smart and inspiring.

Above all, I thank my loyal early reader, my best friend, Lyuba Krasnova, an English language teacher in a Russian school, for her enthusiasm. I am lucky to have Liz Amaral, an author of remarkable books, as my friend. Her thoughtful and astute advice was of enormous help to me personally and in the completion of this book.

I thank Claire Wallace and Linda Bennett Pennell who gave me observations about this novel that were helpful and wise. For their contributions, I thank Enrico Martens and Bob Silberstein.

Much thanks to all those anonymous judges of the RWA-sponsored and other contests for their kind or incisive feedback and sharp advice, their encouragement and the expressed desire to see the story in print.

Finally, I owe more than words can express to my parents who advised me of what every-day life was in the forties and fifties of the previous century and who patiently guided me through the littlest details of that time.

Printed in the United States
By Bookmasters